THE PINK BONNET

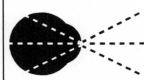

This Large Print Book carries the
Seal of Approval of N.A.V.H.

THE PINK BONNET

LIZ TOLSMA

THORNDIKE PRESS
A part of Gale, a Cengage Company

Farmington Hills, Mich • San Francisco • New York • Waterville, Maine
Meriden, Conn • Mason, Ohio • Chicago

Copyright © 2019 by Liz Tolsma.
True Colors.
All scripture quotations are taken from the King James Version of the Bible.
Thorndike Press, a part of Gale, a Cengage Company.

Thorndike Press® Large Print Christian Historical Fiction.
The text of this Large Print edition is unabridged.
Other aspects of the book may vary from the original edition.
Set in 16 pt. Plantin.

LIBRARY OF CONGRESS CIP DATA ON FILE.
CATALOGUING IN PUBLICATION FOR THIS BOOK
IS AVAILABLE FROM THE LIBRARY OF CONGRESS

ISBN-13: 978-1-4328-6866-6 (hardcover alk. paper)

Published in 2019 by arrangement with Barbour Publishing, Inc.

Printed in Mexico
1 2 3 4 5 6 7 23 22 21 20 19

To my children, Brian, Alyssa, and Jonalyn. You each have your unique adoption stories, but you each demonstrate the beauty that can come from brokenness. I love you more than you'll ever know. You are God's greatest blessings in my life.

CHAPTER ONE

Summer 1933

"Momma, Momma, watch me."

Cecile Dowd turned from the old blackened cookstove where the chicken broth simmered and peeked into the bedroom at her brown-haired three-year-old daughter who jumped on the thin mattress.

"Millie Mae, be careful. You'll fall."

"No, Momma." But at the next landing, her foot missed the edge of the bed, and she tumbled off.

Fat tears rolled down her cheeks, and wails cut the peace of the early afternoon. Cecile rushed to her and cradled Millie in her arms. "That's why you must obey Momma. Then you won't get hurt. Do you understand?"

Millie sniffled. "I be good."

"Why don't you play with your dolly so I can finish lunch?" Cecile kissed the top of her daughter's head.

"Okay." Millie picked up her secondhand, soft-bodied baby. She smoothed down the yellow dress Cecile had sewn for the doll. "My baby pretty."

Cecile smiled. "Yes, she is. But she's not as pretty as you are."

"Momma's pretty."

Could a heart fill and burst with love? Millie followed Cecile into the kitchen and plopped on the floor with the toy, pretending to pour tea for her.

Good. Maybe a few uninterrupted minutes. While the stock bubbled, Cecile cut and buttered bread to eat with it. She wiped her hands on her apron. What was she feeling on it? Oatmeal. From breakfast. Great. She dashed to the bedroom to grab a clean apron.

From the corner of her eye, she caught sight of Millie as she toddled toward the hot oven.

"Millie." She raced to the kitchen, caught the girl with her hand outstretched, and plopped the child into her too-small-for-her crib. Millie tugged on the already-peeling rose-peppered wallpaper. Maybe that would keep her occupied for a few minutes.

Before Cecile could tie her apron, Millie climbed over the crib's rails and headed toward the kitchen. "Millie, no."

The girl stopped for just a second then continued in the direction of danger. Even with only two rooms in the apartment, keeping track of her was impossible.

She scooped up Millie and balanced the little one on her hip. Millie squirmed and hung upside down in an attempt to break free from Cecile's hold.

"Stop it this instant, Millie Mae. Do you hear me?" The child deserved a harsher punishment, but Cecile had no energy to mete it out. Her arms ached from the effort required to maintain her grip. When Millie continued to wriggle, Cecile swatted her little bottom.

The child let loose with an earsplitting howl.

Tears burned the back of Cecile's throat. "Hush, hush, Momma's sorry. But you must behave." Oh, how could Nathaniel have left her alone to deal with all of this?

A year after his death from an infection, they were low on money. Just a few months' worth of rent were left in the bank account. Her part-time job at the nursery school helped, but the savings continued to dwindle.

She glanced at the letter lying on the corner of the worn kitchen table. One she'd sent to her parents in Massachusetts, begging for help. Another one returned unopened.

With Nathaniel's parents deceased, she had no one else to turn to.

She sat the girl on one of two rough chairs at the scarred table and gave her a pencil and an envelope containing a doctor's bill she couldn't pay. "You draw Momma a pretty picture."

"Okay." As she got down to work, Millie stuck out her lower lip. She resembled Nathaniel so much when she did that. "I draw me and Momma."

"That sounds wonderful. I can't wait to see it." Cecile relaxed her shoulders. How long this would last was anyone's guess.

From outside came shouts, a couple having a fight, an infant screaming at the top of his lungs, dogs barking. What she wouldn't give for the peace and quiet of the New England farm where she'd grown up. But Nathaniel was a dreamer, and he'd envisioned making his fortune in Memphis by selling automobiles in the booming market and saving enough money to buy his own dealership.

The summer heat pressed on her, and she wiped the sweat that trickled across her brow and down her temple. Memphis proved not to be a land flowing with milk and honey but a wasteland. What he'd earned, they'd lost in the stock market crash just after Millie's birth.

She picked up a pair of Millie's frilly white socks and went to return them to the bedroom. An acrid odor, something burning, reached her. She hustled to the kitchen. Millie had pulled her chair to the stove and stood stirring the broth, sloshing much of it onto the hot burner.

Cecile grabbed the child. "You aren't supposed to be by the stove."

"I help, Momma."

Someday, the girl would be helpful, but today wasn't that day. "I know you want to help, but you are too little." Cecile stood her in the tiny room's far corner. "You stay there."

In no time, Millie joined Cecile in front of the hot oven. "No, you don't go near the stove. Have a drink of water." She reached into the cupboard for a glass. As Cecile's fingers brushed it, Millie tugged on her. The cup slipped from the cabinet and shattered on the floor.

"Millicent Mae Dowd, look at what you made me do." With each word, Cecile's voice rose in pitch.

Millie opened her mouth and released a wail to rival that of any injured cat.

11

The apartment door swung open. *No, please, no.* A visit from Mrs. Ward was the last thing Cecile needed.

"Cecile, dear, is everything okay?" Stooped, gray-haired Mrs. Ward from downstairs popped in. Not what Cecile needed, an annoyed neighbor snooping on the disaster area they called home. She pulled her lace-trimmed handkerchief from her pocket and wiped her nose.

"I'm sorry. We broke a glass. I'll keep Millie quiet." She lifted the child into her arms and straightened her ruffled dress.

Mrs. Ward surveyed the room in a single sweep. "I'm far too old to do much good, but maybe I can help you in some way." Her honey-smooth Southern accent washed over Cecile.

No. God told you to work with your own hands. "We're fine."

The old woman shuffled toward Cecile, her cane tapping the way. She touched Cecile's shoulder, and Cecile fought the urge to weep like Millie. If only Momma were here. If only Momma still loved her and accepted her.

"You can't do this by yourself, but I have a solution. Miss Georgia Tann is doing wonderful things at the Tennessee Children's Home Society. She'll take this little

12

darlin' in and watch her for you until you can manage. And it won't cost you a thing. Just temporary, you know. Soon you'll have Millie home and everything back to rights."

Cecile squeezed her daughter. "I could never give her up. Not in a million years." Even if it meant Cecile didn't eat or sleep, she'd do what she had to do to keep Millie.

Didn't Mrs. Ward understand? Millie was all Cecile had left of Nathaniel. The little piece of him she adored and cherished. Millie was everything to her. The very breath in her lungs.

"Bless your heart. At least let me get a broom and sweep up this mess."

"No!" The word burst from Cecile's lips with more force than she intended. She struggled to lower her voice. "Thank you. I have everything under control."

Mrs. Ward patted Cecile's arm, her hand gnarled with arthritis and rough from years of hard work. "Of course you do, but think about what I said." She shuffled away and out the door.

"I hungry, Momma."

Cecile brushed Millie's cheek with the back of her fingers. "Lunch isn't quite ready. As soon as it is, we'll eat."

They could do this. They would weather this storm. Hardship was part of life. Once more, she went to the bedroom and sat Millie on the floor. Cecile stopped to straighten the bed's quilt. In seconds, Millie was gone, and great sobbing cries came from the other room.

Cecile rushed to her daughter, who stood in the middle of the shattered glass, blood dripping from her hand.

No, she couldn't do this. She couldn't do it at all.

Cecile's shoes might as well have been filled with lumps of iron for how heavy they were and how her legs burned as she climbed the three stories' worth of creaky, uneven stairs. A sandwich and her mattress called to her.

What a long day. And a fruitless one. No full-time employment. The depression held the country in its grip. Not a single company wanted to hire a woman with no job experience. Not even the cotton company where Nathaniel had found a job after they lost their automobile business. The factory was where he was working when he was injured and got a blood infection, the one that killed him.

She shook away the thoughts before she burst into tears. Right now, she had more pressing problems.

After pausing on the landing for a moment to catch her breath and wipe the sweat from the back of her neck, she turned to the right, to Mrs. Ward's apartment. The elderly woman had agreed to watch Millie for a few hours. If they had both survived the encounter, it would be a miracle.

All was silent. Mrs. Ward must have gotten Millie to take a nap. Cecile would have to ask what her secret was. She knocked at the door.

Mrs. Ward ushered Cecile inside, the bun in her gray hair so tight it kept her wrinkled skin from sagging. "Did you have any success, my dear?"

Cecile shook her head. "All I want now is to snuggle with Millie, although, with this nap she's having, she's not going to want to sleep tonight. You're amazing. She won't lay down for me."

"Have a seat. I'll pour you some tea."

"That's very sweet of you, but I would just like to go home. I'm exhausted."

"Have a seat." Mrs. Ward hardened her gray eyes the same way Momma used to when she was upset with Cecile.

She thumped into the well-worn chair, and Mrs. Ward settled beside her.

"I've seen how hard it's been on you, darlin', since your husband died. Bless your heart, Millie is a handful, and you need more work to support yourself."

"We're managing." They were for now, but how much longer could she go on this way?

"Remember I mentioned the Tennessee Children's Home Society a few days ago?"

"Yes." What was this about?

"It was for the best, dear."

"What was?" Her middle cramped. Where was Millie?

"I couldn't bear to see you struggling. And with you having to work, the child needs to be cared for."

"I'll figure it out." She swallowed hard.

"I called Miss Tann."

Cecile jumped from her seat, her heart doing the Charleston in her chest. "You did what?"

"She'll take care of Millie. Find her a good family, one who can give her the things you can't."

A buzz filled Cecile's head, drowning out the rest of what Mrs. Ward said. "Millie is . . ."

"With Georgia Tann. She does such wonderful work for children."

Cecile again lost track of Mrs. Ward's words. *Millie gone? That couldn't be.* She was Cecile's daughter not Mrs. Ward's. "You had no right. How could you give away my child?"

Now the old lady had the decency to study her short fingernails. "Well, I . . . It was quite easy. And Miss Tann told me it was fine. That we had to do what was in Millie's best interest."

Cecile's chest was about to explode. "Her best interest? What about being with her mother? A mother who loves her more than the sun and the moon? What did you do, forge my signature?"

Mrs. Ward picked at a hangnail.

Cecile grabbed Mrs. Ward by the shoulders and almost shook the stuffing from her. "My baby! My baby! Where is she? I have to get her back."

"I don't know." Mrs. Ward leaned back in her chair.

Cecile released her grip. "How could you? That woman kidnapped my baby."

"Don't get yourself in a fuss. Think of Millie. She's the most important person in this horrible mess."

"She's mine. No one else can have her."

"You're hysterical. Let me get you a drink of water."

"Water isn't going to solve my problems. I need my daughter back. Millie! Millie!" She ran from the apartment, down the stairs, and to the street.

"Millie! Millie!"

No sweet chatter. No big hugs. No snuggles in the night. Nothing.

Cecile fell to her knees in the middle of the walk. "Millie, oh Millie!" She sobbed for a long while. When she'd exhausted her store of tears, she wiped her eyes and raised her focus to the heavens. "I promise, Millicent Mae, I swear to you, I will find you and get you back. I will never give up on you."

She had to act. Fast. Before Miss Tann snatched Millie away forever.

CHAPTER TWO

Little Millie Dowd's screeches made those of a banshee appear tame, and she kicked the seat in front of her as the black Cadillac rolled down the street and out of the slums of Memphis. Percy Vance resisted the urge to cover his ears to drown out the little girl's cries. Instead, he squirmed in his tufted seat and stared out the window.

Why Miss Tann insisted on bringing him today as they removed this child from her unsuitable home, he had no idea, but the child's tantrum unsettled him. He turned away from the scene out the window.

Miss Tann grabbed the child by the upper arm and gave her a glare that could freeze the Amazon River. "That is enough. I will tolerate no more noise. Not a peep."

The brim of the child's pink bonnet hid her face. Just as well. Percy hated the images of the children they'd snatched away from their parents. Images that taunted him.

19

Today, he'd stayed in the automobile with James, the driver.

"Poor mite. The house she came from was awful. The neighbor let me into the apartment. Peeling wallpaper, uneven furniture, warped and worn wood floors." Miss Tann continued, but he didn't listen.

He shuddered and blocked the images that fought to work themselves to the front of his mind. He'd left all that behind, and he'd never return there. "She's a feisty one."

"This is why we remove children from homes such as hers. That mother was so neglectful, the living conditions not fit for a rat. I'll reform the girl and give her a better life. Though with her brown hair and green eyes, it won't be easy."

Percy furrowed his brow. "What does her appearance have to do with anything?"

"Her coloring will hinder us in finding an adoptive home. Everyone wants a blond-haired, blue-eyed child."

"Oh." Because that was the ideal, the standard for beauty in America. He sighed and shifted in his seat.

"We'll do what we can with her." Miss Tann adjusted her round, wireless glasses and stared out the window at the brick buildings rising to the sky, meeting electric wires running overhead.

"The world needs more women like you, Miss Tann." More women who rescued children from despicable places in the world and gave them loving homes. A savior like the one he had needed. Acid ate at his stomach, and he fidgeted in his seat much like the little tyke. "What if the mother loved the child though?"

"Love isn't everything, Mr. Vance. Love doesn't give a child money, comfort, or ease in life."

Maybe not, but love did matter, didn't it? Then again, how would he know?

Miss Tann didn't turn from peering out the window. "And those weren't the worst conditions in which I've found children. It's disgraceful how the poor and wretched treat their offspring."

"Yes, I do agree."

"It's the job of the Tennessee Children's Home Society to provide for the welfare of all children, to give every child the opportunity to know a home of love and of means."

"I concur."

"Good." Now she did turn to him and spoke over Millie's head. "That's why I hired you as my legal assistant. With your background, you understand our mission."

"My background?" He'd told her nothing

21

of it. Instead, he'd skirted his history until the time he won a full scholarship to Vanderbilt Law School. How had she found out?

"I know all, Mr. Vance."

He clenched his hands but gave her a polite smile. Or his best attempt at it.

"I hope you will prove yourself worthy of my trust in you."

"Of course I will."

"That's good. Very good."

He'd do what it took to prove that her faith in him was warranted. "So what happens with Millie now?"

"She'll be placed with a much more suitable family, one who can provide for her every need."

"And if she can't be placed?"

"Don't worry, Mr. Vance, I will find her a placement."

What noble people who took in such children. "That's wonderful. I'm glad to be able to help."

She reached across Millie, who now rocked against the back of the seat, and patted Percy's hand, her fingers like ice. "I'm happy to have you. We train up children in the way they should go."

The Bible reference warmed him through, and he thanked the Lord for bringing him to this place where he could do good for society's most vulnerable.

They rolled into the heart of Memphis, down Madison Street, tall brick and stone buildings rising like canyon walls on either side of them. Cars' horns honked, and the trolley's bell clanged.

The chauffeur pulled in front of a seven-story stone building with arched doorways overseen by lions' heads and pairs of columns supporting the second and third stories. The Goodwyn Institute, as this building was known, housed not only the office of the Tennessee Children's Home Society and other businesses but also a library and an auditorium.

"Here we are, Mr. Vance. If you could leave those contracts we discussed earlier, I will see to them tomorrow."

"You don't want me to come with you to drop off Millie?"

"I can manage quite well."

"But she's so fiery." Despite her size, Miss Tann wouldn't be able to carry and control the child.

"Nothing a little discipline won't rectify."

Percy stiffened. Just how was Miss Tann going to discipline her?

"I can come and get her settled."

"James is quite capable. He's been assisting me for years, long before you ever came along."

"But —"

Miss Tann turned to him. "That will be all, Mr. Vance. You may exit the car."

"Ma'am?"

"We can handle her from here."

"I'm happy to help."

"I said that will be all." Her nostrils flared.

He stepped out of the automobile and onto the sidewalk, waves of heat rising from the concrete. But as he stood there, the car pulling away from the curb and into the flow of traffic, little Millie turned and knelt on the car seat, looking out the back window after him, her face shadowed by the pink bonnet.

By the time Cecile had arrived at the offices of the Tennessee Children's Home Society last night, the building was dark. Everyone had left for the day, so she'd trudged home without her daughter. Sleep had proved elusive, but she wouldn't spend another restless night. Today she would get Millie back. She would locate her and bring her home.

Cecile spun in a circle as she surveyed her small apartment. There in the corner, on the big bed where Nathaniel had died, lay

24

Millie's well-loved pink quilt. One drawer of the battered bureau, now empty of her husband's clothes, was filled with Millie's dresses. Lace-trimmed socks and frilly underwear occupied another drawer. Neither Miss Tann nor Mrs. Ward had packed any of Millie's belongings.

The only item Millie took with her besides the clothes on her back was her pink bonnet, the one Cecile had bought when she'd found out she was pregnant and hoped that she would have a little girl. She opened another of the bureau's drawers and retrieved a length of pink satin ribbon. Along with a few flowers, she'd used the material to embellish the plain bonnet. She looped the ribbon around her wrist and knotted it. It was the one item tying her to her daughter, their one connection.

In the kitchen, a stack of secondhand books stood on the scarred table, waiting for Cecile to read them to her daughter. Beside that sat a pile of paper and a handful of crayons. When she got home, Millie would color beautiful pictures, and they would decorate the rooms with her artwork.

First Nathaniel was gone then Millie. Without them, there was no joy. Oh, when she saw her daughter, she would cry. That was a given. She would try not to, but she would. Maybe they both would. They could stop on the way home for ice cream. What a treat that would be. A smile broke out on Cecile's lips as a picture came to mind of Millie with chocolate all over her face. She wouldn't even scold her daughter for not eating neater. Today was special. Today Millie would have free rein.

Cecile dressed in her best brown wool suit, the one she'd worn the day she buried Nathaniel. Using a hot iron she'd heated on the stove, Cecile crimped her bobbed hair. She had to make her best impression on Miss Tann, show her she had the means to provide for Millie. That she was a good, loving, kind mother.

She had but one tube of lipstick, the one she'd used on her wedding day. She saved it only for very special occasions. She didn't even wear it to church on Sundays. But today deserved lipstick. She ran it over her lips and blotted. Perfect.

A colony of butterflies had taken up residence in her stomach. Why did her hands shake? She had nothing to be nervous about. This was her own flesh and blood, her dearly loved child. She wouldn't come home without her.

She pulled up her stockings and slipped her feet into her spectator pumps. Once she had settled a tan cloche hat on her head and picked up her box bag pocketbook, she left the apartment. When she returned, Millie would be with her.

She kept herself from skipping all the way to Miss Tann's office in the Goodwyn Institute on Madison Avenue, the many buildings of the city's downtown looming above her. By the time she stood in front of the white stone office building, she was winded and warm. She willed her breathing and heart rate to return to normal. An impossible feat. Instead, she drew herself up to her full height, entered the building, and rode the elevator to the fifth floor. There was the office, the gold stenciling on the door's frosted window proclaiming this to be the Tennessee Children's Home Society.

She entered the small office and approached the brown-haired receptionist. "I'm here to see Miss Tann. I'm Mrs. Dowd to pick up my daughter, Millie."

"I'll let her know you're here." The slip of a girl disappeared, and a few moments later, Georgia Tann limped through the door.

"Mrs. Dowd, please, step into my office."

Cecile followed the imposing rather manly woman into a modest office dominated by a large, dark wood desk. Photographs of smil-

27

ing infants and children covered the wall, and a window overlooked the busy street.

"You are here about your daughter?"

"That's correct." Cecile fiddled with the ribbon at her wrist.

Miss Tann settled herself in a straight wood chair behind the desk. She rubbed her whiskered chin. "Do you have a job, Mrs. Dowd?"

Cecile crossed her arms so Miss Tann wouldn't see her hands tremble. She inhaled, long and deep, to steady her voice. "A part-time one at a nursery school. I haven't been able to secure full-time employment, but I'm searching hard. I have enough money to last me until the new year."

"And your husband has passed away." Miss Tann spoke without any warmth in her voice.

"More than a year ago, yes. And all this time, I've been providing for our daughter. Nathaniel left me with some savings, so we haven't been destitute. We haven't gone hungry. We have a place to live."

"Do you have any family in the city?"

"No."

"And I saw your apartment yesterday."

Mrs. Ward had let the woman into her home without her permission?

"It is not a fit place for a child."

"It's not Buckingham Palace, but we have lived there for three years, since right after Millie's birth. I keep a clean house."

"But not a safe one. Mrs. Ward told me about the broken glass."

Of course she had. And here she had trusted the woman. "Accidents happen. Millie wasn't seriously injured."

"But you aren't able to provide the oversight such a strong-willed child needs."

"My daughter and I love each other. Please, I need her, and she needs me." *Oh please, God, please give me Millie.* "She's all I have of my husband. She's a piece of me, my heart, my soul, my everything."

"I'm sorry, Mrs. Dowd. We at the Tennessee Children's Home Society don't feel you are a fit parent."

"What?"

"Besides, you signed her over to us."

"I did no such thing." Cecile's head rang.

"You relinquished your rights." Miss Tann folded her square hands.

"Show those papers to me. Show them to me now."

Miss Tann turned to a large gray metal filing cabinet on her right and withdrew a folder from it that she slid across the desk to Cecile. "See for yourself."

29

Typed across the top of the page were the words *Relinquishment of Child.*

Miss Tann turned the pages until she came to the last one. There, at the bottom, was Cecile's name. "That isn't my signature."

"It appears to be." Miss Tann pointed to the scribble across the paper.

"No." She twisted her wedding ring. "Mrs. Ward must have forged my signature."

"You signed them. Everything is legal."

This wasn't happening. Couldn't be. She clutched the piece of ribbon. If only she could hold Millie. Where was she?

Miss Tann collected the papers. "Your daughter will be adopted by a fine family with the means to support her well."

It was almost as if she heard Miss Tann's words from underwater. "Adopted?" Cecile gripped the ribbon tighter until it cut off the blood supply to her fingers.

"Your daughter will have a much better life than you could ever give her."

"She should have the life I can give her."

Miss Tann cracked her knuckles. "That's not possible."

Cecile's voice rose in pitch, and she raised herself from the chair. "You kidnapped her."

"I would thank you to speak in a civilized tone, or I will have you removed from this office."

Cecile didn't sit, but she spoke in a low growl. "You will not get away with stealing my daughter. I will get her back."

As cool as if she were having iced tea on the front porch, Miss Tann eyed Cecile. "That is quite impossible."

CHAPTER THREE

As Percy reached to open the Tennessee Children's Home Society's office door, it flew open, and a thin young woman rushed out past him. In her wake, the scent of roses filled his senses.

"Excuse me, ma'am?"

She came to a dead stop.

He approached her. "Can I help you?"

Her shoulders shook.

"You seem upset." He played with the change in his pocket. What should he do?

She whirled around. Red rimmed her eyes. "Can you help me get my daughter back?"

He stepped away. "Pardon me?"

"That woman." She pointed toward the office. "She kidnapped my child."

"Miss Tann isn't in the habit of kidnapping children. She has their best interest at heart."

"How do you know?"

"I'm her legal assistant, Mr. Percy Vance."

"Well, Mr. Vance, she conned my neighbor into forging my signature. I wasn't even home when she stole Millie."

"She wouldn't commit such a crime."

Her round face reddened. "Like employer, like employee. I don't need or want your help." She raced down the hall and disappeared into the stairwell.

He shrugged and entered the windowless outer office. The low ceilings closed in on him. Miss Stewart, the perky brunette who sat behind an oak desk clacking away at her typewriter, flashed him a grin and gave him a tiny wave. Nothing but a flirt.

He nodded but schooled his features lest she get the wrong impression. He had no interest in her. "Is Miss Tann available?"

"She's with a client, Mr. Vance. Have a seat. She shouldn't be much longer."

He settled into the buttery-smooth leather couch and picked up the June issue of *Life* magazine from the polished coffee table. The cover pictured a fashionably dressed woman and a list of headlines, including one about a man named Hitler in Germany. He flipped through the pages featuring advertisements for White Star line, Listerine, and Lucky Strike cigarettes.

The black telephone on the desk jingled,

and Miss Stewart answered it. "Yes, Mr. Crump, she's here. Oh. Oh yes, of course, I'll put you through to her right away." The secretary pushed a button on a speaker. "Mr. Crump is on the line for you."

Miss Tann's tinny voice answered. "Thank you. I'll take it."

Of course she would. When Crump had led Memphis as mayor, he'd ruled with an iron fist. Sure, the city was one of the most beautiful in the country, thanks to him, but at what cost? Even though he'd left for national office a few years ago, he still held considerable political sway here. No one crossed Crump or his cronies. Not even Miss Tann.

Miss Tann's client exited. Percy flipped through a *National Geographic* magazine and even a copy of *Good Housekeeping* with a print of a young boy and girl picking flowers on the front. That was the kind of life Miss Tann was giving these poor unfortunates. A good, happy one. Once he'd paged through a few more magazines, he drummed his fingers on the coffee table. He had other business to take care of. Miss Tann wasn't his only client.

At long last, her door opened, and she waved him into her office. She shut the door behind him and took her spot at her desk, seeming to dwarf the large piece of furniture even though she wasn't that heavy. "Do you have those court papers?"

"Yes, right here." He attempted to focus on what Miss Tann was saying to him, but the weeping woman haunted him. "I'm sorry. I passed a woman in the hall who claimed you stole her daughter. Why would she make such an accusation?"

Miss Tann tsked. "So awful. She's an unfit mother, and I had to tell her so in no uncertain terms. She claims she didn't give consent to her daughter's adoption, but she did."

"How awful for her."

"No, Mr. Vance, not awful for her but for her daughter. Imagine growing up in those circumstances." She cast a soft glance at him. "Like you did. Now the child has a chance at a better life."

He reviewed the weeping woman's face in his mind's eye, and a familiarity about her struck him. "I think I know her."

"Perhaps her daughter. She was that wild child we took custody of yesterday."

He couldn't keep his mouth from falling open. "And she's been adopted already?"

"Not quite. But soon. No need to tell Cecile Dowd that. It's a foregone conclusion."

"She claims her neighbor forged her signature."

"Of course not. She didn't comprehend. You know, the poor don't have much education or a whole lot of understanding. You can explain things to them over and over, and these cows just don't get it into their heads. They're nothing more than breeders."

They discussed several documents, and she gave him instructions on what to do. Even still, his mind wandered to the woman in the hall. Dowd was the name, wasn't it?

"Mr. Vance, have you heard a single word I've said?"

He startled and dropped a handful of papers on the floor. "Oh, I'm sorry. My mind wandered." He bent to gather them.

Miss Tann glared at him. "Well, corral it and get down to business."

Mrs. Dowd had dressed neatly though simply. She carried herself with a certain grace, her neck elongated, her chin high, her steps soft.

Yes, his parents had been uneducated, but that wasn't the case with everyone who had financial constraints. Especially since the stock market crash. Men went from living in penthouses on Fifth Avenue in New York to riding the rails to find work and food.

"Just one question."

"What?" Miss Tann huffed the word.

"Yesterday, how did you know without speaking to her that she's an unfit mother?"

"Why do you take such an interest in that case? I've brought you on other home visits. You've been with me when I've removed other children."

He didn't have a ready answer. Something about this situation haunted him. "I'm not sure. Maybe the pepper the child possessed. Maybe the way she cried for her mother. Maybe running into the woman in the hall. Whatever the case, it made an impression on me."

"Forget about her. In a little while, she'll breed other children. That's what her kind do."

"Don't you give the parents some time to change their circumstances? Especially during this depression? There have to be thousands of people in this city alone who have fallen on hard times through no fault of their own."

"And the children should suffer because of it?" Miss Tann rose from her chair and leaned across the desk. "Who are you to question how I run my agency? You're nothing but a small-time lawyer, struggling to make his way in the world, aren't you?"

He nodded, his Adam's apple caught in his throat.

"But you want to be more, don't you?"

Again he nodded.

"Then I suggest that unless you want to return from whence you came, you keep your nose out of my business. I know what I'm doing. I don't need your questions."

Percy clutched the desk's edge, his palms damp. "Just one more. Where is the child now?"

Miss Tann fisted her hand and thumped the desk, her bobbed hair jerking with the motion. "How dare you ask? That is none of your business." She was all but roaring. Then she relaxed her shoulders and softened her voice. "Why are you persisting?"

He couldn't say.

"Then drop it. For good. Now, let's get back to the matters at hand."

They concluded their meeting, and Miss Tann showed him from her office, tight-lipped, without a farewell. When he went by Miss Stewart's desk on his way out, he couldn't force himself to return her sugary smile.

Miss Tann's reaction to his questions had been much too forceful. Something was rotten in Denmark.

■ ■ ■ ■

Shouts of fun and peals of laughter echoed through the lush, fenced-in nursery-school yard as Cecile stood on playground duty watching the ten or so three- and four-year-olds romp on the grass. Some swung high into the blue sky on squeaky swings while others teetered on the seesaw or whirled on the red and silver merry-go-round.

Blond, curly-headed little Faith Thomas ran to Cecile, tears streaming down her cheeks and blood streaming down her leg. "Mrs. Dowd, I fell."

"Oh dear. Let's go inside and get you cleaned up. We'll make it all better." Cecile signaled to Mrs. Quinn to keep an eye on the rest of the children. Cecile scooped up the petite four-year-old and wiped her eyes as she carried her inside. Small round tables cluttered the space, and pieces of childish artwork adorned the bright blue walls.

The girl trembled in her arms. Was someone watching out for Millie this way? Did that someone wipe her tears when she hurt herself or when she was scared? Though it was only two days since she had been kidnapped, she was sure to be terrified.

Overhead, a crack of thunder sounded.

Millie hated storms. Was she frightened now?

As the rain came down, the children poured in from outside. Cecile took Faith to the washroom. "No more reason for tears. We'll clean this out, apply some iodine, and get some gauze."

"No! No! I don't want iodine. That stings." Faith let loose a series of wails.

So much like Millie. Cecile blinked away her own tears. "Shh, it isn't so bad. The sting is good. That means the yucky stuff is going away, and your boo-boo will soon be better."

Faith's cries quieted to hiccups. "Are you sure?"

"I promise. You may hold my hand while I patch you up, and if you are a good girl, I will bring you a Valomilk Candy Cup tomorrow." The treat would eat into Cecile's savings, but she couldn't resist. It's what she would do for Millie. What she prayed someone was doing for her.

"I'll be brave."

"That's wonderful."

As she cleaned out the wound, Faith clung to Cecile's hand. Only a small squeak escaped her tight-pressed lips when Cecile swabbed the iodine. Soon the scrape was cared for, a smile was restored to Faith's face, and the child returned to her class.

If only this crushing ache would lift from Cecile's chest. Did anyone kiss away Millie's tears? Did anyone tuck her in at night?

The rest of the day passed in a flurry of helping little fingers with art projects, wiping runny noses, and mediating scuffles. At last the day ended, parents claimed their children, and Cecile set the room back to rights, ready for tomorrow. She grabbed her brown box bag purse from the hook by the door and made her way into the fading sunshine.

A tall, lean man with wavy raven hair stood across the street in the drizzle, holding the newspaper to his eyes. Strange that he would stand on the walk and not move one way or the other. There wasn't a bus stop in the vicinity. And something about the way he carried himself, his back a little rounded, was familiar. She'd seen him before. No doubt about it. But where?

He peeked above the top of the paper, and she caught sight of his oval face and his memorable deep-blue eyes. With a gasp, she scurried away, her heart moving faster than her feet. He was the man from Miss Tann's office. That lawyer. What was he doing here?

After a half block, she glanced over her shoulder. The man had followed her. She

41

swallowed hard. What should she do? Return to the school? No one was there anymore. Head home? She didn't want him to know where she lived. Why would he tail her? Did this have something to do with Millie?

She continued in the same direction for another block. This time when she turned around, he had disappeared. She released a breath she hadn't known she'd been holding. Silly of her. Here she was, a grown woman, spooked by a man strolling down the street. He hadn't been following her. Just a coincidence.

By the time she hiked the mile or so back to her apartment, every muscle in her body ached, and sweat trickled down her sternum. How had she cared for Millie after school when she often didn't have the energy to open a box of crackers for her own dinner?

She entered the dark, close, hot apartment. Much too oppressive to start a fire to heat soup. She didn't have an appetite anyway. She shuffled to the bedroom to dig out her blue-striped housecoat. On the shelf above the secondhand dresser sat Mrs. Cuddles, the porcelain doll that Papa had given Cecile for Christmas when she was ten years old.

Oh Papa. Did he ever think about her? Wonder if he had grandchildren? What could she do to get him to open a letter? If only she had the money to travel to see him, perhaps . . .

No use dwelling on the past. Today had enough troubles.

She stood on her tiptoes, slid the doll from her perch, and cradled it. Though Millie was too young for such a fragile toy, perhaps Cecile would give it to her. They could leave her on the shelf and talk to her. Cecile would help her daughter sew a couple of outfits, and together they could dress Mrs. Cuddles.

Like she would have carried Millie, Cecile brought the doll to the main room and sat with it on the hard, uneven kitchen chair. She stroked the doll's real brown hair and tied the laces on one of the high-top black shoes. For the longest time, she sat and dreamed about having Millie home, running around the apartment together, laughing until their sides ached, getting into mischief. Cecile must have dozed because she woke with a start and jerked to a sitting position.

Mrs. Cuddles fell from her lap to the floor. And shattered into a thousand pieces.

CHAPTER FOUR

Percy yawned. He hadn't slept well the past two nights, remembering how he'd cased Mrs. Dowd and followed her at Miss Tann's directive. He might as well be at the fishmonger for how this case stank.

By the time he came to the end of today's business with Miss Tann, Percy's head pounded and his jaw ached from clenching it for so long. This time though, he had managed to keep the conversation to the matters at hand. He closed his attaché case with a click.

Percy nodded at Miss Tann's final instructions and gathered his papers. "I have work to tend to at my office. I'll stop by tomorrow with those contracts you wanted." He headed for the door.

"Thank you. And Mr. Vance?"

He stopped and faced her. "Yes?"

"If you value your employment here, put the incident with Mrs. Dowd from your mind. Such situations are part of the job."

This time he strode from the room, closing the door behind him a little too hard. He had to get out of this office, this building, before he exploded. He sprinted down the stairs and burst onto the street, the warm midday sunshine bathing him. And doing nothing to cool him down.

A familiar figure, slight, crimped brown hair, a graceful air, stood on the walk in front of the Goodwyn Institute, staring at the building. Mrs. Dowd. As if his thoughts conjured her.

He stepped closer. A wash of tears cascaded down her cheeks. The poor woman. Though Miss Tann called her stupid, he hadn't gathered that about her in their short encounter. Could her claims be true? How tragic. First husbandless and now childless.

She turned and staggered away, her light brown cloche hat with buttons on the side bobbing as she walked. An invisible force drove him forward.

When the clanging trolley stopped on the corner of Madison and Fifth Streets, she climbed on board, deposited her coins into the farebox, and settled onto one of the wooden benches.

Percy sprinted to catch the trolley at the next stop. As Mrs. Dowd gazed out the window at the towering brick buildings lining the street, he boarded and sat behind her. When the tram arrived at the entrance to the Overton Park Zoo, she disembarked. Percy followed.

Mrs. Dowd bypassed the neat flower beds bursting with red and white blooms that lined the manicured lawns, continued down the sidewalks leading to a white-columned pavilion and beyond it, to a pagoda, American flags on top flapping in the breeze. She didn't stop until she reached the playground. There, she fell to a weathered wooden bench and covered her face, her shoulders heaving.

He reached her and then stood shifting his weight from one foot to the other. Should he intrude on her grief? Surely his coming might make the situation worse. He sat beside her and allowed her to cry for a time. When she straightened, he pulled his handkerchief from his pocket and offered it to her.

"Thank you." She wiped her nose and her eyes. "I'm much obliged." She turned to him.

The moment she recognized him was unmistakable. Her mouth dropped open, and her eyes, as green as the trees' tender leaves, widened. "You. What are you doing here?" She clutched her pocketbook in a death grip, her knuckles white.

"I'm sorry. I followed you from Miss Tann's office. I had to see for myself that you were all right."

She scooted toward the edge of the bench. "Why? Did you think I would throw myself into the Mississippi River?"

"No." Had she been thinking about it? "But I was concerned."

She stiffened her spine until her back was as rigid as his pa's rules. "No need. I'll be fine." Even so, her chin quivered.

"Please, let me help."

"Why? I don't have any more children Miss Tann can steal."

"She's not in the practice of doing so."

"That's where you're wrong." She studied him for a long moment. Her nostrils flared. "You're affiliated with her, aren't you? Her lawyer?"

"Legal assistant." Maybe one day her lawyer. Maybe one day lawyer to many of the rich and powerful of Memphis.

"Legal assistant?" At her shouts, several of the parents and children on the playground stopped and stared at them.

"Yes."

"Why do you question my accusations, then? You know they're true."

"Because Miss Tann said you willingly signed the surrender papers."

"I didn't. I never signed anything. My neighbor did. I didn't even see the papers until I went to Miss Tann's office the day afterward."

"You can read, then?" Even though he suspected she could, Miss Tann insinuated she couldn't.

She stared at him, redness flooding her face. "Do you believe me to be illiterate? Or stupid? Too dumb to raise my own child?"

"Miss Tann believes so."

"Of course she does. She has to have an excuse for stealing my daughter from under my nose. I'll prove to you I can read. Hand me whatever papers you have in your brief-case. I'll read each and every one. And tell you what they mean. I finished high school. In fact, I graduated at the top of my class."

"There's no need."

"No. I want you to know I'm not bluffing. Hand them to me."

"They are confidential." No wonder her daughter was a handful. This woman was a spitfire herself. "I believe you. But where were you that day? Why was your daughter with a neighbor?"

She gazed at the treetops and then at the ground. Deflated just a bit. "I was out run-

48

ning errands. There are places you can't take a child. Why did you come after me?"

"Because I didn't go inside with Miss Tann, I needed to know what went on in your home the day we took custody of Millie."

"You were there?"

He gulped and nodded.

"But you did nothing to stop Miss Tann?"

"She told me your house was a mess. An unfit place to raise a child. That you were uneducated and unqualified to be a mother. And that you had willingly signed the papers." In other words, Tann had lied to him. How many more lies had she told?

Dowd grabbed him by the upper arm so hard there were sure to be bruises. "Did Millie cry? Was she frightened? Did anyone comfort her?"

"Yes, she screamed and wailed like no child I've ever heard before."

"But neither of you sought to soothe her?"

"Miss Tann said she would teach the child manners."

"That's my job. She's stepping in where only I belong."

He rubbed the back of his neck. All around, mothers and their happy children surrounded them. Most of the clothing was faded and worn. But the children's smiling faces and the mothers' doting attention told of happy homes.

"I'd like to help if I can."

"I don't need the help of someone associated with that woman. Leave me in peace and return to your boss."

"She's not my boss but my client."

Mrs. Dowd eyed him up and down. "From all appearances, she's your boss." The words stung mostly because they were true. Georgia Tann held the strings, and Percy danced to whatever tune she played.

As the filtered sunlight danced overhead, Cecile gazed into Mr. Vance's dark blue eyes. They shimmered. Was that with hurt? Had her words found their mark? She sighed. "Please, forgive my rudeness."

With a wave of his graceful hand and long fingers, he dismissed her. "No need. I understand how difficult it is for you to trust me. After all, I do work for Miss Tann and Judge Kelley."

"Judge Kelley?"

He squirmed. "Never mind."

Was he keeping something from her? Had he just dropped a clue? She sat forward on the seat. "You have to believe me. I didn't voluntarily sign away my rights to my daughter. I didn't. She's my life. My everything. All I have left of my husband. My only family."

He leaned backward. "Your only family?"

She nodded and dabbed at a fresh round of tears with his handkerchief. Why had she blurted that? All it did was make her easy prey for him and his ilk. "I'd rather not talk about it."

"Understandable." His voice was soft, almost compassionate.

"The question remains. Do you believe Miss Tann and the Tennessee Children's Home Society kidnapped my daughter?"

"Let me ask you this. Are you prepared to take care of your child? Do you have the means to sustain the two of you for the long term?"

She bit back the words that beckoned to be let loose from her tongue. He had to ask. Had to make sure Millie would be safe with her. That's what a good, responsible social worker and lawyer would do. "Yes. I have employment." No need in letting him know how tenuous her circumstances were. "Times are difficult, but I'm doing the best I can. Millie never went to bed hungry.

"The best part of my job is that I'm able to be with Millie all day. You saw me when I came out of the nursery school." She'd almost forgotten about that. "Why were you spying on me?"

He chuckled. "I wasn't spying. Miss Tann sent me there to watch the students and parents, to be on the lookout for any signs of neglect or abuse among the children."

"That's spying. Does Miss Tann steal other children? Is that how she cases them out and decides who to kidnap?"

He frowned. "Of course not."

"Funny that Miss Tann would tell you to go incognito — see, I do know big words, Mr. Vance — and not have you ask the staff directly. Suspicious, if you ask me."

He shrugged a few times. "I have questions, reservations, many of them, about Miss Tann and her operation. But it's not easy to extricate myself from her network."

"Because she pays you handsomely."

He winced. Another arrow had found its mark. "Because of who her boss is."

"And just who might that be?"

"E. H. Crump."

At the mention of the smarmy politician's name, her skin prickled. "You think he's backing her?"

"I don't think it. I know it. And I know things about Miss Tann and the Tennessee Children's Home Society they don't want me sharing with the world."

If he hadn't had her full attention before,

he did now. "Like what?"

"Nothing I can tell you."

"You can't or you won't?"

"Please, don't push me."

"I believe I see the situation very clearly, Mr. Vance." Cecile stood so she loomed above him. "You enjoy living in Miss Tann and Mr. Crump's back pocket. I can see by the cut of your three-piece suit and the perfect press of your shirt that you like the finer things in life." Heat rushed to her face. "If you dug into what is going on at the home and with those innocent children and families, it would cost you too much. And to you, your luxuries are more important than anything. Or anyone." Her voice rose higher in pitch than she'd intended.

Now he came to his feet and rose above her, clenching his fists at his side. "You, Mrs. Dowd, are out of line. Nothing, and I mean nothing, is more important to me than the welfare of those children. That is what Miss Tann and I and all who work for the Tennessee Children's Home Society have foremost in our minds as we grapple with these issues." He matched the volume of her words.

"Oh, I'll bet it is."

"It is." A vein bulged in his neck.

And she had thought she'd seen pain in

53

his eyes. What a fool she was.

"We ensure that children are being raised in the best environment with parents who can give them anything and everything they need."

"What about love? Isn't that the most important thing of all?"

"Of course. And that's what we give them. Not parents who are too poor or too naive to take care of them."

"Neither wealth nor poverty make a parent. Love. Compassion. Kindness. Those constitute a parent, whether blood or not."

"I couldn't have said it better myself."

A young mother who had been staring at them as they argued pulled her boys from the monkey bars as she kept watch on Percy and Cecile. He sent them a glare, and they hurried off.

Sure, he treated women and children well. "For a moment, you almost had me hoodwinked. I thought maybe you were different than Miss Tann, but I was wrong. You two are just alike. You don't care a whit about the families you tear apart."

She grabbed the back of the bench for support. "You are high and mighty, and you want to stay that way. Until you know what it's like to lose everything in the market crash and then to have your husband and your daughter severed from you, don't talk to me." With that, she whirled on her heel and marched away. Only the rise of heat in her chest kept the tears at bay. Who cared that the people in the park stared at her? Without Millie, nothing mattered.

Near the zoo entrance, she spied a police officer in a blue uniform, a row of buttons down his coat, a star on his chest, and a badge on his billed hat. He would aid her. He had to. With her purse banging against her thigh, she ran to him. "Excuse me, sir. You have to help me. My daughter's been stolen."

The fair officer lifted his light eyebrows. "Just now? Where?"

"No, Miss Georgia Tann from the Tennessee Children's Home Society came to my neighbor the other day when I was out looking for a job and took my daughter. They forged my signature on relinquishment papers. She's already been adopted by another family."

He grabbed her by the upper arm. "Are you feeling well, ma'am? Is there anyone here with you?"

"No. Please, you have to believe me." She couldn't draw a deep breath. "Help me."

"Let me escort you home. You need to lie down."

"What? No, no. I have to find my little girl." She wrenched from the officer's grasp and raced from the park. Down the street, around the corner, in between traffic, she ran and ran until her legs refused to carry her one step farther. She discovered herself at the entrance of the cemetery where Nathaniel was buried, the rusty iron gates swung open. She weaved among the simple stone markers and the wooden crosses. Very little broken sunlight dappled the shaggy grass. She came to Nathaniel's plain gravestone.

Falling to her knees, she wept bitter tears. "Millie. Oh my Millie Mae."

CHAPTER FIVE

The clack of numerous typewriters and the ding of the bells as they reached the edge of the page greeted R. D. Griggs as he wandered into the clerk of court's office, his domain. At one of the desks, the telephone jangled, and the pretty redhead answered with a chipper "Hello."

He could allow himself to relax when the office operated as it should. And that's what he was here to ensure. No need to have Crump's cronies on his back. R.D. sauntered over to his adjustable stool and perched on it in front of the clerk's barred window. From his briefcase, he pulled a recent silver-framed photograph of his wife, Darcy, and their new three-year-old daughter. Pearl. His love, his heart. She didn't have Darcy's blond hair but brown, much like his own.

"How are things?" Jefferson Landers, R.D.'s boss, slapped him on the back, maybe a little harder than necessary, and didn't smile.

He pushed his wire-rimmed glasses up his nose. "Just fine."

Landers leaned in and lowered his voice. "What about that problem from the other day? That upstart lawyer who thought he could go rogue and do things his own way?"

"The one with the lawsuit against Thompson?"

"That's the one."

R.D. shuffled a few papers. "Taken care of." He swallowed. A few phone calls to the right people, and the lawyer had backed off. Thompson, a friend of Boss Crump, wouldn't be bothered. He could encroach on his neighbor's land if he so desired.

"Good, then you've actually done your job." Landers heaved a sigh. "We'd better not have any more trouble with him."

"He'll toe the line from now on. The case he brought was dismissed in a flash, and he was humiliated." R.D. shifted a stack of papers on his desk and avoided eye contact with Landers. As the weight of his boss's stare fell heavy on him, his skin prickled.

"Let's have a chat in my office." Not a request but a demand.

R.D. turned as Landers strode through the maze of clerks and secretaries, desks and wastepaper baskets. Like a meek puppy caught chewing his master's shoes, R.D. followed Landers through the bright, noisy room, the odors of coffee and cigarettes mingling in the air, to his private corner office.

They entered, the sounds and smells from the main room cut off when Landers shut the door. He moved behind his well-polished tiger-maple desk and sat in his gray leather chair.

R.D. stood as straight and stiff as a statue. This might as well be the Spanish inquisition for all the jangling his stomach was doing.

"Take a seat, Griggs. This isn't the army. You don't have to stand at attention."

R.D. settled himself on the edge of the brown club chair, his gaze on the white carpeting with orange and purple fans printed on it. "What is this about?"

Landers cracked his knuckles. "About you."

R.D. flicked his gaze upward. "Me?"

"Not having qualms about your work, are you?"

"Of course not." R.D.'s voice squeaked.

"Because I wouldn't be happy about that. Neither would Crump."

"I know full well." Everyone in this building did.

"What is it, then?"

"Nothing, really." R.D. couldn't meet his boss's eyes.

Landers leaned across the table and settled his voice into a softer, more soothing tone. "You can tell me. I'm not a cold, heartless man."

And that was the truth. No one much enjoyed messing in dirty politics with Crump, but if you wanted any position of power in the city, the county, even the state, you had to play nice with the boss. If you didn't do what he said, he would ruin you in a second.

And Darcy, R.D.'s beautiful debutante wife, wouldn't stand for that. Neither would R.D.'s father-in-law, who had bought him this position and enough money to care for Darcy in the way she'd become accustomed.

"I know that about you, Griggs. I've seen you with your child."

A child he would fight to keep.

"And that's what this pertains to."

"My child?"

"Not yours specifically, but children in particular."

"You're talking in riddles. Come out with it."

Landers drew a folded sheet of pink paper from his suit coat pocket and handed it to R.D. R.D. smoothed it open.

To Whom It May Concern,

On June 13th of this year, as I was searching for a job to support myself and my three-year-old daughter, Miss Georgia Tann from the Tennessee Children's Home Society and Mr. Percy Vance, her legal assistant, paid my elderly neighbor a visit. In short order, they deemed my apartment unsuitable for children and removed Millicent from my custody. Miss Tann forced my neighbor to sign papers she was led to believe were giving permission for Millie to be handed into their temporary care.

June 13th. A few days before Pearl came to them. He perused the rest of the letter where the woman further explained her situation.

I am begging you to help me locate my daughter. Though Miss Tann cites my inability to adequately provide for my child, nothing could be further from the truth.

Please, help me. No lawyer or law

61

enforcement officer has been willing to assist me. If you are a parent, you can understand the agony I've faced since her loss. Please, I beseech you, help me.

Sincerely,
Mrs. Nathaniel Dowd

Like a window ahead of a summer storm, R.D.'s mind slammed shut. Of course, for years there had been rumors about Miss Tann's methods of obtaining the hundreds of children she adopted to various families around the country. And one day, she had shown up unannounced at R.D.'s home with a brown-haired, green-eyed angel and announced she was theirs. In that instant, R.D. and Darcy, who had despaired of ever having children, became parents. And Miss Tann took every opportunity she had, every time they met, whether by accident or on purpose, to remind him of her gift and how easily she could rip it from him.

R.D. inhaled a steadying breath. "This woman is fabricating the story. What a crazy pack of lies."

"There have been others."

"I'm well aware. Parents who can't take care of their children but hate the world to know what terrible mothers they are. Trust me, these children are better off adopted than with a single woman who can't provide for them. The poor wenches, traversing the city's streets at night by themselves, no supervision."

"I just wanted you to know."

"Why, because I have a three-year-old daughter from the Tennessee Children's Home Society? Sir, Miss Tann places hundreds of children a year. Many of them, I suspect, are around the age of three."

"Again, I wanted you to be informed. These women are searching for their children."

"Women like this Mrs. Dowd have no business raising a family. Those kids are better off with Georgia and will be better off in adoptive homes." R.D. tore the letter into tiny shreds and dropped it into the wastebasket beside the desk, his ears ringing. Then he huffed from the room. As soon as he shut the door behind him, he slumped. What if his daughter . . . ?

Absolutely not. She was his and had a better life with him and Darcy. End of story.

Cecile stood on the courthouse steps, peering at the Greek-style, white-columned stone building. Around the perimeter stood numerous statues. This was a place of important people, important happenings.

Justice. Every policeman she'd inquired of, every lawyer she'd spoken to, every letter she'd written had not brought a single spark of hope. No one cared to listen to her. No one cared to help her locate Millie. So today she came to the place where truth and right were supposed to prevail. Her one last chance.

She stepped into the cool interior and to the list of all the building's offices on the board posted on the wall. She scanned them. There was the one she wanted. Armed with the information she needed, she headed to the elevator. The black operator, his curly hair whitened with age, slid the metal bars to the side and ushered her in. "What floor, ma'am?"

"Third."

He shut the cage and pressed the button. As they rode upward, the tiny space closed in on her. She panted. Prickles of sweat broke out on her arms. She couldn't do this. Shouldn't be here. Who did she think she was, going to a powerful judge like Camille Kelley to petition her to open Millie's adoption records? A judge who had refused to take her repeated phone calls day after day.

She twisted the length of ribbon on her wrist.

"Ma'am? Ma'am?" The elevator operator

tapped her on the shoulder. "Is you okay?"

"What? Oh, I'm fine. So sorry."

"We're here. Who's you going to see?"

"Judge Kelley."

"Turn right then, and her office be the first on the left."

"Thank you."

"Good day."

She exited the lift and followed the man's instructions and soon stood in front of the judge's chambers. A simple gold plaque screwed into a large oak door proclaimed she'd found the correct office.

What did people do? Knock or just enter? To be on the safe side, she rapped on the door.

"Come on in."

She did as bid and discovered a young man behind a desk, his light brown mustache twitching. "Can I help you?" The room was small and spartan. File cabinets and stacks of papers and books occupied most of the space.

"I would like to speak to Judge Kelley."

"Do you have an appointment?"

"No. But I won't take up much of her time. I have one small favor to ask, that's all."

"I recognize your voice. You're the woman who calls every day asking for the judge's

65

help with your daughter."

Found out already. She dropped the pretense. "Please, I know I've come unannounced, but if I could just talk to her, just for a little bit, to make her understand, to plead my case."

"For that you have to go to court." The aide, tall and broad-shouldered, came to his feet. He'd probably been a football player at some point in his life. "I must ask you to leave."

"I'm not going anywhere until I speak to the judge."

"I will call security and have you removed from the premises."

"Go ahead. By the time they arrive, I'll have spoken my piece and left."

"Mrs. Dowd."

Good, he remembered her name.

"Be reasonable."

"It's unreasonable for me to be denied access to one of our government officials."

"I'm warning you." The color in his cheeks deepened. He took a step in her direction then another.

Perfect. She skirted by him and barged into the office. Before she shut the door, he was on the phone with the building's guards. She didn't have much time.

Again, the office was spartan. Nothing

here that wasn't utilitarian. A desk with a typewriter and a phone. File cabinets. Shelves that stretched from floor to ceiling and laden with leather-bound books with gold lettering. Amid it all sat the judge whose name Cecile had spied on several papers on Miss Tann's desk. The name Mr. Vance had dropped at the park.

Judge Kelley wore her curly hair short, and a strand of pearls hung around her reddening neck. As she rose, she adjusted her round glasses. "What is the meaning of this?"

"Please, Your Honor, I have to speak to you for just a moment. You see, I'm Mrs. Cecile Dowd. Miss Tann came to my apartment two weeks ago and kidnapped my daughter from me then gave her to another family to adopt. My neighbor forged my signature on the relinquishment papers."

"What does that have to do with me?"

"I believe you may have approved her adoption."

The judge clenched her jaw and bellowed, "How did you find that out?"

Though Mr. Vance was a cad, it would be wrong of her to single him out and get him in trouble. "That's not important. What is vital is that I get my daughter back. For that, I must have her records unsealed."

"Not a chance."

"But, please, no one else will help me."

"And for good reason. You are an unfit mother. That's why you lost your daughter. And that's all I have to say on the matter. Good day, Mrs. Dowd." Judge Kelley turned her back.

Cecile scampered in front of her. "Have some compassion. I love Millie. I have the means to take care of her. Help me." No matter that she'd resorted to begging. Whatever it took to get Millie.

"Good day."

A commotion sounded from the outer office, and two security guards in navy-blue uniforms entered. They each grabbed her by an arm, their grips like clamps.

"You're hurting me. Let me go."

"You are causing a disturbance." They dragged her from the chambers, out of the office, and down the stairs. The entire way, she fought, squirmed, and wiggled like Millie. All in vain.

When they came to the main level, a police officer, the one from the park, waited in the hushed marble lobby. The fight drained from Cecile. She'd lost. Her one last, best chance vaporized.

"Disturbing the peace?" The officer nodded at the guards, his brimmed hat bobbing.

"Yes," Judge Kelley's aide answered from behind Cecile. She hadn't heard him following probably because she was making such a fuss. He proceeded to describe what transpired.

"Very well. Mrs. Dowd, I'm citing you for disturbing the peace." He pulled a notebook from his pocket and wrote the ticket. "You can pay the fine down at city hall." He ripped the paper from his book and handed it to her.

When she saw the amount in black and white, she sucked in her breath. "I can't afford this."

"Probably why you lost custody of your daughter."

She itched to slap the smart-mouthed aide. Instead, she clenched her fists, digging her fingernails into her palms to keep from lashing out at him. The last thing she needed was another fine she couldn't pay. Then again, it mattered very little. She'd run out of options for finding Millie. Except for one.

CHAPTER SIX

Percy stood beside Miss Tann's desk. The woman's face glistened as she sweated in the early summer heat, and he scrunched his nose at the rotten-egg stench emanating from her. Though the sun shone in the clear blue sky today, she kept her blinds drawn, the room dark, close, and foul.

"Just one more paper for you to sign, Miss Tann, and that will conclude our business for the week." And lift a weight off his shoulders. Every time he entered this office, it pressed heavier on him.

With a flourish, she scrawled her name and slid the paper in his direction. He picked it up, thrust it in his briefcase, snapped it shut, and headed for the door.

"Where are you off to in such a hurry?"

He stopped as he grasped the metal doorknob. "I'm not."

"No chitchat today?"

"I do have matters to attend to, other

clients I must complete work for."

"But you're dying to talk to me. I watched you, watched you grinding your teeth and clenching your lips. So spit it out."

He whirled around and strode to her desk, plunking his briefcase on it. "There is a matter that has been bothering me."

"And it has to do with that Dowd woman, doesn't it?"

Was he that transparent or was she that perceptive? "Actually, it does. When she left here that day, I followed her."

"You did, did you?" Tann pushed her chair back and crossed her legs in a less-than-ladylike fashion.

"And I had a conversation with her. An interesting one."

"Do tell."

"The first thing I discovered is that she's far from uneducated. Mrs. Dowd is very intelligent, articulate, and astute." A little too much for his taste. She saw right through him.

"And the second thing?"

"I also learned she loves her daughter a great deal. When we took the girl, Mrs. Dowd was going through a rough patch. Like we all do from time to time. She was out running errands and left Millie with a neighbor for a short time."

71

Tann raised her mud-brown eyebrows. "And that's something a smart woman would do? No. She can't be trusted to handle her own affairs."

"You preyed on her in her weakest moment."

As she came to her feet, color rose from her neck and suffused her face. "I don't care for what you're insinuating."

He worked to keep his breathing steady and even. "My heart goes out to the woman."

"Feelings are for weaklings. In this business, you learn how to be calloused and jaded. Otherwise, the things you're forced to do, like separating children from their mothers, would be too painful. You're too invested in Mrs. Dowd's case. What is it? Do you fancy her?"

Fancy her? No. The stirrings in his heart were nothing more than compassion for his fellow human being, a vulnerable woman with no one to watch out for her or to help her. "You took advantage of her."

"Beware of the accusations you are leveling, Mr. Vance." Her nostrils flared. "They could land you in serious trouble." She rounded the desk as he backed against the wall. "You like your life now, don't you? And you don't want to lose the luxuries you enjoy. Your spacious home. Your Packard automobile. Your tailored suits."

The very same words Mrs. Dowd had used against him. After coming from such humble beginnings, where a chicken on the table on Sunday was an unheard-of feast, his living quarters, his car, his clothes were nice. Very nice.

His father's shouts and his mother's screams rattled in his mind. Hadn't he longed to be delivered from that situation? "All I'm saying is that I believe Mrs. Dowd was a loving mother in a bad position. One who deserved a little time to learn how to provide for herself and her daughter."

Beet-red took on a whole new meaning in comparison to Tann's face. "And now you are a licensed social worker? Thank you for enlightening me on how to do my job. The state of Tennessee believes I'm capable of making these decisions." She jabbed herself in the chest. "Me not you. And what about the child? Isn't that who should be foremost in this situation? Was it fair to make her live without a loving family while her mother may or may not be able to get a full-time job and suitable living arrangements?"

"She should never have been removed from the home in the first place." He almost gasped as the words passed his lips.

"You have no right to question what I do. I control your destiny, Mr. Vance. I made you what you are. I can ruin you. Is that what you want?" She reached for her telephone.

"Who are you calling?"

She twisted her lips into a smug smile and gave an almost imperceptible nod. "Miss Stewart, would you please get the Tennessee Bar on the phone for me?"

Percy stepped closer to Tann and raised his voice. "What are you doing?"

"Thank you. I'll hold."

"Why are you calling the bar?" His tongue went dry.

She covered the mouthpiece. "It has come to my attention that you are engaging in some rather unethical practices, sir."

"Unethical practices?"

"Yes. You take cases that are clearly conflicts of interest, you've been known to accept bribes, and there's the matter of that tryst between you and one of your clients."

"Tryst!" Percy fought to control his words. "You wouldn't dare. You can't substantiate any of it."

"Oh, but I can."

"How?"

She tipped her head.

Oh, by whomever she paid off.

74

She clutched the phone to her large bosom. "Back off, Mr. Vance. Do your job and nothing more, or I will notify the bar. Have nothing more to do with Mrs. Dowd or her daughter."

With a single call, she could ruin him forever. He'd never again practice law in this state or any other. He'd lose everything. He held up his hands. "Fine. You win. I'll drop it. We won't speak of it anymore."

She returned the receiver to its cradle. "Good choice, Mr. Vance."

He left the office a whipped puppy with his tail between his legs.

Had he just sold his soul to the devil?

"Momma, Momma."

Darkness enveloped Cecile. Not a single sliver of light pierced the heavy blackness. But Millie's voice resonated loud and clear. Despite the tightness in her chest, Cecile answered, "I'm here, Millie Mae. Momma is here. I'll never leave you."

"Momma, I can't see you."

She couldn't see Millie, either. Where was she? Cecile screamed, "Here! In front of you!"

"But it's so dark."

"I know. I can't see you. But I'm here. Reach out. I'll find you." *Please, God, let me find her.* The blackness threatened to consume her.

"Where are you?"

Blood pounded in Cecile's ears. She had to locate her child. Had to help her. "Just grab for me. I'll get you."

"You're not here!"

Millie's cries tore a hole in Cecile's heart. "I am, sweetie, I am." Though she gestured high and low, she couldn't touch Millie. Where was she? Dear God, where was she?

"They're hurting me, Momma. Make them stop. Please! Help! Help!"

Cecile awoke with a jerk, sitting straight up in bed. Though a blanket of blackness covered the bedroom, a thin stream of moonlight filtered through the window overlooking the alley. She wiped a band of sweat from her forehead. Beside her rumpled mattress, the little alarm clock ticked away the seconds. Quite a number of them passed before her heart's rhythm slowed to match that of the clock.

She threw aside the bedsheets and padded barefoot through the thin stream of moonlight, across the tiny room to the crib in the corner. Millie had been too big for it when she'd been here, but it had been a godsend when she'd been nursing Nathaniel in his final days, before Millie learned how

76

to climb out.

She picked up Millie's little pillow and held it to her nose. The lingering scent of talcum powder and baby shampoo filled her nostrils. Was there anything sweeter than the smell of a child?

Millie should be here. She should be sleeping in the big bed beside her.

The dream was so strange. Had it meant something? Was Millie trying to tell her that she was in danger? Being harmed?

Cecile flipped on the kitchen light and glanced at the clock on the wall. Four o'clock. She was wide awake. There was no point in going back to sleep. Even if there was, she wouldn't. If she closed her eyes, the nightmares would start again as they had every evening for the past week.

Instead, she brewed herself a cup of strong, black coffee and sat at the little table and sipped it. She fingered the satin ribbon at her wrist, and for a moment, her daughter was nearer. Almost a physical presence. "When, Lord, when are You going to restore her to me? I beg You to give me back my daughter."

The silence of the empty apartment was her answer. All that long, long day, though the laughter of small children circled her like a hug, the dream haunted her. Where

77

was Millie? Her heart crushed. What if someone was hurting her? Her poor, poor baby.

Cecile should have demanded Miss Tann return Millie. Done her bodily harm if necessary. No matter what the consequences. Well, she would remedy that.

Today, because she had come into work early, she left the school by three o'clock. On a normal day, she would take care of her laundry and grocery shopping but not today. No, an invisible force, strong, compelling, unable to be ignored, pulled her to the Tennessee Children's Home Society offices.

This time, she didn't stop to admire the building's impressive facade. She didn't allow the butterflies to infest her stomach. She didn't think at all. Instead, she marched right inside the building, up the stairs so she wouldn't have to speak to the elevator operator, and straight to Miss Tann's office.

When she entered, the much-too-cheery secretary peered up from her paperwork. "Can I help you?"

"I'm here to speak to Miss Tann. About my daughter."

The slender young woman pushed her chair back to stand then hesitated. "Wait a minute. I remember you. Mrs. Dowd, right?"

"Yes."

"I'm sorry, but Miss Tann isn't in the office at the moment."

From beyond the inner door came the slamming of a drawer. "Don't fib. She's here, and I will see her."

"She's with someone now and has a full itinerary for the rest of the day. I can schedule an appointment next week if you'd like."

Cecile stood straighter and aimed her narrow gaze at Miss Stewart. "No, I don't want one next week. I will speak to Miss Tann. Today. Right now, in fact." Her pulse pounded in her neck. Cecile stomped toward the office.

Miss Stewart moved in front of her and blocked the door, arms and legs splayed. "I cannot allow you in there."

"Help me, Momma."

Millie's pleas from the dream propelled Cecile forward. "Out of my way." She growled like a lioness about to spring on her prey.

"I will call security."

Just like at Judge Kelley's office. Fine. Let her ring them. Cecile could speak fast. With a single thrust, she shoved the secretary to the side and burst into the office.

Miss Tann, in a gray tailored shirt, sat

behind her desk. Mr. Vance stood beside her, a sheaf of papers in his hand.

"Get her out of here." Miss Tann pointed a crooked finger at Miss Stewart.

Cecile lengthened her spine and raised her chin. "No need. This won't take long. Tell me where my daughter is. Now. Or I will turn this place upside down to find the file."

Miss Tann honeyed her voice. "Have a seat, Mrs. Dowd. Miss Stewart, please leave us and hold off on that phone call." She returned her attention to Cecile. "Now, what can I do for you?" Like a Dr. Jekyll and Mr. Hyde.

At the change in disposition, Cecile lost a bit of her wind. "My daughter. Millicent Mae Dowd."

Mr. Vance stood by, silent.

"Mrs. Dowd, do you remember the conditions in which we found your living quarters the day we took custody of Millie?"

Yes, all too well. "Those weren't my usual circumstances."

"Do you have a new place of residence?"

She shook her head.

"And what about your job? Will you have the energy to care for such a demanding child after your shift?"

Would she? Even now, her feet throbbed inside her white T-strap shoes.

"If Millie were returned to you, how would you manage to care for her? Children are so energetic. And she is a rambunctious, wild child, into everything, never giving you a moment's peace."

"But she'll learn. Grow up."

Mr. Vance swallowed hard but didn't come to her defense. Not that she expected him to.

"When you had a husband, you weren't able to see to her needs. What makes you think now that you're on your own, you'll be able to do any better?"

Hadn't she been a good mother to Millie? Maybe not. Millie was full of mischief and into everything. Scolding her or spanking her was difficult for Cecile. Especially once she'd lost Nathaniel's guidance. Maybe it would be too much for her. Perhaps Millie was better off without her.

CHAPTER SEVEN

Percy paced between the headstones in Elmwood Cemetery in the dying daylight. Mist and fog cloaked the crooked, chipped, and weather-worn headstones. Moss covered many of them.

In a tree above him, a screech owl screamed. Off in the distance, its mate answered. Despite the cloying humidity, Percy's flesh broke out in goose pimples. The half-dead tree branches stood as skeletons against the pale pink sky. The rancid taste of death lingered on his tongue.

Though he had struggled to put Cecile out of his mind and get some sleep last night, it proved impossible. Her story, her pain, her desperation to find her daughter resonated with him. Drove him to ask her to meet him in this place today. Despite Tann's threats.

Perhaps this wasn't the best choice of sites to meet Cecile. When he'd sent the note, he'd only thought of privacy, somewhere Tann was sure not to see them together. But he could have picked a jazz club on the edge of town.

Instead, here he paced in front of Kit Dalton's grave. Everyone in Memphis knew the famous outlaw's final resting place. The man had ridden with Frank and Jesse James. Five governors had once put a price of $50,000 on his head.

He turned from the marker. He didn't have any assurance Cecile would even show up. Because of his association with the Tennessee Children's Home Society, she had no reason to trust him. That much, she'd made clear. And judging from the glares she shot him yesterday in Tann's office, she hadn't forgotten.

Why was he even here? He must be a dog who liked to be kicked. Probably why he still worked for Tann.

But then an image of Cecile's countenance that day in Overton Park flashed in front of his eyes like a picture show. Her round face, deep-set eyes, and sweet, almost innocent mouth. And the tears streaming down her face, those tears that brought out a side of him he thought extinct after the death of his sister. Or maybe it had been there all along but lay dormant to protect himself

83

from the pain of losing Tenny. Hard enough as it was to lose a sibling, the pain must be magnified a hundred-fold to lose a child. And in such a manner. No wonder Cecile was frantic. He couldn't allow a mother and child to be separated from one another for no good reason.

Through the gloom, there she came, her gray dress blending in with the lead-colored markers, her brown purse swinging by her side, the veil on her black hat pulled over her eyes.

He gulped. Never in his life had he seen such a beautiful woman, one who stirred him deep inside. He shook his head. No, she was his client. Nothing more. If he allowed himself to become involved with her, it would complicate the case. Muddy relationships that should be well defined. And give Tann all the ammunition she required to place that call to the Tennessee Bar.

He waved at her. She frowned. No worry about a relationship between them. She couldn't stand the sight of him. That much was clear.

"Mrs. Dowd. I'm glad you came."

She approached him then stopped short as if afraid to get too close. "Seems a fitting place for you. Did Miss Tann arrange this?"

"No, she doesn't know I'm here. If she

did, I would lose my job and my law license."

"Then why did you ask to meet me?"

"Since your visit to the office yesterday, I've been contemplating you and your plight."

"Oh yes, my plight. Well, Mr. Vance, I'll have you know that I've given up. I have no husband, and when I did have one, I wasn't a very good mother. Besides, I thought you didn't believe me."

"No one said you weren't a good mother."

She gave a half-chuckle. "They didn't? Weren't you in the same room yesterday?"

"You were, are, in a difficult situation."

"And perhaps Mrs. Ward and Miss Tann were correct. Maybe removing Millie from my care was best for her. Might still be best for her."

Why this sudden switch in her thinking? Yesterday, she'd been ready to storm the Bastille for Millie. Today, she'd called off the search. "Please, don't stop seeking her."

"And if I do locate her, how will I raise her? I have very little money, time, or energy to devote to her. Maybe she deserves a better home, one where she can wear lacy dresses, play with a multitude of toys, and attend the best private schools."

"Those are Miss Tann's words."

Tears formed in the corners of her seafoam-green eyes, and she turned her head. "I'm tired, Mr. Vance, and scared. Frightened that I'll never find my daughter and that, if I do, she won't love me anymore."

"You were her world. I saw that the day we took her. She screamed and fought with a strength I didn't know children possess."

She turned to him again, a smile crossing her face, and in it, he caught a certain radiance. One that had his heart tripping over itself. He shook his head. Had to stop this nonsense. "She'll never forget you. Don't forget about her."

"I could never forget her funny laugh, her silken hair, the feel of her soft body in my arms."

"Fight for her with the strength she fought for you." Why did he push the matter? In the long run, it would be better to let the situation alone. His involvement was risky at best.

But Tenny had not given up on him. He couldn't allow Cecile to give up on Millie.

Cecile hugged herself. "She is a handful. You never knew my Nathaniel. He possessed boundless energy, a dreamer always on the move, could never sit still, always had something to do, somewhere to be.

Millie reminds me so much of him. I have to do what he would agree is best for her."

"Would he say that living without you was the right thing to do?"

She shrugged, her mouth working up and down. "How am I supposed to know what that is?"

"Were you managing before?"

"Yes. Barely."

"Do you love her?"

"With all my heart."

"I can help you bring her home."

"And then what? How do I raise her?"

"With all the love you can give her. You, the woman who gave her life."

A cloud passed over her face, snuffing out the light. "You operate under Miss Tann's thumb. If I search for Millie, how do I know you won't block me at every turn?"

"Would I be here if I didn't mean to help you? I wasn't kidding when I said I could lose my livelihood."

She rubbed her forearms. "Then why do you want to help me?"

He couldn't relive that pain. The pain he'd labored so hard to dull, to leave in the past where it belonged, untouched, forgotten, nonexistent. "Let's just say I can't stand to see little ones hurt. Every child deserves happiness."

She parted her lips. "Do you have information that Millie is in danger? That her adoptive parents are cruel?"

"No, no, that's not what I meant. My apologies if I alarmed you. I just meant that . . ." He couldn't explain without touching that very tender place inside. "That Millie deserves to be with the mother who loves her."

She touched his arm, her fingers light against his suit coat. "Thank you." Some of the hard lines around her eyes softened, and her mouth relaxed.

"Does that mean you'll allow me to assist you?"

Even in the dim light, he couldn't mistake the steeliness that returned to her eyes. "I don't know."

"I'm on the inside. I have access to information you won't garner any other way."

"Or you could deceive me. Point me in the wrong direction. Or worse yet, let Miss Tann know I'm searching."

"I don't know what to do to make you trust me, but I can tell you that I'm questioning Tann's tactics at great personal risk."

"And when you decide it's not worth the cost?"

"There are some things, Mrs. Dowd, that are worth any cost."

She bit the corner of her lip for a moment. "I don't have much of a choice, do I?"

"I'm your best hope." Why was he so insistent with her? Just because she was beautiful and vulnerable? Or because it would mean redemption from his inability to come to Tenny's rescue? Whatever the reason, she needed help, and he could provide it.

"Well, I suppose, thank you."

"Don't thank me until we find her."

"If we do."

"I'll try my level best to make that happen."

"I'm still scared."

"Just take it one step at a time."

She straightened her shoulders. "Do you have a plan?"

"I do. I have to get into the records in Miss Tann's office. Have a peek at Millie's file and see what I can glean. That might be enough to at least give us a clue as to her whereabouts. Which orphanage Millie might have been sent to, if she was sent to one. A starting point, if nothing else."

"I'm going with you." She set her mouth in a hard, straight line.

"No, I can't allow you. There's too much risk. All you need is a criminal record for breaking and entering, and you'll never see your daughter again."

She licked her lips and drew in a deep breath. "This is my child we're talking about. Don't you understand? Any risk I have to take to bring Millie home is worth it. She's everything to me. Besides, how do I know you'll really look? You might say you did and then never follow through. Until I can trust you, Mr. Vance, you're going to have to put up with me. And I'm willing to do it, no matter the cost."

"While I like this side of you better than the one that listened to Miss Tann's lies, I still don't want you to come."

"I have to. This is my child. First and foremost, it is my search." Her voice cracked.

"Is there nothing I can say that will dissuade you?"

"Absolutely nothing." She straightened her shoulders. "Like I said, I don't trust you."

He swallowed. "I'll do whatever I can to protect you, but I cannot guarantee your personal safety."

"I know you can't."

The heat and humidity enveloped him, sending a trickle of sweat down the side of his face. "Let's go now, then, while the office is vacant."

■ ■ ■ ■

As Cecile and Mr. Vance left Elmwood Cemetery, a misty fog clung to the graceful elms and abundance of magnolias, shrouding them in a hazy film. Not a breath of wind stirred the branches, not an animal howled in the night.

Underneath her feet, the debris of last year's leaves squished. Her fingertips tingled.

He guided her through the graveyard by pressing on the small of her back. The heat of his hand sent warmth radiating throughout her.

"Are you okay? Sure you want to go through with this? I can do it alone."

No, she'd go, even though her heart sped along in her chest. "I'm fine." But when a branch snapped behind them, she just about jumped as high as the treetops. "What was that?"

"Probably nothing more than a squirrel."

Yes, he was right. No one followed them. No one watched them. The branch snapped again. She grabbed Percy by the arm. "That was more than a squirrel."

"Do you want me to check it out?"

"No." She'd answered too fast. He'd think

her a coward. Then again, he'd leave her alone here if he went to investigate. And that she couldn't have. She slowed her tongue. "No, probably another squirrel."

"Yes."

Did his voice warble? Her imagination had to be getting the better of her. "Let's just get out of here as fast as possible."

He chuckled, rich and deep, so different from Nathaniel's tenor laugh, and patted her hand as she clutched his bicep. "I'm in total agreement."

She released her grasp.

As they approached the entrance, a breeze stirred the fog around their feet. They crossed the bridge and strolled underneath the wrought-iron sign supported by two large pillars.

Cecile puffed out a breath as they exited onto Dudley Street.

"Nervous?"

"Are you?"

He nodded.

"Thanks for the reassurance."

"Anytime."

His attempt at levity didn't manage to melt away any of her tension.

"If you'd like, there is still the chance for you to go home. I'll meet you in the morning and let you know what I discover."

"No. I'm coming." Once she pulled her cloche down on her head, she ambled beside him. A Buick rumbled down the road and passed out of sight, but nothing else stirred on the street. The night deepened. Here and there, a few men who'd had a little too much to drink, despite Prohibition, stumbled onto the street. Mr. Vance drew her to his side. She hadn't been this near a man since Nathaniel died. She breathed in his scent, a musky cologne, and huddled a little closer. And that was nice. A little too nice. She pulled away.

"I'm sorry. I overstepped." His voice was deep.

"No, not at all." But yes.

"It's late, and I don't want anything to happen to you."

"Thank you. I do appreciate that." And she did.

They arrived at the Goodwyn Institute, a place she'd become too familiar with the past few weeks. From across the street, they studied the darkened building. The mist now turned into a light drizzle. A small light bobbed by one of the ground-level windows.

"How do you propose we get in?"

Mr. Vance fiddled with the knot on his tie. "There's a night watchman. That's his flashlight." He pointed at one of the win-

93

dows. "I'll spin a yarn that will allow us access."

"And when we're inside?"

"Do you know how to pick a lock?"

She leaned away from him and raised her eyebrows. "Do I look like the kind of woman who would have such a skill?"

"One thing at a time then." He led her across the street and up to the front door, where he knocked.

After several minutes of rapping on the glass, the guard appeared. "Can I help you?"

Mr. Vance cleared his throat. Cecile wouldn't have been able to speak if she'd wanted to. "I work for Miss Tann and the Tennessee Children's Home Society. They have offices on the fifth floor here."

"I'm well aware of that." The rotund, bulgy-eyed man spotlighted them in his torch. She stepped behind Mr. Vance.

"I left an important file in Miss Tann's office. My girlfriend and I are on our way home from the picture show and stopped by so I could retrieve it."

"I'm sorry, sir, no one is allowed in the building after hours."

Cecile's heart thrummed in her ears so that she had a difficult time making out Mr. Vance's words. "Can't you make an exception this time? I must have that file to study

94

tonight. It's very important."

"I don't care how important it is. You shouldn't have left it."

"You're right, I shouldn't have. I've learned my lesson. That's why if you could just let us in —"

"I said no, and that's what I mean." The watchman moved to close the door.

Cecile couldn't allow this opportunity to slip through their fingers. If Millie hadn't been adopted yet, she soon would be. And once that happened, all hope of finding her would vaporize. She pushed on the door to keep him from shutting it. "Please, sir, it's crucial to my husband's career."

He quirked his gray eyebrows. "Husband, you say?"

"Uh-huh."

He turned to Mr. Vance. "I thought you said she was your girlfriend."

All the stiffness seeped from Cecile's bones, and she leaned against Mr. Vance for support. What had she done?

"Get out of here before I call the police. There's been enough trouble at Miss Tann's office lately." Caused by Cecile.

Mr. Vance leaned in. "We'll go. But please, don't tell Miss Tann we were here."

"It's my job to report any incidents during my shift. You bet she'll find out."

CHAPTER EIGHT

Heat permeated the house even though Gladys Knowles had only just stoked the fire in the stove. It would be a scorcher today, for sure. "Fanny, come get breakfast."

The brown-haired child shuffled her way in from the lean-to Willard had turned into a room, such as it was, for Fanny when they adopted her a few weeks ago.

"I made you oatmeal. Eat up."

The child's permanent frown didn't change. Instead, she stomped her little foot. "No oatmeal. I wanna go home."

Gladys slopped the gruel into the bowl and, with a sigh, returned the pot to the stove. "For the millionth time, this is your home. We're done with this nonsense. I won't abide it no more, Fanny."

"I not Fanny."

"Do you want another whoopin'? Don't let Pa hear you say that."

"He's not Pa."

"One more word from you, and there won't be no breakfast. Now hush your mouth and eat."

With her green eyes wide, Fanny stared at the bowl then at Gladys and back again.

"You'll want to eat it all. We have washing to do today. That's hard work."

Fanny struggled to pull the chair from the table and at last sat. At least she didn't mouth off while she ate. Gladys allowed herself to relax. If Willard caught Fanny saying this weren't her home and that weren't her name, he'd beat her for sure. Gladys couldn't stand no more of that. After all, it wasn't the kid's fault if she was all mixed up. She'd been living on the Memphis streets, fending for herself for a long time. Poor mite, she was so itty bitty for five. She'd probably long ago forgotten her real name. If she'd ever had one.

Gladys cleared the empty bowl and the drained glass of milk. "That's the way to be good. Go put on your overalls on and let's get to work."

Shoulders slumped, Fanny dragged on the way out as much as on the way in. While she dressed, Gladys boiled the water for the washing and shaved soap into the pot. Fanny returned to the room within a few minutes, her pants on backward and the

97

straps not looped over her shoulders.

At the same time, Willard blew through the back door, the screen slapping behind him. He took one look at Fanny and went red in the face. "What's this?" He yanked on her overalls. "Can't you even dress yerself? What good are you?" He raised his hand to strike her.

Before he could land the blow, Gladys grabbed him. "Leave her be. She don't know no better. I'll help her."

"She's supposed to be helping you. I got Quinn in the barn for me, and we got Fanny for you. If she can't dress herself, what use is she? We spent a lot of money for her." He spat a stream of tobacco on the floor. Another chore for Fanny.

"Lemme worry about her. You got enough on your mind with the farm. She's fine and smart as a whip. In no time, she'll get the hang of things. Give her a chance."

"Don't coddle her, Gladys. She ain't here to be a plaything. She's here to work."

"I know. Don't you worry none. You sit and have a cup of coffee, and I'll take care of her. The washing's ready to be done."

He took a seat at the table, calm for the moment. If'n it could only stay that way. She filled his mug with strong black joe then took Fanny to the lean-to. Nothing in here other than a thin mattress, a blanket, and a few hooks with a couple of items of clothing.

"Now you gotta learn how to get dressed. A big girl like you should know how to do this." For the third time that week, Gladys showed Fanny how the clasps needed to be on the front and how to hook them. She finger-combed the child's short, straight locks. "There you be. Let's get that washing done."

She set Fanny to scrubbing the clothes on the washboard. It sure was nice to have a helping hand. Willard and that Tann lady were right. It was good for everyone. Gladys got someone to work with her, and Fanny got a roof over her head and a family, something she hadn't known before.

"My arms hurt." Fanny's whiny voice echoed off the rustic cabin walls.

"We just hardly got started. Better keep scrubbing. Pa and Quinn get their clothes mighty dirty working all day like they do."

"Owie."

Gladys gazed at the child and narrowed her eyes. "No more bellyaching. You're a big girl, all of five years old."

"I'm three."

"You ain't no such thing. Miss Tann told us you're five." Though Fanny was very tiny for a child of that age. Had Miss Tann lied to them? No, there weren't no reason for her to. They'd asked for a girl about five or so, and that's what they'd gotten.

"Momma says I three."

"That's enough. You don't want Pa to hear you."

Fanny pinched her lips shut and kept on scrubbing. Once they had all the clothes cleaned, Gladys piled them in a wicker basket and carried them outside. A warm wind sliced through her thin dress. The child wore those hot pants. Willard done said she'd be fine.

Gladys knew when to keep her mouth shut. Been many a time when she hadn't, and she'd learned the hard way Willard didn't tolerate no back talk from no one.

"You hand me Quinn's pants." Gladys pulled two clothespins from a bag.

Fanny struggled with the pair of dungarees she pulled from the basket. They were longer than she was tall. The cuffs dragged in the bare ground.

"Fanny, what're you doing? Now we gotta wash those again."

Willard popped out of the barn and strode across the yard. He whacked the child on the back of the head. "Do your work right, you hear me?"

Fanny stared at the ground, but her eyes watered. "Yes."

He pulled her by the arm. "That's 'yes, sir' to you. And I'm gonna teach you to remember that from now on. Gladys, get me a switch."

"Really, Willard, it ain't a big deal. Won't take but a minute to clean."

"You'll have to redo all the laundry the way she's going." His blue eyes turned cold. "I said to get me a switch, woman. And don't wait for the Second Coming to fetch it."

Gladys's mouth went dry. No child should be beaten. But unless she wanted the sting of the branch on her back, she had to obey. With the knife in her apron pocket, she cut a thin twig from the willow tree near the creek behind the house and brought it to Willard.

He dragged Fanny toward the barn, the child already kicking and screaming like a wild bronco. Once he shut the door, a bunch of *thwacks* came from inside. Fanny screeched like a rabbit got by a hawk. What had Gladys done?

"Good afternoon, Griggs."

R.D. startled from the ledger where he'd been scheduling court cases, his pen leaving a line across the page. Bother, he'd have to start over. He peered through his glasses and the teller-like bars across his window. "Mr. Vance." They'd grown up together. Vance was nothing but poor white trash who'd gotten an education and sold his soul to the highest bidder. And now R.D. was hearing plenty about the trouble the young lawyer was getting himself into. "What brings you by?"

"I have a matter to discuss with you, one of some importance and delicacy."

"I can well imagine."

Vance glanced around and jingled a few coins in his pocket. "Is there somewhere we can speak in private?"

This man was out of his mind if he thought R.D. was going to get sucked into his dealings. No one wanted to be on the wrong side of Tann and Crump. Especially not someone in R.D.'s position. He'd had nothing to do with Percy Vance when they were growing up, and he'd have nothing to do with him now. "I have no interest in what you have to say."

"I'll make it worth your while. Just hear me out."

The worth-your-while bit caught R.D.'s attention. Having a child was an expensive proposition, especially with a mother like

Darcy. "Fine. Just give me a minute." R.D. closed his schedule book and wove his way through the maze of desks where secretaries of various sizes and ages plunked away on typewriters. The ding of the machines' bells followed him out of the office.

"Come with me." R.D. led the way down the hall. He didn't get far before Vance yanked him by the arm into a small janitor's closet and closed the door.

"What on earth?" The walls threatened to press in on R.D., and a bead of sweat broke out on his forehead. The eye-watering odor of cleaning solution and musty mops churned his stomach.

"When I said it was a private matter, I wasn't kidding. No one must know of this, no one at all. Do you understand?" Vance's breath was hot on R.D.'s cheek.

A small tremor passed through R.D. He braced himself against the wall in a vain attempt to keep it from closing in on him. Vance's pa had been a bully. Looked like it ran in the family. "Get to the point."

"I'm trying to locate a missing child."

"Why would I be able to help you with a runaway kid?"

"Miss Georgia Tann from the Tennessee Children's Home Society forced a woman's neighbor to forge her signature relinquishing her daughter for adoption. Kidnapped a child. Took her without the mother's permission. Refuses to disclose Millie's location. The girl should never have been removed from the home. A loving one, I might add. We want to find her. I need to get into the records."

"Are you out of your ever-lovin' mind? No one can see those."

Percy pulled out a picture of a woman and a very young child no more than a year old. R.D. leaned closer. His breath clogged his throat. Round face. Darkish hair. It couldn't be. Just couldn't be. No, the child in the photo was much too young. Pearl was three.

He forced himself to breathe out. R.D. had had enough of this. Couldn't afford to get involved. Couldn't afford to know the truth. He moved to leave.

Vance blocked the door. "Not so fast." The words hissed between his teeth. "You aren't going anywhere until you agree to get those records."

R.D. made a vain attempt to push Vance to the side. "Let me by."

"I'm not releasing you until I have your promise."

"This is blackmail." Just how men raised like Percy turned out.

"Nothing worse than what Tann did to

Mrs. Dowd. Are you going to assist us?"

"I can't get them." He grabbed Vance by the arm but couldn't get the man to budge.

"You'd better find a way. What if you lost your only child?"

At Vance's quiet question, R.D. ceased his struggle. What if something happened to Pearl? He'd be frantic, would do anything he had to in order to get her back.

But the resemblance. Maybe it was an old picture. No, he couldn't allow himself to even think such a thing. He'd do anything to protect his precious Pearl.

"I'm waiting for your answer. Will you help us?" Vance's words were deep and strained, like a dog waiting to be let off a leash.

What could he do? This was the woman from the letter Landers had him read. What Miss Tann had done to Mrs. Dowd was wrong. How awful to lose your child in such a tragic manner, especially when also mourning your husband's death.

On the other hand, how could an adoptive couple give back the child they believed to now be theirs? What if . . . ? "How old did you say the girl was?"

"Three."

R.D. struggled to keep from wetting himself.

Pearl was three.

No, no way they could be the same child. Though the resemblance was strong, it was too much of a coincidence. It couldn't be so. He squeezed his eyes shut as if he could shut out the thought. If someone came to take Pearl away, he wouldn't be able to stand it.

"I'm waiting." Vance's breath sent a shiver skittering down R.D.'s spine.

Bile rose in R.D.'s throat. "I told you, no one has access to those records."

"That's not quite the truth, is it?"

R.D.'s mouth went dry. What would Vance do to him if he didn't agree to cooperate? What would Landers and Crump do to him if he did? He gulped. "You don't expect me to break the law, do you?"

"I expect you to do whatever is necessary. The way I see it, the law has already been broken."

Pearl's laughter rang in his head. To lose that would rip his heart from his chest. And she'd only been with them a few weeks. How could he yank a child from a loving home?

"I can't help you. I could lose my job, my home, my family. Even my life."

Vance now stood toe to toe with R.D. "No one said it would be easy or without risk.

But sometimes, sacrifices must be made for the right cause."

Was this the right cause?

"You're a father. How would you feel if your child were stolen from you?"

He pushed back against Vance's shoulders. "That's all I'm thinking about." His voice raised in pitch with each word. "Do you believe Crump or his gang will let me get away with snooping? There are secrets in there."

"Secrets that deserve to be uncovered. Not only for her but for countless other women and children over the years. If you don't help them, who will?"

Why did it have to be him?

CHAPTER NINE

The floral fragrance of chamomile tea wafted from the cup on Percy's coffee table. Whenever Pa went on a tirade, Tenny would brew Percy a cup of chamomile and tell him it melted away troubles. He set aside the mystery novel he'd been reading and sipped the hot liquid. His sister had been right. With each mouthful, the worries of the day slipped further away.

His shoulders tightened. At least he had the clerk's assurance of help. What remained to be seen was if Griggs would follow through.

Percy gulped the tea and burned his tongue. He clicked on his Tiffany lamp, the warm, rich red and green colors spilling over the words in his book. His stomach rumbled. Maybe it was time to dip into the pot of chicken soup his housekeeper, Lola, had made and was keeping warm on the back of the stove. The savory, salty odor drew him to his spotless kitchen, which even boasted a Westinghouse refrigerator.

From the pot sunk into the back of his Hotpoint range, he ladled a bowlful of the chunky, carrot-laden soup then cut a slice of warm, crusty french bread. Before he could enjoy a mouthful, his doorbell rang the Westminster Chimes. He sighed.

He moved through his paneled formal dining room, the living room, and the screened front porch and opened the door to find Tann and her dark-skinned chauffeur, James, standing on his step. The doorman had made good on his promise.

Percy widened his eyes and put on his best surprised face. "Miss Tann. I didn't expect the pleasure of a visit this evening." Could she smell the soup? Should he offer her some or would that encourage her to stay?

"Cut the bologna, Vance. It doesn't become you." Tann pushed by him and into the house, her pants whispering as she walked, James on her heels. "I'm here on business."

Was there any other reason? "I thought we had covered everything we needed to get through for the next few days."

"So had I. But I heard you paid a visit to the office after hours the other night."

He left her and James standing in the

middle of the living room, but she didn't need an invitation. She settled herself on his brown and white cowhide sofa.

"Yes, I was there." No use in denying it. "As I told the watchman, I left a file. Or I thought I did. Turns out, I had it with me the entire time, stuffed inside another folder."

"Is that the case?"

"Of course." And plausible, at least to him.

"And why would you have a woman with you?"

"With all due respect, Miss Tann, my personal life is private and not a matter I wish to discuss."

"So you are involved with Mrs. Dowd?"

He clenched his jaw to keep from opening and closing his mouth like a fish. The guard was thorough. He must have given a good enough description of Cecile to Tann that she managed to make the connection. "There must be a mistake."

"Come, come, Mr. Vance. Don't play games with me." She rose from the couch and wandered around the room, examining the pink cherry blossom Japanese vase on the mantel and his collection of art deco cigarette cases in his built-in bookshelves.

There was no use in trying to hide anything from the woman. Somehow, she always found out. "Fine, it was Mrs. Dowd with me. We have formed, yes, a relationship. Just a friendship, mutual companionship, nothing more."

Tann swirled around so fast she almost toppled over. With a deep breath, she retained her composure. "Your association with the lady is of concern to me. I believe I warned you to stay away from her."

"Again, it's my personal business."

"Not when it affects mine."

"How so?" Percy strode three steps in her direction as she fingered the brass candlesticks on the table behind the sofa.

"She is attempting to interfere with the adoption of a child. That is no small matter. Is that why she was with you the other night at the office?"

"I told you, I believed I'd forgotten a file."

"Rather convenient, isn't it? I thought I'd taught you to be a better liar."

Is that what an alliance with Miss Tann and her ilk required? Not a good understanding of the law or excellent communication and argumentation skills but the ability to lie and cheat and steal? He grimaced.

"Does that make you uncomfortable, Mr. Vance?"

During the dark, long nights when Pa went on his drinking binges, Percy and

111

Tenny would often seek shelter in the hayloft. She would calm him by telling him Bible stories she'd learned when the family still attended church.

Part of his brain screamed at him to run from the immorality of associating with Tann. The other part of him surveyed every well-appointed corner of his home and screamed at him to do whatever it took to become a success.

"What do you expect of me?"

"To do what I tell you and not an iota more or less. And no more questions. You must cut off all ties with Mrs. Dowd. Our business with her is concluded. There is no need for you to see her."

Percy gulped. "What if I enjoy her company?" Which he did.

Tann waved him away. "Memphis is a large city. There are plenty of other, more deserving women. Why do you want to be tied to a woman of her rank? She's nothing but an uneducated rat."

Percy crossed the room to where Tann stood beside the brick fireplace. "She is nothing of the sort. More of a lady than you are."

Tann slapped him across the face, and he staggered backward. "How dare you."

"I could have you brought up on charges

of assault." His eyes watered as his cheek stung.

"You wouldn't dare." She ducked around him and over to James. "I'll take my pistol now."

The man with an ebony face reached into his coat pocket, produced a dull iron hand revolver, and passed it to Tann, who slipped it into her large black purse.

As she exited the front door, she turned and spoke over her shoulder. "Watch your step, Mr. Vance. Watch it very carefully."

Usually bustling with activity, people coming and going, proceedings taking place behind closed doors, the mausoleum-like marble courthouse was unusually quiet tonight. R.D. had never been here alone. And never at night. The stillness of it all was like a shadow following him. He tried to shake it off to no avail.

Darkness covered the long hallway, thin slivers of moonlight snaking underneath the office doors enough to light his path. His footsteps echoed in the silence. His arms broke out in gooseflesh. Losing the dim moonlight, the blackness of the stairwell was palpable. Something he could grasp and hold in his trembling hands. Here, he had to switch on the flashlight. He missed the bottom stair, tripping and dropping the light. It clanked to the floor. Even though he reminded himself that no one was here, he held his breath.

No noises.

Good.

With a *whoosh,* he released the air. He unlocked the door to the giant records room. Decades upon decades of birth, marriage, and death certificates. Census records. And adoption records. Perhaps even his own daughter's papers.

Dust floated in front of the light beam and tickled his nose. He sneezed. And froze. Again, no one came.

He moved on, sweeping the light before him as he searched through the sections of files. When he found the correct aisle, he steadied himself against the end of the shelf. Then he turned the corner. Boxes and boxes were lined up by year. Each box was wrapped in red tape. When they said the records were sealed, they meant sealed.

The box marked June 1933 was shut, impossible to investigate without breaking the tape. And he wouldn't go that far. When it was discovered that the box had been opened, an investigation would follow. And as clerk of court, the blame would come to him at some point.

Tann and Crump and the rest were much more of a force to be reckoned with, one he didn't want to tangle with.

But July 1933 had yet to be sealed. He reached out to slide the box from the shelf. Something clinked. Was there someone in the hall? He switched off his flashlight and stood without making a sound, keeping his breathing shallow. No more noise. Still, he couldn't take the chance that someone lurked outside the room. He crept to the door. Tiny bit by tiny bit, he turned the knob then pulled. The door creaked, so loud in the stillness. R.D. winced. Tensed. Waited. Nothing. He relaxed and peered through the crack. No one about. The long, dark hall was quiet. Deserted.

He closed the door without making a sound and hurried back to the files. No more gadding about. He pulled out the box. Even the files inside were wrapped in tape. He fingered through them, but there was no Millicent Dowd. What he found at the end though, stopped his heart.

Pearl Raylene Griggs. His daughter.

So the names on the records were the adoptive names. The birth names must be on the inside. He wouldn't be able to locate Mrs. Dowd's child without unsealing each and every record. Far, far too risky.

But in his hands, he held Pearl's history. Dare he open it?

His entire body quaked, his knees weak. What if she was Mrs. Dowd's daughter? Did he even want to know? He couldn't swallow. Her name blurred in front of his eyes. What should he do?

"That child can't do nothin' right. We're sending her back." Willard stomped around the kitchen, his face red.

Gladys poured him a cup of coffee and handed it to him.

"Even the beating I gave her didn't do no good. And all that money I spent on her, down the drain. If'n you haven't heard, woman, there's a depression on."

"Sit and let me get you some breakfast." Best thing to do when he was in one of his moods was to not get him riled up even more. Stay calm.

He thumped into one of the cracked kitchen chairs. Would he ever fix it? Gladys sighed. Likely not.

"I'm telling you, that Tann woman duped us. Said Fanny was a good worker, but she ain't nothin' of the sort."

She sprinkled a drop of water on the griddle to check if it was hot enough and then poured the pancake batter. "She'll learn. Give the child time. She's only just come to us."

"Should've never listened to you. Griping about not enough help in the house and how Quinn worked with me and why couldn't you have someone with you. That's why men are to rule the home. Womenfolk don't know what they're talking about."

When he stopped for a breath, Gladys flipped the pancakes. Something deep inside of her resisted the idea of sending Fanny back. Maybe it was those big green eyes or her innocent round face. Maybe it was that Gladys had always dreamed of having a girl of her own.

"I see what you're thinking." Willard jabbed his fork in her direction. "Don't get too attached. She's going back."

Gladys lifted three cakes from the pan and placed them on her husband's china plate. "She's not. Give her time. She'll learn. That one's a smart one, for sure."

She turned to go back to the stove and caught sight of Fanny standing in the kitchen doorway, her chin trembling. But today, she'd put her overalls on correctly. "See what I mean. She's already dressing herself just fine."

"Should've been able to do that from the start," Willard mumbled as he shoveled his breakfast into his big mouth.

He scarfed down three more pancakes, scraped back his chair, and marched to the barn. Quinn had been in there working for an hour already. Poor kid. Quiet. Gladys didn't know him well. She'd slip him some pancakes later.

Gladys turned her attention to Fanny. The little girl's mouth turned down, but her eyes remained dry.

"Would you like a pancake?"

Fanny shook her head, her brown hair bouncing with the motion. She stared at the dirty wood floor.

Gladys knelt in front of her. Sorry mite. She'd been through so much. "What's the problem?" Willard'd likely have a fit if he caught her speaking to the child so nice and all.

"I want my momma."

"Fanny." Gladys touched her cool, bony hand.

Fanny flinched and backed away. "I not Fanny."

"Of course you are. You're being silly this morning. Come on, if'n you have some breakfast, you'll feel better." Gladys grabbed Fanny by the wrist and dragged her to the table.

"I don't wanna eat."

"Course you do. You love my pancakes."

"I want my momma."

Gladys leaned close and hissed in Fanny's ear. "If Pa hears you, you'll get another whoopin'. I know you don't want that."

"I want Momma. I be good. I go home."

"That's enough of that. Now eat. I'm your ma, and your pa is in the barn doing chores. You'd best hush and fill up. Today is bread-making day, and we need to get to it."

But Fanny only took three bites of her breakfast. After much pleading with her, all of which did no good, Gladys cleared the plate. "Waste of food. And during the depression, no less. Best not let your pa catch you not cleaning your plate."

Gladys motioned to Fanny. "Get washing then if you ain't gonna eat. There's gonna be nothing but skin and bones left of you pretty soon." Gladys took her coffee mug and sat at the kitchen table.

Perhaps they needed to call a doctor. Fanny hadn't eaten much since she'd arrived, and the tiny child had gotten even smaller.

Fanny pulled a chair over to the sink and pumped in the water. She took each dish and slid it into the water. The last one slipped from her grip and splashed in with a great crash.

Gladys rushed over and pulled out pieces of plates. Heat built into her chest and exploded like a volcano. "What've you done?" She shook the broken dishes in Fanny's face. "They're busted, each one of them. Nothing left. What are we supposed to eat off of?" She towered over the child. "We ain't got money for more. These were my mimi's."

Fanny jumped from the chair, ran to the far corner behind the table, and cowered in a little ball. Still boiling, Gladys rushed toward her. "You stupid, careless child. How're you gonna make this right? Are you gonna buy new ones?"

Fanny stared at her.

"Well, are you? You got the money for more? Cause your pa's gonna be awful mad when he comes in and finds out what happened. You think the beating you got the other day was bad, you just watch out. Ain't gonna be no mercy for you this time. And he'll be meaner than a bull with me. How could you do this to me? Can't you do nothin' right?"

Fanny's eyes widened.

"Answer me, girl."

She pinched her lips shut.

"Answer me now."

Fanny shrank farther into the corner.

"You naughty, naughty girl." Gladys yanked her from under the table and squeezed her forearm. She raised her hand to strike Fanny.

The child whimpered.

Gladys froze.

What had she been about to do? She released Fanny and stroked her arm, a big black and purple bruise marring the fair flesh. "Oh baby, I'm so sorry. So sorry for what I done to you. Don't you worry about nothin'. I'm gonna take care of it all. It'll be fine, you'll see. You just go on to your room. Ma'll clean up the mess."

Without a backward glance, Fanny scampered away behind the curtain that separated her room from the rest of the house.

Her innards in knots, Gladys pulled the pieces of china from the water and threw them in the trash bin. She'd almost beaten Fanny herself. But it was up to her to protect the child.

Tonight, she'd have to confess to Willard that she'd broken the dishes. And take Fanny's punishment.

CHAPTER TEN

"What did you say?" Percy stood in front of Tann's oak desk, crushing the handle of his leather attaché case, his mouth gone dry.

She slid the newspaper across the desk to him, the page folded so he could make out the headline with no trouble: WILLIAM KEARNY, LONG-TIME MEMPHIS COUNCILMAN, MISSING.

He skimmed the article. According to the reporter, Mr. Kearny had fallen out with those in power and had made more than one enemy in the city's political machine. Many more than one.

"How does this pertain to me?" He tossed the paper in Tann's direction.

"It's a shame what happened to him."

"What happened? He's missing. Possibly on vacation in the mountains."

"I fear a more sinister fate."

Feared or knew of? The room closed in on Percy. "Why?"

Tann pushed away from the desk and lumbered to the single, small window, parting the almost-always closed curtains. "Making enemies in this city is detrimental to one's health."

Did she have any involvement in Mr. Kearny's disappearance? Percy stepped backward, ready to dive for the door if necessary.

"You've angered some influential people, Mr. Vance."

Namely, her. "That was never my intention."

"Intention or not, there are those in power around here who are most unhappy with your antics."

Yes, she spoke nothing but the truth of a risk he knew he was taking when he offered to assist Mrs. Dowd.

He gazed at her desk, rings from coffee cups marring the surface. Did she keep her revolver in one of the drawers? Was it in her purse somewhere in the room? He gulped. Or in her pants pocket?

She broke off gazing out the window. "I don't know how much longer I will require your services. Mr. Waldauer is capable of handling my affairs."

"But he is a busy man. I lessen his load." Losing this position would devastate him.

No more Packard. No more home on Poplar Avenue. The room swirled. And it would complicate the investigation into Cecile's missing daughter. How would he get information about her if he was no longer in Tann's employ?

"Mr. Kearny also believed himself to be indispensable, but he was wrong. Just a bit player that Memphis could do without." She ambled to her desk, the rotten-egg stench of her drifting toward him.

Rotten not only on the outside but also on the inside. "Then I suppose I have to work to make you see you can't do without me."

"Don't flatter yourself." Tann snorted. "I like to keep my friends close and my enemies closer. Have a good day, Mr. Vance."

Even those most innocuous words, when spoken from her mouth, composed a threat. "Thank you."

Once he stood on the street, breathing in the stale summer air clogged with car fumes, he loosened his tie and slung his suit coat over his shoulder. He hadn't taken full advantage of his time working for Tann. File cabinets lined one wall of her office. There had to be information in there. Well, he couldn't stand on the street corner all day. He planned on meeting Cecile on one of the wooded trails in Overton Park at noon. Seeing her sweet, trusting face would brighten this dreary day.

Storm clouds brewed overhead, rising as the foam on a choppy sea, the bottoms dark and heavy with rain. In the distance, thunder rumbled.

He rode the streetcar, much as he had done the day he followed Cecile to the park. This time, however, their meeting had to be clandestine. He disembarked a couple of blocks from his destination and made his way there on foot, meandering down several side streets instead of taking a direct route.

Once he reached Overton, he headed for the walking trails. For a while, he left the path and hiked through the bramble. Thorns scratched his flesh. A vine tangled itself around his ankle, and he tripped. He caught himself, scraping his tender palms.

The air hung still. Motionless. Like the world held its breath. Another peal of thunder, this one closer and longer. A breeze blew up, rattling the leaves above him.

"Mr. Vance?"

Cecile's voice behind him weakened his knees. He locked them to keep from slumping to the ground. "You startled me."

"I'm sorry. I suppose with the storm you

didn't hear me coming. Do you have information on Millie?" She widened her green eyes and leaned forward.

"No. Not yet. But I'm working on it. Trying to get into that office alone to have a glimpse at the files."

"Oh dear. When you called, I got my hopes up, I'm afraid. I thought . . ." Cecile, pretty in a pink polka-dotted dress, deflated. A single tear sparkled like a diamond on her eyelashes.

"But don't worry. I will get into that office. Alone. And I will get the information we need."

"I'm coming with you. I insist."

"Haven't we had this argument once before?"

She laughed, transformed from just moments before, the music of her giggle like the rain now pattering on the canopy above. "Then let's not argue. I won then. I'll win now."

"You still don't trust me?"

"Not yet."

He chewed the inside of his cheek. "An accomplice would be handy." Especially one as beautiful as she, the day's warmth bringing color to her cheeks.

She smiled, a dimple appearing in her right cheek. Funny how he had never noticed that before. She touched his arm, only his thin, white cotton shirt between them. Even so, a bolt of electricity raced up his arm, and it had nothing to do with the lightning flashing overhead. "Thank you for understanding."

"Your insistence on being included has given me an idea." He shared with her the plan he'd devised for getting into Tann's office.

"Perfect." Her eyes glittered in the dim light. "Let's go. I don't have much time before I have to be back at work."

"Tann always takes a lunch break right on the dot of twelve."

They dodged raindrops as they scurried from the woods toward the tram. He waited several minutes after she disappeared from sight, took a different path out of the forest, and caught a later tram. So far, so good. No one followed him. At least, that's what he counted on.

By the time he arrived at the Goodwyn Institute, it was ten minutes past twelve. Perfect. He strode up the stairs, taking them two at a time, praying all the while their plan would work. It had to. There was no other option.

With Miss Tann out for lunch, the key to the operation was to get Miss Stewart from the office. That's where Cecile came in. While she entered the office, Percy waited down the hall from the Tennessee Children's Home Society, plastered against the wall. Not that it would do any good. If anyone came out of the elevator or one of the doors, they would spy him. But the strength of the wall supporting him helped him keep his breathing steady and even.

Miss Stewart's shriek emanated from the office. "What have you done, you lazy oaf? Look at my blouse. Ruined, for sure."

Percy couldn't stop the smile that teased his mouth at Miss Stewart's outburst. So far, so good.

"I'll take it to the lavatory and wash it out."

"I'm not going to trust my silk blouse to you. Look at the mess you've already made. You shouldn't be here, Mrs. Dowd."

"Of course. My apologies for my clumsiness."

Both ladies exited the office. Percy scooted around the corner to be sure Miss Stewart didn't catch a glimpse of him. When the washroom door clicked shut, he popped out of hiding. "Let's go." He motioned for Cecile to follow.

"She locked the door." The breath of her whisper tickled the back of his neck.

"Do you have a hairpin?"

"No, but I have a hatpin."

"That will do."

She pulled the long, slender pin from her blue hat. Though it took him a moment longer than he'd hoped, he jimmied the lock. He ushered Cecile inside. "Hurry. We don't have much time."

Cecile held her breath as Percy shut Miss Tann's office door behind them. The bittersweet odor of coffee and creamer lingered in the air, churning Cecile's stomach. Flashes of lightning from the window in Miss Tann's office sent their shadows writhing on the wall.

Any moment, Miss Stewart might return. Any moment, they could be caught. She gulped down breaths to keep from screaming. The life of a criminal was not for Cecile.

As Percy entered Miss Tann's office, Cecile stood rooted to the spot as if her limbs had turned to stone. "Come on." He motioned to her.

The throbbing in her head just about drowned out his words. Though it was the only way to get information about Millie, this was insanity. He returned to her and clasped her hands, his grip strong and warm. Some of that energy flowed from him to her, driving away a bit of the iciness.

"We have to be quick. This is for Millie. Keep that in the front of your mind."

For Millie. Yes, that's why she had broken into this office. That's why she stood here quivering like a bowl of Jell-O. That's why she risked her livelihood and even her freedom. Whatever it took to bring her daughter home. "What do you want me to do?"

He motioned her deeper into the office and pointed to the wall on their right. "I'll search this cabinet. You look through the one next to it. I don't know what she keeps in each drawer. Just search for anything that might have to do with the adoption of a girl around Millie's age about the time Tann snatched her."

"Okay." Cecile could do this. She took the time to inhale and exhale once and steel herself.

Only a green and brown art deco lamp lit the office. Outside, the sky blackened and shimmered green. Every now and again, a flash of lightning provided a bit more illumination. The building creaked in the wind.

She tugged open the top drawer, the metal cabinet's handle cool in her hand. Neat manila folders stretched all the way back, and she thumbed through them, the tabs labeled in precise block handwriting. Nothing but receipts for office supplies.

With a bang, she slammed the door shut. She jumped back.

"Shh." Percy gestured for her to be quieter.

"Sorry." She hadn't meant to do that, but the handle slid out of her grasp. Her hands now sweating, she opened the drawer beneath. Payroll information and financial records. They didn't have time to comb through these.

"Anything?" Percy searched his third drawer.

"Nothing. You?"

He furrowed his brow. Shook his head. "This is taking too long. We have to be faster."

Cecile also searched through her third drawer. Picked up speed. Read each label as fast as possible. One folder near the back was marked *letters.* She pulled it up. Skimmed the contents.

Dear Miss Tann,
You told me my son was stillborn, but I heard him cry. Please, help me find him.

Dear Miss Tann,
I was groggy from anesthesia when I

131

signed those adoption papers. But I don't want to give away my daughter.

Dear Miss Tann,
Please return my children to me. My father had no authority to sign those papers on my behalf.

Cecile gasped. On and on the letters went. Each one tore away another piece of her heart.

Rain slashed against the windows. The wind howled outside, rattling window panes.

Cecile flipped through a few more. Her chest tightened with each she read. A few had pictures stapled to them. One of a young girl with long braids caught her eye. Such a sweet, beautiful child. Every single one of these letters claimed Georgia Tann had stolen a woman's child. Among them, in Cecile's own shaky handwriting, was Cecile's cry for help.

"Percy." She elbowed him.

"Hmm." He didn't glance from his work.

"I've found something."

Now he turned his attention to her.

"Letters. Just like the one I wrote to Miss Tann. Several dozen of them, all saying their children were snatched from them." Her voice broke. There were so many. Just like

132

her. She hadn't been the only one.

He grabbed the folder and scanned it. "Let's see if we can find adoption records for any of these children."

With the clock on Miss Tann's desk ticking away each precious second, they flung open drawer after drawer. Soon, Percy located one containing some records, but none of the names matched. "Falsified, is my guess."

Tiny hailstones tinkled against the panes. Bolt after bolt of lightning streaked across the sky.

"Or in another spot, maybe? Millie's papers have to be here. Keep looking." She wasn't going to give up. They were so close to the answers.

They scanned a couple more drawers. No matches. The clack of heels on the hall's tile floor brought them to a standstill. Cecile's heartbeat came to a screeching halt.

Just then, a bolt of lightning split the sky. At the same moment, such a roar of thunder rolled that it shook the windows. The office lights flickered then snuffed out.

CHAPTER ELEVEN

R.D.'s head pounded and every bone in his body ached as he climbed the steps to his gray bungalow. Coming from an average family in Mississippi, he'd worked hard for everything he had. And it had been worth it.

Overhead, a crack of thunder split the peace of the neighborhood. He made it home just before the storm hit. He inhaled a deep breath and huffed it out then swung open the door. "Darcy, I'm here."

"I'm in the kitchen. You have a phone call." Her sweet voice carried through the house.

Pearl ran to greet him, her chubby little legs carrying her through the living room and into his arms. "Daddy, Daddy, you're home!"

He tossed her in the air and caught her, sending her into a peal of giggles. "Of course I am. Wild horses couldn't keep me from my girls. Let's go see who's calling."

With Pearl still in his arms, he crossed through the living room and dining room to the kitchen. Darcy stood at her new electric stove and stirred something in a pot, her blond hair loose, a curl falling over her shoulder. And she was all his.

He kissed her cheek and picked up the receiver that sat on the round kitchen table. "This is Griggs."

"I've had an interesting phone call."

"Mr. Landers?"

"Not Santa Claus," the man growled. "That lawyer I spotted you with, a Percy Vance, has been nosing around where he shouldn't regarding Tann's adoptions. The woman he's helping to get her child returned showed up at the office today."

"I don't know what this has to do with me."

"Everything." R.D. held the phone away from his ear as Landers bellowed. "You disappeared together the other day for a good amount of time. Makes me wonder what you might have been discussing."

"Absolutely nothing. I refused to help him and sent him on his way. Nothing worth reporting to Tann."

"She wanted to know if anyone in my office might have been giving Vance a hand.

What could I say? Had to tell her something. I value my career. And my life."

R.D. thumped into the white, rounded-back kitchen chair. "And put mine on the line."

"Memphis is a rough city."

Pearl and Darcy both stared at him, their eyes wide. No need to alarm them. "Thank you for phoning." He ended the call.

"What did your boss want?" A *V* appeared between Darcy's eyebrows.

He kissed her forehead to ease it away. "Nothing. Just a small matter at the office." The tangy odor of onions and the sweet smell of roasting beef overtook him. He lifted the lid of the pot on the stove. "Stew. My favorite lunch." Another roll of thunder sounded, and rain pinged against the window pane.

"You say that no matter what I make." There was a hint of teasing in her voice, but her blue eyes didn't gleam like they usually did.

"Is something wrong?"

"Pearl, honey, go play upstairs. I'll call you when lunch is ready." Darcy paused until their daughter trotted out of the room. "Earlier today I had a call from Miss Tann at the Tennessee Children's Home Society."

A lump formed in R.D.'s throat. "Really?

Maybe they have another child for us." But his stomach turned rock hard.

She gripped the wooden spoon until her knuckles turned white. "No, that's not at all what she wanted. Miss Tann would like to come today and check on Pearl, see how she's adjusting to our home. The woman who called, Miss Tann's assistant, said that they've received reports that our home is not up to standards and that Pearl isn't happy."

Just what he had feared. That lawyer, Vance, called every other day, badgering him to break into the sealed adoption files. There was one file they wouldn't find. Because he had it. And Percy could upset everything R.D. had labored to build.

One mistake. That's all it took to ruin a man in this town. Crump didn't easily forgive. Neither did Tann.

"I'm sure it's nothing."

"She'll be here within the hour." With a clatter, Darcy dropped the spoon on the floor and flung herself into R.D.'s embrace. "What are we going to do? We can't lose Pearl."

The tot, who must have returned to the room at some point, tugged on R.D.'s rumpled suit coat. "Why's Mommy crying?"

"No reason." He glanced at Pearl over

Darcy's shoulder. "Please run upstairs and play with your doll for a while. Mommy will be better soon, and then we'll eat."

"Okay." Pearl trotted off, her brown curls bouncing as she went.

How was it possible to love a child so much after just a few weeks? He rubbed his wife's back. "Sweetheart, I'm sure you don't have anything to worry about. How can they object to us when we've given Pearl such a comfortable home? She has toys, a room of her own, two parents who love her. What more could a child ask?"

"Are you sure?"

"I am. I don't know who's spreading these vicious rumors, but when Miss Tann visits, she will discover they are baseless." He handed her his handkerchief. "Dry your eyes, and I'll check on our girl. We'll be down to eat in a minute."

Darcy kissed his cheek. "Thank you. I love you."

"And I love you." He left her working on her crusty bread, the yeasty perfume of it urging him to hurry, and climbed the stairs to Pearl's room. When he pushed open her door, he found her perched on her pink chenille-covered bed, a crayon in her hand. And her artwork scribbled all over the plastered wall.

"Pearl! What have you done?"

"I colored." She grasped the blue crayon in her chubby fingers.

"Not on the walls. You have to ask Mommy for a piece of paper." He moved forward to catch her, but the imp scampered away and hid under the bed.

He lifted the bedspread and peeked underneath. "Come on out, Miss Muffet. Lunch is almost ready. You don't want burned stew, do you?"

"No, I wanna color."

He dropped the bed covering and rounded to the other side. But when he went to his knees and peered underneath, Pearl had moved across from him. "Let's go, sweetheart. After we eat, we'll get you some paper for coloring."

"No. I wanna color now."

He would wait it out. Over the past days, he and Darcy had discovered that was the best way to handle Pearl. Eventually, she came around.

As he lay on the floor and examined her, he studied her features, searching for any part of her that resembled the photo of Mrs. Dowd's child. Did she and Pearl have the same nose? How about the same mouth? The chin rang a bell of familiarity.

But really, he was no good at this. When

parents gushed over their children and proclaimed them to have their father's forehead or their mother's eyes, he never could see it.

What if Miss Tann took Pearl? Or what if she turned out to be Mrs. Dowd's child? The loss would kill Darcy. And him. No matter what, he had to protect his little family and do everything in his power to keep them together. No matter what, he couldn't allow Vance and the woman to ever see Pearl or find out she was adopted through the Tennessee Children's Home Society.

The doorbell chimed a two-note *ding-dong.* Footsteps raced across the house downstairs. A moment later, Darcy climbed the stairs and into the room. "Miss Tann is here."

As Percy and Cecile stood elbow-deep in adoption files, a great crash of thunder shook the entire Goodwyn Institute, and the lights flickered and faded.

He licked his lips. Cecile gasped.

From the hallway, Miss Stewart screamed.

He turned to Cecile, silhouetted against the window. "Stay quiet."

She nodded.

This might be the perfect opportunity to get out unseen.

"Hello? Hello? Does anyone have a flash-light? Or candles?" Miss Stewart's voice came from the hall.

No one answered.

A moment later, the click of her heels faded away.

"Grab that folder, and let's get out of here." Percy shut the drawer with as little noise as possible.

Cecile stuffed the folder in her purse. "I hope they don't miss it."

"Don't worry about that." Thankful for the carpeting that silenced their footsteps, Percy led her through Tann's office and the secretary's to the main door. He clung to her hand, delicate and warm.

He cracked open the door and peered into the hall, not that he could see much in the darkness. If only his heart didn't pound so, he might hear if anyone moved about.

As far as he could tell, all was silent.

The tile floors outside the office presented more of a problem. He led Cecile as they tip-toed down the hall. At one point, he stepped flat on his foot, the heel of his wing-tip connecting with the marble tile.

"Is someone there?" Miss Stewart was on the opposite side of the building.

Percy didn't dare breathe, didn't dare move. Cecile squeezed his hand, and he

141

squeezed back. He wouldn't let anything happen to her.

Miss Stewart giggled. "This storm is getting to me. And now I'm talking to myself." She opened a door, took a few steps, and shut the door.

"Now." Percy made tracks, dashing the rest of the way down the hall and into the ghoulish blackness of the stairwell.

Behind him, Cecile huffed. "That was close."

"A little too close. But we made it. We can wait out the storm here."

"What if Miss Tann returns from lunch?"

"Have you seen her? She won't take the stairs."

"But with the electricity out, she may have no choice."

"She'll wait for service to be restored. We can't chance meeting her in the lobby."

"Good point." Cecile sat on the step, and he took his place beside her.

"I can't believe it." Her words were little more than a whisper. She leaned against him.

"That we escaped from there?"

"That I'm not the only one to lose a child to that horrible woman."

A pain radiated from behind Percy's left eye. "Unfortunately, you aren't."

"It's almost too much to bear."

He touched her hand. "I know. Her wickedness knows no bounds." If Tann discovered what he just did, she would blackball him for sure, and his clientele would evaporate until he had no practice left. When that happened, he wouldn't be able to afford his mortgage. Or his car. Or any of the fine amenities he'd become accustomed to. Life would change. And not for the better.

He would have to figure that out later. Right now, Cecile needed him.

"If all those other women are searching, that means no one has been able to locate their missing children."

"We don't know that." He couldn't allow her to give up hope, though the extent of Tann's deception was staggering.

"Will any of us ever see our children again?"

"How can I answer that? I wish I could gaze into the future and tell you that you will, but it's a promise I'm unable to make."

"My poor, poor baby." Cecile sniffled. "All those poor, poor babies. God help every one of them." She turned into the crook of his arm and sobbed, her shoulders heaving.

He stroked her silky hair. As more thunder and wind shuddered the building, they sat on the steps, and he allowed her time to weep.

A lump grew in his own throat. Tann probably sold the children to the highest bidder. So many families destroyed by one woman's greed. So many children harmed by her deceit. And this woman beside him, her life ruined by a cruel, unfeeling despot.

He rubbed Cecile's back until her sobs subsided then ceased. "Something good might come of this, you know."

She slid out of his hold. "I don't see how."

"We can reach out to these women and see if any of them have been searching for their children. Perhaps together we can locate them and reunite some families."

"Oh, we could. This might be the break we've been waiting for." She kissed his cheek. "Thank you."

"For what?"

"For giving me a sliver of hope, small as it may be."

What he kept from telling her was that the hope was very, very tiny.

CHAPTER TWELVE

With Pearl in his arms, R.D. descended the stairs to the living room, where a rather damp Miss Tann sat on the navy-blue wing chair, the walnut coffee table and end tables polished to a high shine, the hardwood floors gleaming. Even the blue and mauve Oriental rug beneath her feet was spotless. Tann wouldn't be able to fault his wife for a messy house.

Pearl squirmed. "I wanna play."

No chance he was going to let this imp loose. "Remember, we're going to talk to Miss Tann for a while, and you must behave like a lady."

She stuck out her lower lip but nodded. Perhaps he and Darcy were making headway in taming the child.

He turned his attention to Miss Tann. "I must say, this is a surprise."

She smoothed her shirt over her midsection but narrowed her eyes, her round glasses resting on her hawkish nose. "You should have been expecting me."

Darcy entered the room, carrying a teapot and cups painted with purple violets atop a silver tray. She set it down, poured the spice-laden tea, and handed a cup to Miss Tann before settling on the sofa beside him and Pearl.

He cleared his throat and prayed his voice wouldn't break. "What can we help you with?"

"You know why I'm here." The tundra in January was warmer than her words.

"I'm afraid I don't." Hail clinked against the windows.

Pearl wriggled between him and Darcy. "I wanna go play. Please?"

Miss Tann leaned forward in her chair. "You go on, sweetheart, and let us grown-ups talk in peace. Play quietly, now."

Beside him, Darcy stiffened. Miss Tann shouldn't be telling their child what to do.

R.D. clenched his hands together. "Come to your point, Miss Tann, as soon as possible. I have to return to work."

"A work that now involves Mr. Vance, does it not? What did he want with you?"

"To get a case of his moved back on the docket. He needed more time to prepare."

"And that had to be discussed in secret?"

146

She leaned forward.

"He thought it did." R.D. clung to the edge of the sofa cushion. "I don't see how what I do as part of my job is any of your business."

"When it affects the children I place for adoption, I make it my business."

R.D. worked to keep his words polite but firm. "As I said, this didn't involve adoption records."

"But you did go to the courthouse in the middle of the night."

How did she know? Had he been followed? Impossible. He'd been so careful, cautious, glancing over his shoulder every few steps. These goons had spies on every street corner. That was the only way anyone could have known what he was doing. He wiped the beads of sweat from his upper lip.

"Come, come, Mr. Griggs. Don't play me for the fool." Miss Tann set her teacup on the end table. "You and I both know what went on in that records room. And it will cost you. Greatly."

Goose bumps broke out on his arms.

Darcy stifled a sob. "Please, Miss Tann, I have no idea what this is about, but I don't appreciate your threats. My husband works for the courts and has every right to pull whatever records he needs. It all sounds perfectly innocent."

"Innocent?" Miss Tann gave a single guffaw. "Hardly." She directed her attention to R.D., and her tone turned stony. "Were you trying to get into your daughter's adoption records? Or someone else's?"

Darcy grabbed him by the arm. "Were you?"

"No. I swear to you, I wasn't. Why would I do a thing like that? I — We love our daughter. Pearl is ours and no one else's. I would never do anything to jeopardize her position in our family."

Miss Tann crossed her arms over her ample bosom. "I gave you Pearl, and I have the power to take her away."

"No, you wouldn't." Darcy shook him by the arm. "Tell her you would never let that happen. Show her what good parents we are. That we're teaching Pearl good manners. We're civilizing her. Isn't that the goal of adoption?"

Miss Tann hoisted herself from the chair. "Perhaps I should see for myself."

Darcy jumped up. "Take a look around. You won't find anything amiss."

Tann lumbered around the first floor, and his wife was correct. You couldn't find a single flaw in the way she kept house or in the food she prepared. Everything was just as it should be.

The woman proceeded to the stairs, winded by the time she reached the upper landing. "Which is the child's room?"

Darcy pointed to the first door on the right. As Miss Tann turned the glass knob on the three-panel door, R.D.'s heart came to a full and complete stop. The coloring on the wall. He hadn't had a chance to tell his wife about it or to clean it. He slid between Tann and the door. "You can't go in there."

Darcy puffed out a breath. "Why not? This is where Pearl sleeps and plays. Miss Tann will see she has plenty of toys. That her adoption is what is best for her."

"I'll determine if it is." Tann pushed R.D. to the side. He allowed her to enter the room.

She took a moment to study the drawings on the wall. In the time they'd been downstairs, Pearl had added to them. She now stood in the middle of the room, a big brown crayon grasped in her little fingers.

"What is this?"

R.D. tsked. "Pearl is a work in progress."

Tann turned to him, nose to nose. She reeked of garlic.

"This may be cause for removal of the child from your home. Obviously, you cannot properly supervise her. She isn't safe here."

"No!" Darcy pushed Tann by the shoulder to turn her to face her. "You will not take my daughter from me. She's not perfect. None of us are. But she's loved and cared for. As she grows, she'll learn right from wrong. I'll never let you take her."

"We'll have to see about that."

Pink had yet to streak the eastern sky when Cecile locked her apartment and made her way down the building's old, creaky stairs. Hundreds, thousands of hand rubbings had left the varnished banister smooth as glass.

Some may groan and complain about rising so early, but it mattered little to her. Sleep came hard and left fast.

Percy was going to meet her at the nursery school this morning with the phone number of one of the women they discovered in the file. Her heart fluttered at the thought of having to call the mother and speak to her about her loss. But from the letter, it was clear she wanted her daughter back. Perhaps together they could find the answers.

At this early hour, the streets lay desolate and deserted. Off in the distance, a cat screeched, and a dog howled. The click of her two-toned oxford shoes on the pavement resounded in the quiet. She rounded the corner onto the main street and bumped into something. No, someone, who stumbled backward. She grabbed him by the arm.

"Hello, little lady." His body reeked of sweat. His breath reeked of alcohol.

She let go and sidestepped him.

"Where're you going?"

Cecile hurried on her way, trembling all over. She hustled down the street, away from him, and didn't stop until she rounded another corner and leaned against the building's rough brick. Her insides caught up with her a few minutes later. As the milkman passed her in his Ford truck, he waved to her. She managed a small smile. Steadier now, she continued the few blocks to the nursery school.

When she approached the white brick building that had once been a home, Percy was nowhere in sight. No matter. She'd go inside and wait for him. She unlocked the black front door and entered. At the sight inside, she clutched her throat. Tables lay overturned, chairs thrown around the room, drawers pulled from Mrs. Quinn's desk. Like a layer of confetti after a ticker-tape parade, papers covered the floor.

Who did this? And why?

She stepped over broken crayons and upset glue bottles. The children's artwork had been torn from the wall. Her stomach jumped into her throat. Was the person who vandalized the room still in the building? Maybe it wasn't safe here.

As if playing leapfrog, she hopped around the obstacles and out the door. If her heart kept pounding at this rate, she would pass away from cardiac arrest sooner rather than later.

She darted across the street, a car hoot-hooting its horn at her. Breath coming in ragged gasps, she clung to the light pole for support.

"Cecile?"

At the sound of her name, she just about jumped as high as the building. "Percy. What are you trying to do to me?"

"What's wrong? You're as white as a mountain's snow."

She turned to him and held him tight. How good to have him near. To have his strength to depend on. "It's awful. I went in there. Who could have done such a terrible thing?"

"Okay, take a deep breath."

She obeyed.

"I didn't understand any of what you just said. Start from the beginning."

"I can't describe it. Someone, someone ransacked the nursery. Maybe he's still inside."

"Let's have a look."

"No." She tightened her hold to keep him from leaving her. "Please, it's too dangerous. We need to inform the police."

"Just a peek inside. You stay here, and I'll let you know if the coast is clear."

She couldn't allow him out of her sight. Couldn't bear it if anything happened to him.

He was the only hope she had in the world of finding Millie. "I'm coming."

"You said yourself it might be dangerous."

"That's probably true. But if you can go, so can I."

"You're a plucky dame." He untangled himself from her grasp and held her at arm's length. For a forever-long moment, he gazed at her, all the laughter gone from his storm-cloud blue eyes. And just like that, the moment ended. He cleared his throat. "Come on."

She followed him across the street and into the nursery yard. He stopped without warning, and she ran into his back. "Sorry."

He swung open the door to reveal the full horror. "Oh no."

The early-morning humidity pressed

153

against Cecile, and she broke into a sweat. Much as she had done, he picked his way through the mess in the classroom. He halted in front of the bulletin board.

She sidled next to him. "Oh my goodness."

The vandal had tacked a note to the board with a long-handled knife. He'd spilled red paint down it to resemble blood. Most chilling of all were the words.

You'll be next.

Cecile covered her mouth to stifle her scream.

Percy rubbed her shoulder.

"This was left for me?"

"No way to be sure."

But she had no doubts. The message was her warning. "I won't let it stop me."

"I know you won't, but are you sure?"

She nodded.

He righted the rolling wooden teacher's chair. "Have a seat before you faint."

"I'm not the swooning type." But she sat anyway.

"You might be when you see what's in this morning's paper." He withdrew a copy of the *Memphis Commercial Appeal* from his jacket pocket and spread it on the desk in front of her.

She fisted her hands in front of her face, unable to draw a breath. "Because he . . ."

"Read the first paragraph. It will tell you all you need to know."

William Kearny, a member of the Memphis city council and a champion of social welfare reform, was found dead in a wooded area of Overton Park last evening by a passer-by. He had been missing for almost a week.

"And you believe he was on Tann's wrong side."

"If not hers, someone close to her."

"And this might be connected to what happened here?"

"As we and others close in on the truth, these politicians and their friends are running scared. And they will do whatever they have to in order to protect their secret."

Even murder.

CHAPTER THIRTEEN

Gladys settled into the chair at the kitchen table, a cup of coffee steaming in front of her. She didn't even have the energy to lift the mug to her lips, though the bitter aroma enticed her.

With the intense heat in the house, it was a wonder she'd even poured herself a cup, let alone thought about drinking it. Maybe it was more about having a few minutes to rest.

With the garden coming in, she and Fanny were busy putting up stores for the winter. Pickles, sweet corn, chowchow, green beans. The list went on and on. Every bone and muscle in Gladys's body ached. Even with Fanny's help.

The mite tried her best; you had to give her that. But all that picking and canning and hard work was just about too much for her. Sure, she'd grown some and gotten a good bit stronger, but she was still tiny.

Much smaller than any five-year-old Gladys knew.

When they'd come in from the yard, all hot and sweaty like, Fanny curled in a ball on the hard floor in the corner of the warm kitchen and fell fast asleep. She snored, a little whiffle. Sweet thing. She did her best, bless her heart.

Boots pounded on the porch.

Willard.

He didn't usually come in this time of day. And if he caught Fanny napping . . .

Gladys jumped from her seat to wake the child. But not in time. The door flew open, and there stood Willard like the devil himself. Right away, he turned to where Fanny napped. "What's she doing? Why ain't she working?"

"Please, she was so tired. The poor thing worked hard this morning. We both did, so we're taking a break. There's no fault in that."

"Don't you tell me how to run my home. She didn't come here to loaf around. She could be washing the dishes or sweeping the floor if'n you're done outside. She's young and strong. That's why we got her."

Fanny startled awake and sat up, scooting farther into the corner.

Gladys shook her head. "We got her 'cause

we been wanting a girl."

"With her background, she should thank her lucky stars she even gots a home. Coming from a neglectful family, poor to boot. They can't help the way they are." Willard spit a stream of tobacco.

"What're you talking about?"

"You know these children aren't quite the same as others. You wouldn't understand even if I explained it to you. They're different, is all."

"Willard, the child's right here."

Fanny almost disappeared into the plastered wall.

"She don't know what I'm saying. But she's been bred for work, and that's what she should be doing." He made a move in Fanny's direction.

Gladys jumped in front of him and steered him toward the table. "We've all been working hard. Why don't you get Quinn from the barn, and I'll make some sweet tea. A treat on a hot day like this."

"Quinn's out doing what he's supposed to be doing. Unlike this little loafer."

Quinn deserved better too. Gladys would try to find a way to slip him a glass of something cool.

Again, Gladys steered Willard away from Fanny and toward the table. "Fine. Then three of us for a drink."

"How about two? Fanny, get up and get the broom. You get this place swept. And I don't want to see a crumb left." He turned to Gladys. "And make mine some hooch."

"It's the middle of the day." If he started drinking now, he'd be three sheets to the wind by dinner.

He pounded on the table. "If I say I want rotgut, that's what I expect you to get, woman. Don't you go sassin' me again." His words echoed in the room.

Fanny scampered away, and the utility closet door opened and shut. Soon, a swishing noise came from the hall.

"Fine, bathtub gin it is then."

He watched her every move, so she couldn't even water it down. He'd notice the difference anyway.

She poured the illegal, home-distilled drink and slapped it on the table, picked up her own mug, joe down the sink. Though it was a bit early, she might as well get supper started. Maybe some food in Willard's stomach would keep him sober a mite longer.

By the time she had the stew meat and carrots chopped and in the pot and the biscuits mixed, Willard had three more drinks in him. "Girl, you'd best get in here and get these floors swept. Now. I'm going to inspect to make sure you got the parlor clean."

As Fanny scuttled in, Willard staggered out and, as they passed, he knocked her upside the head.

"Willard, stop it. She ain't done nothin' wrong."

"That's for sleepin' when she should be workin'. And she deserves a whole lot more."

The broom handle was twice as tall as Fanny, but she persevered and managed to pull the bristles across the floor.

"Dagnabit, the floor in here's a mess. Dirt everywhere. Get in here, girl."

All the blood drained from Fanny's face. She knew as well as Gladys did what was coming next.

"Stay put. I'll calm him down." As if there were any reasoning with him so drunk.

Gladys found Willard on his hands and knees beside the piano against the far wall in the sitting room. "What on God's green earth are you doing?"

"Look at this dirt." He pointed to something.

She moved to see what Fanny might have missed.

The floor was spotless. The little mite had

managed to sweep it clean. "There ain't nothing there. You're seeing things."

He came to his feet and swayed. Before she knew what was happening, he spun around and slapped her across the cheek. "Don't you contradict me. Just wait'll I get my hands on that good-for-nothin' girl. I have half a mind to return her to Tann." He slurred his words.

"Don't hurt her. She's a baby."

"Then she shouldn't be here."

Gladys raced ahead of her husband to where Fanny once again cowered in the corner.

"Out of my way, woman."

She flung herself on top of the little girl, who was now whimpering.

"Hush now, Momma's gonna make it all right." Gladys peered over her shoulder. Willard picked up a kitchen chair. What was he going to do with that?

A moment later, he swung it and hit Gladys in the back of the head. Pain exploded behind her eyes. She fought for consciousness and clung to Fanny. Never, never would she allow him to hurt her again.

"Mr. Vance?" Miss Connors, his efficient secretary with a high forehead and curly hair, popped into his office.

He glanced from the case study he was reading, the red, leather-bound volume heavy in his hands. "Yes?"

"I've finished all the paperwork and billing you requested."

In other words, she had no more work for today, even though it was not yet noon. His caseload, even his work for Miss Tann, had dwindled to almost nothing, and that he owed in large part to the Tennessee Children's Home Society's director.

No, she may not have fired him outright, but she was willing to strangle the life out of him figuratively and maybe even literally.

"Thank you, Miss Connors. If you'd like, you can go home for the day. I'll pay your full salary." Even though affording it would be a good trick.

"Are you sure? I hate to leave you alone if the phone should get busy."

He tilted his head and stared at her. They could only pray business would pick up. "I'll be able to handle it. Enjoy this beautiful afternoon."

"I will." With a soft click of the door, she left.

His law degree, framed and hanging on the wall, his lawbooks, even his letterhead, all mocked him. If this kept up, he would be forced to let Miss Connors go in the coming weeks. And by Christmas, he might have to take down his shingle. He slammed the book shut, pushed out of his chair, and wandered to the window overlooking Front Street, just blocks from the mighty Mississippi. Perhaps he would end up in a hobo jungle, fighting for scraps, begging for work.

He rubbed his aching forehead. An oscillating fan blew a breeze, ruffling the papers on his desk but not really breaking the heat. Being a lawyer was supposed to be his ticket out of poverty, out of that difficult and abusive life. But he was headed right back there. Would he end up like his father, addicted to the bottle? He shuddered. *Please, God, no.*

The telephone on his desk rang, the chime startling him from his reverie. Three more rings. Why wasn't Miss Connors answering? Oh, right, he'd sent her home.

He returned to his desk and picked up the receiver. "Percy Vance."

"Mr. Vance, this is R.D. Griggs."

Percy worked to keep from seeming too eager. "About time you got back to me. I hope you have some good news."

"I did get into the file room at my own peril. Tann is threatening to remove my daughter from our home if I continue assisting you."

"Who saw you?"

"Who's to say? All I know is that I was spied despite the great lengths I went to in order to remain unseen. Gracious, you'd think the woman had a pair of eyes in every nook and cranny of the city."

"She most likely does. Be more cautious next time."

"There won't be a next time. I can't help you with the records. They're all sealed. Every one of them. If I open them, I can't seal them again."

"Maybe —"

"Absolutely not. Losing Pearl would break my wife's heart. I refuse to allow her to endure that kind of pain."

As the breeze from the fan crossed him, Percy huffed out a breath. "There has to be some way."

"That's the reason I'm calling." The tinkling laughter of a young child floated through the line. Mr. Griggs must be home for lunch, and that must be Pearl in the background.

That would be Percy's guess, anyway. "Oh?" He turned and perched on the edge of his expansive desk.

"Before I give you this information, I want your assurance that this will be the last time you will involve me in this sordid business. I want no more part of it. This is too risky for me and for my family."

"And if I don't agree to your terms?"

"Then you will never find out what I know."

If they needed help in the future, he could always return to Griggs and see if they could work out an agreement. "Fine."

"I had to pay a visit upstairs to the registrar's office. On his desk, he had a stack of court orders from Judge Camille Kelley."

Percy gripped the edge of the desk. "Adoptions?"

"Yes."

This could be the break he and Cecile needed. "Did you get a peek at any of them?"

"Just the top one. There was a sheaf of them. Maybe ten or a dozen or so."

"Tann sells these kids in batches."

R.D.'s voice tightened. "I wouldn't go that far."

Okay, no need in riling him up. This was the kind of information Percy had been waiting for. "What did you see?"

"The paper on top was for a girl, three years old."

"And?"

"Brown hair. Adopted by a Jewish family in Chattanooga."

So close. Almost within touching distance. Percy clutched his midsection with one hand and the phone with his other. "Do you have a name for the family who has her?" He hardly dared to breathe.

"Adolph and Miriam Friedman."

A three-year-old girl with brown hair. Sure, there were plenty of them. And with the hundreds of adoptions Tann churned out each year, many of them were sure to match Millie's description. But there was a chance. "Thank you very much, Mr. Griggs. You've done well."

"Remember your promise to stay far away from me."

"You've got it." Percy dropped the telephone receiver into the cradle.

Wait until he told Cecile. If this wasn't Millie, she would be crushed. But they had to investigate. This was their first real lead. They had a trip to make to Chattanooga.

CHAPTER FOURTEEN

Though R.D. kept his focus on the stack of papers on his desk, Landers's cold stare sent shivers down his back. The man never took his attention from R.D. It was a wonder that either of them got any work done.

A haggard woman stepped to the window he worked behind. She must not have run a comb through her wild blond hair in several days or washed it, for that matter. Dark half-moons hung underneath her eyes, and wrinkles radiated from her pale, pinched lips. She could have been twenty-three. She could have been fifty-three.

"Can I help you, ma'am?" He used the polite greeting despite the lack of a wedding ring on her finger.

"I hope you can," her alto voice rasped. She glanced behind her and all around before leaning closer. In addition to shampooing her hair, she needed a bath. R.D.'s eyes watered.

"My child has been stolen."

He kept himself from sucking in a big breath. "Stolen? You mean kidnapped? You'll need the police for that. You can find them —"

"No, I don't mean kidnapped. No one is holding him for ransom. I mean stolen."

He gripped the edge of the desk and raised himself to the woman's eye level. "Go home. There is nothing we can do for you here."

"But —"

"Go home and forget about your child. You will never find him. And if you know what's good for you, don't come snooping around here again."

"Please, listen to me." Tears glistened in the woman's blue eyes.

R.D. turned from his barred window. His skin tingled. Landers was approaching, his footfalls soft on the carpeting.

From the other side of the window, the woman continued her tirade. "I don't have anywhere else to turn. You have to help me. I'm a good mother. I didn't deserve to have him taken away. Please, I'm begging you, for the love of everything good in this world, help me."

R.D.'s throat tightened and threatened to close all the way. Since he couldn't cover his ears, he worked to close his mind. Yet another woman who had lost a child through no fault of her own. Just like Mrs. Dowd. Just like all those whose letters he'd received. What about the girl with the Friedmans in Chattanooga? Was she stolen? Could she be Mrs. Dowd's child? And what about Pearl? Could she belong to Mrs. Dowd? All he had to do was break the seal on the file and find out.

No. Never. Pearl belonged to him and Darcy.

At last, the woman's voice went hoarse, and her words died off to a whisper. When she couldn't speak anymore, she banged on the counter. R.D. kept his focus on his work. After a fruitless hour, the woman walked away. R.D. relaxed his shoulders. Within moments, Landers was at his side. "Don't ever think about helping a single one of these crazy women." His words were like the hiss of a snake.

The hairs on R.D.'s arms stood up straight. "Of course not."

He'd never been happier to have a workday end. He cleaned up his desk and made his way home. Ah, home. His safe haven. Darcy would have supper ready. Pearl would run into his arms. He would unwind in his favorite brown armchair. He climbed the porch steps and opened the front door. "I'm home."

Instead of being greeted by Pearl, he discovered Darcy curled up in a corner of the green davenport. He dropped his briefcase on the floor and went to her. As soon as he sat beside her, she reached out to him and clung to him.

He stroked her long, silky hair. "What's wrong, darling?"

For the longest moment, she held him and sobbed as if she would drown if she let go. He shushed her, and she finally ceased weeping. When she peered at him, her blue eyes were red-rimmed. "I can't lose her. Do you know what it would do to me if they took her away?"

He did. All too well. He remembered the nights he spent at her bedside in the hospital after they lost their stillborn son. He begged the doctors not to commit her. Instead, he remained next to her and nursed her back to health little by little.

And today marked five years since the death of their son. By now, her heart should have healed, but it hadn't. Would it ever? Would his? If Tann took Pearl away, it would devastate them both.

What if this child in Chattanooga turned out not to be Mrs. Dowd's child but Pearl was? Darcy would never recover. "There's nothing to do but to pray."

She gazed at him. "But there is. We can run. It's the perfect solution. We'll go far away where no one knows us, out of Tann's reach. Start fresh with no more fear for our daughter's security."

"I can't pick up and leave. This is where my job is. Where our home is. Our church and our friends."

"I would give all that up, all our security, in a second for my daughter. I would sacrifice anything to keep her. Wouldn't you?"

Of course. But not this. If they ran, Tann would hunt them down. "Miss Tann hasn't been back, has she?"

Darcy shook her head.

And she hadn't contacted him either. "See, then she wasn't serious about taking Pearl. A good social worker will follow up on her placements. That's all she was doing. She has enough experience with children to know that sometimes they are mischievous."

"Are you sure?" She crinkled her slender nose.

"I wouldn't take any chances when it comes to our Pearl, you know that."

She rested against his shoulder, still sniffling. "Promise me though, that if there is the slightest hint from Miss Tann that she is

171

coming for Pearl, we will leave here and go far away."

Maybe she was right. Maybe they did need a plan just in case. "I promise, darling."

Throughout the long, hot afternoon, Cecile rode beside Percy in his dark green Packard, the wind whipping her hair and cooling her cheeks as they raced across the plains, then climbed the tree-covered mountains and whizzed down the other side. She clung to the door handle until her fingers burned.

This had to be Millie. Just had to be. With her free hand, she rubbed the bonnet ribbon on her wrist, now frayed, discolored, and worn from how often she grasped it. God had dropped this lead into their laps. Wasn't that the way He worked? Cecile was just hours away from holding Millie in her arms.

How she ached for her daughter. Once they were together, Cecile would be complete and would have everything she needed.

She dared to peer at Percy, who was intent on the winding mountain road in front of them. Another one of God's blessings. Through his work, they had come this far. When this ordeal came to an end, she would miss him. Miss his strength, his camaraderie, his tender care for her. The only truly good thing about this city. Because there was no way she was going to stay in Memphis, within Miss Tann's reach.

Perhaps she would go home. Maybe Momma and Daddy would welcome her with open arms and accept their grandchild. Who wouldn't be swayed by Millie's sweet, round face and her beautiful green eyes?

Tomorrow, they would go to their apartment and grab their few items. Cecile would empty her savings account and purchase two train tickets to Massachusetts. Maybe Percy would even come with them. Since he was helping her regain custody of Millie, he was sure to lose his job with Tann.

No. What was she thinking? That was crazy. But she would miss him.

She glanced over her shoulder.

"No one's following us." Percy didn't break his concentration on the road.

"How do you know?"

"Because I've been watching ever since we pulled away from my house. No one is back there. No one knows where we are going or why."

"Ever since that note at the school, I can't stop myself from looking behind me every couple of minutes. I've even been dipping into the money I had set aside for a new dress to take the tram to work, so I'm always in public."

"Good idea."

"And you're sure there's no one back there?"

"Positive. You can release your grip on the handle. You won't have feeling in your fingers by the time we arrive."

She chuckled and forced herself to relax her hold. "How much longer?"

"A few more hours. Why don't you get some rest?"

"I could never sleep. I'm too excited."

For a second, he switched his focus from the road to her. "Don't get your hopes too high. We have no guarantee this is Millie."

"But it could be. Hope is what I live, breathe, and eat these days. It's all I have." And in the last few hours, it had blossomed, perhaps more than she should have allowed it to. But she might be able to get Millie. To hold her, kiss her, tell her again how desperately she loved her.

"I understand, but I would hate to see you disappointed." He stroked the top of her left hand, Nathaniel's thin gold wedding band still encircling her finger. "I'll pray this child is yours."

Could it be that Percy cared about her? And why did that send her heart into a schoolgirl pitter-pat rhythm? She was being silly, nothing more. Right now, she had to concentrate on Millie, on rebuilding the life she had with her child.

"You said once Millie was your only family, but you weren't ready to talk about it. Are you now?"

"Not really. My parents disowned me. They didn't like Nathaniel, but he was a good man. His only crime was being a dreamer. And that's all I really want to say."

"Thanks for sharing that with me. I won't press you." A good number of miles passed before Percy broke the silence. "How are things at the school?"

"Nice way to distract me."

He grinned. "I try."

"Fine. The mess is cleaned, and we've reopened. I'm thankful to still have a job, since there was talk about closing it." With any of God's grace though, she wouldn't need it after tonight.

"Glad to hear it."

"Do you think whoever did it will return?"

"Let's pray not."

So she did.

The miles passed with excruciating slowness. Why did Memphis have to be so far from Chattanooga? She'd never been there but had always imagined it to be much closer than this.

Talk about storming the gates of heaven. For the rest of the drive, that's what Cecile did, begging and pleading with God in every conceivable fashion to let this child be her Millie.

Would she be scared? Confused? Happy? What an upsetting time it might be for her. *Lord, let her remember me. Don't let me frighten her, but fill her with joy at seeing me again.*

In the midst of her petitions, she must have dozed, because Percy shook her awake. "We're here." He'd parked near a street corner, in front of a filling station, a wooden phone booth with glass doors leaning against it.

She blinked a couple of times to get her bearings. The glass globes on top of the gas pumps glowed in the dying light. In a diner, patrons seated next to the windows spooned in mouthfuls of the daily special. Scattered businesses dotted the area, few people left inside to work as the evening drew near. The neighborhood wasn't residential, that was for sure. "This is where the Friedmans live?"

"No. We'll look them up in the telephone book and then find their house. I'll be right back."

176

True to his word, Percy flipped through the phone directory, scribbled on a piece of paper, studied something in the front of the book, and returned to the car. "Got it."

Her breath caught in her throat. "You have it? Can I hold it?" She cringed at her own strange request.

But Percy gave her a soft smile and handed her the paper. "They aren't too far. I think I know where they live." He turned over the engine, and they motored through the lamp-lit streets for a while before turning onto a tranquil, tree-lined street boasting Crafts-man and porch-fronted Southern Colonial homes.

"This is a nice area." Millie will have been well cared for here. Maybe she wouldn't want to leave. Perhaps it was wrong for Cecile to take her away from the privileges she would have growing up in a home like this.

Percy squeezed her hand. "She'll be so happy to see you. Remember what you once told me?"

She shook her head, her throat too thick to speak.

"Love is the most important thing."

She squeezed his hand back. "Thank you. I needed that."

He didn't release his hold on her as he

177

drove down the peaceful road, one man out walking his little white poodle. The area offered spacious two-story homes set on larger lots at the base of Lookout Mountain. Such a beautiful area.

Percy braked in front of one of the homes. A red front door cut through the evening darkness, beckoning them forward. Percy came around to her side and held the door open.

And she couldn't move, like she was paralyzed. "What if —"

"Don't play what-if games." Though soft, his voice was stern. "You don't need the ticket until you get to the train."

She filled her lungs with oxygen to keep from fainting then slid from the auto. He clasped her hand, and together they strode up the walk.

He pressed the bell, and in short order, a man with straight, dark hair and chocolate eyes opened the door. "Can I help you?"

Percy, ever the lawyer, took over. "Please forgive the lateness of this visit. I'm Attorney Percy Vance from Memphis. I believe you adopted a child through the Tennessee Children's Home Society recently."

The man gave a slow nod. A young woman, her raven hair in waves around her shoulders, came up behind him. "What is this about, Adolph?"

"Ma'am." Percy tipped his walker-style hat. "I'm a lawyer with the Tennessee Children's Home Society. I must see your daughter."

"Daughters. We adopted two. And you want to see them at this hour?" Mr. Friedman frowned.

"This is a routine follow-up."

He stuck to the script they'd devised together on the way here. "Didn't you get a phone call?"

Mrs. Friedman stepped aside. "Please, won't you come in? Let me get you some coffee. And no, we didn't receive a telephone call about any visit."

Percy nudged Cecile inside ahead of him. "My apologies. There must have been some sort of mix-up. And my apologies for the lateness of the hour. We had some issues with the car."

The gracious home was neat and well kept. Light-colored area rugs covered the dark wood floors. End tables flanked a deep red davenport, which faced a brick fireplace. A brass menorah held sway over the mantel.

Cecile rubbed her upper arms. Maybe Miss Tann was correct. Maybe it was best to leave Millie where she was.

While she was lost in her thoughts, Percy

179

must have been speaking, because she came out of them as Mr. Friedman said, "We understand. I'll get the girls."

Cecile sat on the edge of the well-cushioned sofa then stood, then sat once more. She wiped her damp palms on her straight, blue skirt.

And then, at the top of the stairs, appeared a sleepy-eyed, brown-haired girl in a white nightgown.

CHAPTER FIFTEEN

"Are you sure about this?" Gladys leaned out the window of the Chevy pickup truck, her best light blue Sinamay weave cloche hat perched on her head. She eyed Willard and Fanny as they stood on the side of the dusty road in front of the house. Was she doing the right thing leaving them alone together?

Willard tugged on his blue overalls. " 'Course I am. You already done fed us breakfast, and Fanny can make us some lunch." He pulled the scrawny, wide-eyed child close to his side.

"I don't know. Are you sure you two will get along while I'm gone to Miz Brewster's tea?"

" 'Course we will. It'll give me a chance to get to know the girl better. Won't it, Fanny?" He squeezed her till she squeaked.

The girl chewed her lip and stared at the man towering above her. For weeks now, she hadn't uttered a word other than yes ma'am and no sir.

Then again, Willard had behaved better these past few weeks. He had stayed away from the hooch and not given either Fanny or Quinn a licking in as long a time. He'd even managed to be gentle with her.

Perhaps he had changed. Perhaps God could work miracles in the worst man's heart. "Well, if'n you're sure."

"I am. You'd best be goin' afore you're late."

She started the automobile and steered down the dirt road toward the small town, a smile she couldn't stop spreading across her face. Good thing last night's wind had calmed and wasn't kicking up dust like it had been. Yes, if'n God could change water into wine, He could change her husband's heart. Everything would work out in the end. They could be a real family. Maybe Fanny would even break out of her shell and talk and smile. Now wouldn't that be a miracle?

She bumped along the sun-packed rutted road, and soon the small town rose from the Mississippi cotton fields. In short order, she pulled in front of the white clapboard home of the pastor's wife and parked the car. A stream of other women arrived and made their way inside.

The young, slender brunette welcomed Gladys at the door. "So good to see you. I'm glad you could make it."

"Wasn't sure if I could get away, but Willard done told me to come, and you're supposed to obey your husband."

Miz Brewster tipped her head and flashed half a grin. "I — well, I suppose that's right."

Most of the women gathered together on a grouping of fancy chairs in the far corner of the parlor and a settee in the middle of it all. A gleaming silver tea service sat on a shiny walnut coffee table. The only other unoccupied chair was opposite the table, kitty-corner from the gaggle of ladies.

Gladys plunked into it and worried the hem of her best black dress with a simple white lace collar. The dress was fine for funerals and church services but not for such an elegant gathering. The other ladies wore filmy pink and yellow and pale green dresses and even snow-white gloves that came to their elbows. Who knew tea was such a formal affair?

Laughter rose from the group across from Gladys. How she would love to giggle along with them. Not since Ma had died when Gladys was fourteen years old had she laughed with a friend. Just had a good time.

Miz Brewster entered the room and stood on the red and blue and green rug and clapped her hands for attention. The speaking died to a whisper then stopped altogether. "Good morning, ladies. I'm so pleased y'all could be here today. Hasn't the Lord blessed us with a fine day?"

A murmur rose from the group. Gladys nodded.

"Shall we pray? Dear Father, we thank You for this gathering of women. May You be in the midst of us today and bring us to know each other and You better. Thank You for the food You've provided for us and bless it to our bodies. We ask this all in Your Son's name. Amen."

The noise of women's chatter rose again. Gladys studied her cracked hands and broken fingernails. She should have taken the time to at least cut them, but last night, same as every evening, she'd fallen into bed bone-weary.

"Mrs. Knowles? Here's a cup of tea for you. And do help yourself to the sandwiches and goodies."

Gladys brought her attention to Miz Brewster, a white cup with a red-painted design in her hands, steam rising from the tea's surface. "Thank you."

"You're welcome. Why don't you join us?

184

We're discussing the fall missionary luncheon we're planning." Miz Brewster stepped into the kitchen.

But the talk coming from the group of ladies was nothing about no missionary lunch. They thought Gladys couldn't hear, but she did. "Do you see her dress?"

"Doesn't she have a pair of gloves? Imagine coming to a tea with bare hands."

"What does she know about polite society? I'm surprised she stepped foot off that farm."

"And that girl they have living with them. Wherever did they find such a scrawny, stupid kid? Wild ones like that belong in an institution."

Gladys bit her tongue until the metallic flavor of blood filled her mouth. She should never have come. She didn't belong here. Wasn't wanted here. Wasn't wanted anywhere but home and only then to cook and clean.

She placed the tea on the coffee table, the rail around the edge carved in swirls. And that's just what her stomach was doing right now — swirling around in her middle. She stood and headed for the door.

"Mrs. Knowles, are you leaving so soon?"

"I — thank you, but I must go."

"You've only just arrived."

185

"Yes, I'm so sorry. Willard'll be wanting his lunch. Thank you for the lovely time." Heat searing her cheeks, Gladys fled from the room, from the house, and into the security of the truck. Not until she was three-quarters of the way home did her face cool and her hands stop shaking. She'd never fit in with those women. Her place was on the farm.

She parked the car in the yard and opened the door to screams coming from the house. Screeches of terror. *No, not Fanny!*

She raced across the grassless yard, twisting her ankle on a clod of dirt, falling to the ground in pain. Another yell. Gladys came to her feet and limped-ran to the house and flung the door open.

The cries came from the kitchen. Willard leaned over Fanny, a willow lash in his hand. "I'll teach you to talk back."

He lifted the whip.

Fanny screamed.

Gladys leaped between her husband and the child. "Stop it." She yanked Fanny from Willard's grasp. "Don't ever touch the girl again, or I will get the law after you."

He struck Gladys across the mouth. More blood.

"Don't ever interfere with me again, or I will get my gun after you."

Cecile stared at the child standing at the top of the staircase. Her long, brown hair flowed around her shoulders. She rubbed her blue eyes. Like she'd been punched in the stomach, Cecile collapsed. "That's not her. That's not her." Her body went numb.

Percy took over. "You said you adopted two girls. Where is the other one?"

Mrs. Friedman turned away, while her husband swallowed hard. "When Kate came to us, she was very underweight and ill. We took her straight to the doctor, and though we fed her and nursed her, she passed away last week."

"No, no, no!" The screams ripped from Cecile's throat. Not her beautiful, vivacious little girl. *God, don't let it be true. This is too much to bear.*

The Friedmans stared at her. Tears coursed down Mrs. Friedman's cheeks, mirroring those racing down Cecile's.

Mr. Friedman leaned forward. "What's wrong with her? What's going on? You said you were from the home."

Cecile rocked back and forth, unable to breathe. Her last connection to Nathaniel severed. Forever. She'd lost the last bit of her family.

"I am associated with it. This is Mrs. Dowd. Her three-year-old daughter was kidnapped by Miss Tann a couple of months ago. We're afraid that your daughter, the one who passed away, was Mrs. Dowd's child."

All the color drained from Mrs. Friedman's face. She wiped away her tears and sat as straight as a ruler-drawn line. "Miss Tann would never commit such a crime. She works hard for the children. I must ask you to leave right now."

Cecile worked to contain her sobs so she could speak. She pinched the bridge of her nose and stemmed the tide of tears. "Please, I need to know for sure if it was my child. Do you have a picture? Anything?"

Mr. Friedman touched his wife's shoulder. "We have to give this woman the answers she wants."

"Who is she to come into our home at this hour of night and disturb us? To falsely accuse someone of such a hideous crime."

Percy pulled Cecile close. His touch radiated strength, which flowed into her. "She's a mother just like you. And the charges aren't false. I know. I was there when it happened."

Mr. Friedman stood. "I'll get the only

photograph we have of her."

His wife followed him out of the room but not so far that their voices didn't carry to Percy and Cecile. "I want them gone from this house. Do you hear me, Adolph? They shouldn't be here." Her voice faded away.

The wait for Mr. Friedman to return with the photo might have been two lifetimes. Percy held Cecile. At least she wasn't alone. Without him, this wouldn't be bearable. What would she have done these weeks without him beside her? Her insides tumbled and tied themselves into a knot. How would she go on if this was Millie? Losing her would be equivalent to ripping off one of her limbs. She wouldn't be able to function without her. Her head pounded, and her shoulders ached.

At long last, footsteps heralded Mr. Friedman's return. His wife wasn't with him. "I apologize for my wife. You have to understand how upset she is to have lost Kate. She wasn't our daughter for very long, but she was our daughter."

All Cecile could do was nod.

Percy, her rock, answered for her. "We do. And we're so sorry for your loss."

"Thank you." He held out the picture with a deckle edge.

Cecile couldn't make herself move. Percy

took the photo and showed it to her.

Though the black-and-white image was grainy, it showed a pencil-thin young child, her face long, her braided hair reaching to the middle of her back.

She recognized her.

Cecile dropped the photo and covered her face. "That's not Millie." From head to toe, she trembled like grass in the breeze. It wasn't Millie, but it was one of the girls whose photograph they found in the file.

When she uncovered her eyes, Percy was handing the picture to Mr. Friedman. "Thank you for sharing that. We are sorry for having troubled you."

"Miriam doesn't want to believe that the woman who gave us the girls would harm them. But Sarah too came covered with scabies. She has awful nightmares. If you can do anything to help the children remaining in her care, please do so."

"You won't contact the home about our visit, will you?" Percy's voice trembled.

"No, we'll keep it quiet. Just help these children."

"We'll do our best."

"Good luck to both of you."

Percy and Cecile shook Mr. Friedman's hand. As they headed out the door, Cecile turned to face him. "I hope your wife recovers from this grief. Nothing is more terrible than losing a child."

Mr. Friedman gave a small smile then shut the door behind them.

Standing there on the front porch, Cecile went to Percy and pulled him close. He embraced her as she quivered, his coat smelling of pipe tobacco. How good to be nestled in his arms. Her heart beat in time to his. "That could have been Millie. Might still be. She could have met the same fate. What if my little girl is gone?"

"Don't torture yourself. The only answer we have is that the child who came to live here isn't Millie."

"So we've eliminated one home out of the millions in the United States. We're no closer to discovering where she is. What if we never do? How am I supposed to move forward with my life when I'm stuck in the past?" She couldn't live without knowing. The possibilities would drive her insane. Her soul would not be still until she found Millie.

"Don't worry." Percy's tender words washed over her. "We won't stop until we know. I promise. I'm not going to let this matter rest until you have all the answers you need. Until you have peace."

She leaned back and gazed at him. He

191

bent to her and kissed her, his lips gentle
against hers.

And she didn't stop him.

CHAPTER SIXTEEN

Percy sank into the supple dark brown leather chair in the paneled library of his club. Cigar and pipe smoke swirled about him, intoxicating him with their rich odors. He closed his eyes and allowed the music of men's low voices to lull him.

After driving home from Chattanooga all night, he and Cecile had informed the mother about her child's fate. The worst thing he'd ever had to do in his life. Even if he lived to be one hundred, he'd never erase the echo of her soul-crushing sobs.

After a few hours of sleep, he'd gone into the office, but he hadn't managed to get much work done. Every time Miss Connors came in to give him papers or ask him a question, she caught him staring into nothingness. Because what was left after you lost a child?

At last, Miss Connors convinced him to leave and commanded him to unwind.

Across the room he caught sight of Griggs standing near the full-length window, chatting with an older man, a cigar in one hand and a brandy in the other. Griggs eyed Percy but made no move in his direction.

All the better.

A dapper, white-haired man wearing a light tan suit and a string tie approached Percy, bringing a smile to his face.

"Is this seat taken?" The old man motioned to the matching chair beside Percy.

"It's good to see you, Mr. DeJong. Please, have a seat."

Percy's boss back when he first passed the bar lowered himself into the chair. "These old bones creak and groan worse than a door that needs to be oiled. So, what have you been up to? I'm surprised to see you here when it's still afternoon. You always worked such long hours. Or is the practice going so well it runs itself?"

"Ha." Percy spit out the word. "I'm on the wrong side of Memphis politics, and there are hardly enough cases to keep me afloat."

Mr. DeJong raised both of his gray eyebrows.

"Don't ask."

"I've heard rumors about you and Georgia Tann."

"I can only imagine."

"Don't lose heart, my boy. You have this knack for falling into a dung heap and coming out smelling like a rose."

The chances of that happening this time were tiny. Teeny tiny.

A disturbance broke out behind him. "I demand to be admitted. I have business with one of your members."

Percy clutched the chair's armrests. That voice. There was no mistaking it.

"I'm sorry, but I can't let you in there." The poor young man at the desk had his hands full.

"And I don't care what you say." A moment later, Georgia Tann herself strode into the room wearing pants and a loose blouse, the young man trailing her, shrugging as if to say he had done his best.

He probably had.

"There you are." Like an arrow aimed at his heart, Tann pointed at Percy.

He rose. "Please, don't cause a commotion here. This is a private club."

"One you enjoy because of my generosity and tolerance. But no more. I've reached the end of my patience."

At her words, the hairs on Percy's arms stood straight. The stares of a dozen men weighed on his shoulders.

"How dare you interfere with a legal adoption? Of all the nerve. I have half a mind to speak to the district attorney about charging you."

How had she discovered this information? Someone at the courthouse must have tipped her off. Griggs himself, maybe. "Can we talk about this in private?"

"Absolutely not. I want all the world to know what you've done. You believe yourself to be above the law. You are arrogant and headstrong."

He swallowed hard. "Please."

"You go to track down an adoptive family. How dare you?"

He stood mute before her.

"I asked you a question. How dare you?" Her face bloomed red.

He shoved his trembling hands in his pockets.

She stepped closer and whispered, "Did you read in the paper about Mr. Kearny?"

The chair behind him prevented him from moving away. He nodded.

"Good. Then you know what happens to people who cross me. I have influence in this town, and I'm not afraid to wield it."

"Are you threatening my life?" He did not keep his voice low.

She pulled him by the arm into the lobby.

He would have a bruise there in the morning. "I'm warning you. I'm not an enemy you want to make. And I will not have you dipping your sticky little fingers into my pie. You have brought your own ruin upon yourself. Do you like this club? Your house? Your automobile?"

When he was a child, he would sit on his family's cabin's tilted front step and dream of life away from the Mississippi farm. No more early-morning chores. No more back-breaking work for a pittance of subsistence. No more having the money the crops earned poured down his father's gullet. He hadn't known hunger or pain or fear for years. His gut twisted with the idea of begging for food and a place to sleep. He forced the words through his lips. "Yes, I enjoy all of them."

Tann turned to the kid at the podium. "Get me Mr. Simonson on the phone." The head of the state bar.

The telephone was brought to her.

"No. Wait." He lunged to snatch the receiver from her hand. He'd been foolish. Rash.

But she pressed on his chest and kept him at bay.

"This time you've gone too far, Mr. Vance." She put the receiver to her ear. "Charlie. Georgia Tann. I have a problem I need taken care of immediately."

Indistinguishable chatter came from the other end.

"Percy Vance. Disbarred. Today. You will be rewarded."

More tinny words.

"Thank you." She hung up the phone. "You will be getting notification in the mail, Mr. Vance, but from this point forward, you are no longer allowed to practice law in the state of Tennessee." With that, she marched from the building.

He peered over his shoulder at the group of men gathered behind him. Griggs gave a crooked smile. He could never forgive Percy for being born on the wrong side of the tracks.

Mr. DeJong shook his head.

Percy fled the building. The life he'd worked so hard to build crumbled around him.

Cecile rolled over in bed and stared at the face of her alarm clock — 5 a.m. She rubbed her gritty eyes and threw back the blanket.

Once she had pulled her robe around her middle, she padded from the bedroom to the apartment's small main room and sat in the rocker without turning on the light switch. She didn't need illumination to know what the place contained. On the corner of the battered kitchen table stood a white and pink frosted cake. And beside it was a gift for Millie, wrapped in pink paper with white polka dots. Millie should be here to open it. To play with the stuffed teddy bear inside the box. To hold it close when she went to bed.

God, what am I going to do if we never find her? Like happened much too often these days, the heavens remained silent. Didn't He even care about her plight? About the precious daughter He had given her and Nathaniel?

Millie would have been four.

No. She couldn't allow herself to think of Millie in the past tense. Today, her daughter did turn four. The longing in her chest became a physical ache. She twisted the tattered ribbon around and around her wrist. The action didn't ease the pain. Nothing did.

In the semidarkness of the late summer morning, she dressed in a lightweight blue skirt, a black blouse, and her stockings. She slipped her feet into her black Oxford shoes. After consuming a dry piece of toast, she exited the apartment. As she left the building and wandered down the street, the humidity wrapped itself around her, a blanket she couldn't throw off.

Thoughts and memories of Millie flitted through her mind, a new one coming with each footstep. Millie's first cry. Her shiny brown hair. Her face the day she'd left her with Mrs. Ward.

Oh, if she could only go back and relive that day.

She glanced up and found herself marching through the entrance to Overton Park. How had she gotten here?

Since it was Saturday, she didn't have to be at work. She meandered through the park and to the bench where she'd first met Percy. Because of the early hour, no children yet swung on the swings or slid down the slide.

The leaves overhead formed a canopy, a shelter for her to hide away from the world. A covering and protection from all the hurt and evil around her. A place of peace and good. A place where God still saw and heard her.

Someone, a man with tan pants, stepped in front of her, blocking her view. "I had a feeling I'd find you here."

She gazed upward into Percy's eyes, startling in their blueness. "Why are you out and about so early on the weekend?"

"I couldn't sleep."

"Neither could I."

"I remembered what today is."

Her eyes watered. "You did?" What man remembered the birthday of another man's child?

"Millie's fourth birthday. If you came anywhere, it would be here." He sat beside her and swiped away the tear that trickled down her face.

All the gesture accomplished was to make more tears fall. "That is so sweet. Nathaniel always had to ask me when Millie's birthday was, and he was there the day she was born. I can't believe you remembered, especially since I only told you the date once or twice." Part of her heart, deep inside, a piece that had been dead for as long as Nathaniel, sprang to life.

"I thought you might want some company. But if you'd prefer to be alone, I can go."

She took him by the hand, a spark passing between them. "No, please stay. If I'm by myself, I'll get too melancholy."

"We can be melancholy together." He rubbed the top of her thumb, an odd stirring in her chest, in her limbs.

"But you must have plans for today."

"Just to clean out my office."

She slid to face him, her knee bumping

his. "What? Why?"

He chortled. "You must be the only person in Memphis who doesn't know. Miss Tann fired me yesterday in dramatic fashion at my club, in front of my peers."

"Oh dear. How awful. And yet you came here to wallow with me in my problems. After I did this to you. It's because of me you ended up on her wrong side."

He shook his head, the pomade keeping his dark waves in place. "No, the trouble began before I met you. I already had qualms about her dealings."

"So, you were always a crusader for justice?"

"I would fight the bullies who stole the pretty girls' lunches."

She couldn't help the laugh that burst from her. "I can just see you, Mr. Vance, coming to the aid of the damsels in distress."

He winked, and warmth flooded her. "Only the pretty ones, like I said."

Her temperature rose. Was he flirting with her? And was she enjoying it? "I believe you exaggerate. But I do feel guilty. Is there anything I can do to make it up to you?"

"You can help me pack boxes."

Though she had come here to seek solace, she'd found it in Percy instead of in the place. Perhaps being busy, working hard

202

with her hands, would ease the pain in her heart. Help her to forget for a little while the emptiness of her apartment.

He offered her his elbow, and she slipped her hand around his arm. Together, they strolled by the fountain, the water gurgling, out of the park, and down the block toward the trolley stop.

As they stepped into the street to catch the tram, a midnight-blue car careened around the corner. Its tires screeched. The stench of burning rubber filled the air. "Percy!"

He pushed her out of the way.

She fell to the ground.

A sickening thud.

"That should teach you." The car squealed away.

Nauseated, she came to her hands and knees. Percy lay on the road. A gash on his forehead gushed blood.

"No! No! Someone help us!"

CHAPTER SEVENTEEN

A jostling on the bed awakened R.D. long before he was ready for the day to start.

With her small hands, Pearl patted his cheeks. "Get up, Daddy. Today is zoo day."

Then again, how could he be grumpy when he opened his eyes to the sight of his daughter leaning over him, her brown hair brushing her shoulders, her green eyes sparkling. "Yes, Miss Muffet, it's zoo day."

"And we see lions and giraffes and monkeys."

"I see one monkey already."

He tickled her until her peals of laughter rang off the walls. "Stop it, stop it."

So he did.

"More, Daddy."

He joined his chuckles with her giggles.

"What a commotion we have in here." Darcy stood in the doorway, already dressed in a mustard-yellow dress, a pink apron tied around her waist. "You'd think the zoo was right here."

Pearl hopped from the bed. "No, Mommy. We go now to the zoo?"

"First, we have to have breakfast." Hand in hand, the two women R.D. loved most in the world left the room. He would protect them with his life.

For hours on end last night, he'd lain awake, replaying yesterday's incident in his mind. Tann barging into the club, screaming at Vance, ruining him in front of everyone. The woman had nothing but nerve. And she was not to be messed with.

At least R.D.'s affiliation with Vance had ended. And now that Vance had lost his job, he likely wouldn't be a club member much longer. Perhaps they would never see each other again. That suited R.D. just fine. Always had.

As soon as Darcy finished the dishes, the trio left the house. His wife had Pearl togged to the bricks in a frilly pink dress, lacy socks, and a pink bonnet. He tugged on the hat. "You look like you're about to cross the prairie."

Darcy gave him a playful swat. "Stop it. The sun will be hot later, and Pearl is fair. We don't want her nose to freckle."

"Yeah, Daddy, no freckles. I be pretty."

He tweaked her nose. "Freckles or no

freckles, you're the prettiest girl in all Memphis."

"Mommy pretty too."

"She's the prettiest lady in the city."

Pearl squealed with delight and chattered the entire trip on the tram, right up to the zoo's entrance. Or near to it, anyway.

The driver halted the trolley about a block away from the usual stop. "Folks, there's an accident ahead so I'm going to have to let you off here. Sorry for any inconvenience."

A few people mumbled about the trouble, but since it was Saturday, many had been planning to end their trip at the zoo anyway. The brief walk did nothing to dampen Pearl's enthusiasm for the outing.

They happened upon the scene, several people crowded in a circle around a woman who bent over a person lying on the road. All R.D. could distinguish were the soles of a man's shoes. He turned to his wife. "Take Pearl to the entrance. Let me see if I can help. I'll join you in a moment."

"Hurry, darling. I'm not sure I can contain our daughter too much longer."

He threaded his way through the crowd to the accident and peered over the woman's shoulder to get a look at the victim.

No, it couldn't be. Griggs bit on his fist. Vance lay battered and bloody in the middle of the street. The woman kneeling beside him sobbed. "Oh Percy, no, don't die. Please, don't leave me alone again."

Griggs turned to one of the other onlookers, a man dressed in overalls. "What happened?"

"From what I hear, a car came out of nowhere, hit the man, and took off, but not before the driver shouted something about teaching the man a lesson."

The slender woman beside Percy wept. "Where is that ambulance?"

R.D. slipped from the crowd and hustled to his waiting family.

Darcy touched his arm. "You're as white as the courthouse stone. What happened?"

"A man hit by a car. Nothing I can do. Let's go and enjoy the day." But he wiped his hands on his pants. This is what happened to people who messed with Tann.

Cecile knelt on the hard, warm road, giving Percy's scraped cheek a gentle rub. "Please, please, wake up." At least he had a pulse. At least his chest still rose and fell.

Blood gushed from his temple. With her embroidered handkerchief, she worked to stem the flow of crimson. His eyes remained shut.

The insistent beep of a horn intensified

and then stopped. The crowd around them parted. One of the white-clad stretcher bearers touched her shoulder. "Ma'am, we have to ask you to step aside."

"But I can't leave him."

"He's in good hands."

He wasn't though. This was no accident. Someone wanted to harm him and had been successful. At least partially. Who was to say they wouldn't find him and return to finish the job?

And she was the one who had put him in this danger.

The nurses, also dressed in white, tended to Percy, but the scene blurred in front of her eyes. She couldn't catch her breath.

She turned to one of the medics. "Can I ride along with you?"

"Are you his wife?" The man smoothed his dark mustache.

"A friend. Please, he doesn't have anyone else here. He's not married."

He nodded. "Very well." He and his counterpart lifted Percy onto the stretcher.

Percy moaned. She stroked his arm. "You're going to be fine. And I'm going to be right here with you."

The medics loaded Percy into the ambulance, curtains covering the three back windows. She climbed in behind him. With the horn screeching, they raced off to St. Joseph's Hospital just down the road. The ride took a matter of a few minutes, but it might as well have been a lifetime. All the way, she never let go of her grasp on his hand. His steady pulse beneath her fingertips helped her keep her composure. Nothing else. She couldn't lose him, couldn't imagine her life without him. In a short amount of time, he'd become so dear to her, so important to her. But what they were doing was fraught with peril that she'd brought upon him.

At last, they reached the all-brick building. A statue of the patron saint stood guard, and crosses adorned the peaks of the multiple roof lines. She had never been here with Nathaniel. They had no money for treatment at such a place. A simple doctor and her home nursing had been all they could afford.

What if Percy died like Nathaniel had? Why were all the men in her life torn away from her? She fanned away the burning in her eyes.

The caustic odor of antiseptic assaulted her as she entered the building. The medic with the mustache pointed toward a door. "You are going to have to wait on the sun porch so the doctor can assess him. The nurse will come to see you as soon as they know something."

Though she had to rip herself from his side, it was the best for him. She retired to the bright room, dark wicker chairs scattered around the room's perimeter, a couple of large area rugs covering the tile floors. The bitter smell of coffee brewing somewhere sent waves of nausea through her. She raced for the lavatory and retched away her small breakfast. After rinsing her mouth with water and washing her hands and face with the disinfectant soap, she returned to the sunny room. In an office inside the main building, a telephone rang. With a beeping of the horn, another ambulance arrived.

Back and forth, she paced the room. No family came to sit with her. She'd had no answer to the letter she sent to her parents weeks ago after Millie disappeared. Were they even praying for her? If only she had someone to talk to, someone to confide in. Someone to be here to hold her hand and tell her Percy would be okay. But even if he pulled through this time, what about next time? Whoever did this wouldn't be satisfied until Percy lay in Elmwood Cemetery. And his blood would be on her hands.

There was only one way to ensure his safety. That way would leave a wound in her heart. Then again, so would his death. Lights flashed in front of her eyes as pain exploded in her temple. There had to be another way, a different path that would keep him from harm. But there wasn't.

She'd just about worn holes through the soles of her shoes by the time a nurse in a starched white hat entered the room. "Are you here for Mr. Vance?"

Cecile hurried to her. "Yes. How is he?" Like the waves on the shore, her blood whooshed in her ears.

"He's awake. Other than a nasty bump on his head and a gash on his face, he'll be fine."

Cecile sank into one of the cushioned chairs. "Thank the Lord. When can I see him?" One last time.

"Right now, if you'd like."

"Yes. Yes, please." She followed the nurse, whose shoes squeaked on the polished tile floor, into a room much like any bedroom. A spindled table sat beside the bed, and a mirrored dresser huddled in the corner.

Percy lay on the bed, a bandage wound around his head. She rushed to his side. "Percy?"

His eyes flickered opened. "Hi."

"Hi yourself. Don't ever scare me like that again."

"I'll try not to." He chuckled then winced. "Just lay still."

"What happened?"

She lowered herself to the hard wooden chair beside him. "You don't remember?"

He shook his head and groaned. "The zoo."

"Yes, we were leaving there. A car came around the corner and hit you. The driver yelled something about teaching you a lesson."

He shut his eyes. "Man or woman?"

"Man."

"Tann?" He slurred his words, likely groggy.

"Perhaps associated with her."

"It wasn't enough to fire me."

"If it was Tann, do you think it means we might be getting close to the truth?"

"Don't know." He yawned, his eyes still closed.

He was right. But maybe whoever was after them believed they were. The nearer they got to Millie, the more dangerous it would become.

And despite her vow to be there for him, she couldn't bear it if he lost his life because of her.

"I'm sorry."

She blinked three times. "What do you

212

have to be sorry about?"

"My fault."

"You weren't driving the car."

"This mess."

"I think that knot on your head scrambled your brains." She was the one to blame. Because of her, he'd lost everything and almost his life. She would rather have him alive in the world than dead beside her. She no longer hated him. Walking away would hurt, but she had to do it before anything worse happened.

How would she go through with it though? And how could she convince him not to pursue Millie's search any longer?

She bit her lip. "I just realized that I know the voice of the man who ran you over."

"Who?"

"My father." Would he believe her lie?

"Father?"

"He must have resealed my letters when he returned them. He's the one who took Millie. I have to go home. To Massachusetts. Tonight."

"I'll go." His eyes flicked open.

"No." Her words were harsher than she intended, but maybe that would be enough to stop him. "You're in no shape to go anywhere. Besides, I have to do this alone. No telling what my father would do to you if you came. I thank you for your help, Mr. Vance. And I pray for a speedy recovery for you." Her throat burned. She turned to leave.

"Wait."

She halted but didn't face him.

"Are you coming back?"

She shook her head and walked out of the room.

Now, she was truly alone, and she would have to find Millie on her own.

Once on the street, she meandered away from the hospital. From the corner of her eye, she spied a green DeSoto driving beside her, matching her pace. She walked faster. The car drove faster. She slowed down. So did the car. She came to a corner but didn't dare cross the street. The car idled at the stop sign. A cafe's entrance was to her right. She ducked inside.

"Can I help you, ma'am?"

Ignoring the waiter, she sprinted through the restaurant and into the kitchen.

"Excuse me, you can't be in here."

She dashed out the back door and into the alley. By now, night was falling. She zig-zagged her way through the city. Every now and again, she caught sight of a car the same color as the one from earlier. Farther and farther she ran until she arrived at her apartment building and scrambled inside.

A single bare bulb lit the hallway. Two at a time, she raced up the stairs. Once inside, she bolted the door. At the edge of the table sat the cake. She smashed her hand into the middle of it. "Why, God, why?"

CHAPTER EIGHTEEN

A soft September breeze flowed in through the screens on Percy's front porch, and he took a deep breath. A week had passed since his so-called accident. If he took life easy and didn't move too fast, his head didn't pound too much. His injuries could have been so much worse.

The police hadn't yet found the hit-and-run driver. But nothing compared to the pain in his heart. When Cecile had walked out of his hospital room and out of his life, he'd lost his taste for everything. The sun had ceased to shine on him.

Her story didn't ring true. He'd been too groggy at the time for it to process, but the more he pondered it, the more he wondered. All of a sudden, she figured out her father took Millie? Why would he do that when he had disowned his daughter? Despised Millie's father?

No, Percy didn't believe a word she said.

Since he'd been released from the hospital a few days ago, he'd been holed up in his home, doors locked. Cecile's father hadn't gotten Tann to abduct Millie. Danger continued to lurk in every shadow. But today's beautiful weather beckoned him outside. Still, he kept constant vigil. Any cars slowing down. Any people strolling by, casing the house. Anything out of the ordinary.

So far, nothing. A couple of girls sat under a shiny-leafed magnolia tree across the street and threw a tea party. A team of boys gathered together for a game of stickball. All the time, the cicadas sang. From down the street came a family out for a Saturday afternoon walk. A mom and a dad with a little girl skipping ahead of them, behind them, between them.

As they approached, Percy furrowed his brow and leaned forward. The family passed the front of the house, but this wasn't just any family. This was Griggs, his wife, and his daughter. His young adopted daughter with bobbed brown hair. From his lookout, he couldn't identify the color of her eyes, but from the way Mrs. Griggs continued to call to her to keep up with them, she was a handful.

Percy's mouth went dry. Could it be? Could she have been under their noses the entire time? An idea that could right this entire situation struck him. Perhaps it would bring Cecile home. If she'd even quit the city.

Three hours later, Percy had left the shelter of his house and had done a bit of shopping. He shifted the package in his arms as he pressed the doorbell at the Griggs's residence. While staying home was his safest option, he'd been careful not to be followed and had driven his car instead of walked. Driving had been better for his head too. This was the only way he could think to get a better look at the child. Pearl was her name, wasn't it?

Just as he was about to press the button again, the woman he'd seen with Griggs came to the door. A half smile crossed her face. "May I help you?"

"I'm Percy Vance, a friend of your husband's. Is he at home?"

The woman bit her lip, her face rather pale. She glanced over her shoulder and back around. "Can I ask what this is about?"

"I'm so grateful to your husband for all he's done for me the past few months. Without his help, I don't know where I would be."

She crossed her arms, her smile disappearing. Still, she maintained her facade. "That's kind of you. We heard of your accident and trust you are on the mend."

"Yes, I am, thank you. In gratitude for all your husband did for me, I've brought a small birthday gift for your daughter." He held out the square package wrapped in pink paper with yellow butterflies dotting it. "A little birdie told me it was her special day just about now."

Actually, it was nothing more than a hunch.

If possible, more color drained from her face. "It's next week."

"Four, I believe."

"Y–y–yes. But you can't be here. You have to leave."

"If I can just give it to her. As I was shopping, I spied this in the window and knew a little girl had to have it."

"Isn't that thoughtful?" She reached out to take it.

He pulled back. "I'd like the pleasure of presenting it to her myself."

"Oh, well, oh, I see." The woman futzed with the corner of her yellow and green ruffled apron. "I don't know."

"I won't stay long." He remained on the porch.

She shifted her weight from one foot to the other. "I would rather you didn't."

"I won't take no for an answer." He flashed her his most charming grin.

"Wait in the living room. I'll get R.D."

She granted him access, and he made himself at home on the long, green couch. He got up to meander to the french doors that led to a pleasant backyard loaded with roses of every hue. He fingered the change in his pocket then wandered to the ebony baby grand piano in the far corner. Did Pearl take lessons?

"He's what?" R.D.'s voice boomed from the back of the house.

Soft little footsteps sounded on the stairs and then across the floors. He turned to greet a brown-haired child with a cherubic face. No wonder Cecile's heart was breaking.

"Hello, are you Pearl?"

She nodded, her curls dancing in time.

"I'm Mr. Vance, a friend of your father's."

R.D. appeared behind her. "What the devil —"

"The birthday fairy made a terrible mistake."

At that, Pearl made eye contact with him, her green eyes round. "She did?"

R.D. continued to blubber. He reached out to nab Pearl by the shoulder, but she darted from his grasp.

"Oh yes. She brought me this package with your name on it."

"She did?"

Like an out-of-control barnstorming plane, his heart spiraled in his chest. "She came a little early." No surprise that Tann had fudged the birth date just a little. "Had so many presents for you, she couldn't bring them all in one trip."

Now a huge grin cut across her face, and she stepped toward him. "What is it?"

"Vance, I'm warning you." R.D.'s face was redder than any Percy had ever seen.

"You'll have to open it and find out."

While Pearl worked at removing the bow and ripping open the paper, he studied her. Cecile had said Millie's hair was bobbed, but this girl had sausage curls that brushed her shoulders. Then again, several weeks had gone by since Cecile had last seen her daughter. Hair grew. And so did children, and a three-year-old photo didn't do him much good now. Her face wasn't as round as Millie's had been at a few months old, but again, children thinned out. She might have lost her baby fat.

A gasp from Pearl cut short his observation. "A top!"

R.D. snatched the box from the girl. "Really, Mr. Vance, you shouldn't have."

"It would mean the world to me if you would allow her to have it. It will never make up for your help, but I hope it will go a small way toward paying my debt."

"Please, Daddy."

R.D. tapped his toe and studied the box. He huffed. "Fine. But consider your obligation more than paid, Mr. Vance." While polite on the outside, his words carried a chill. "Remember, you promised to stay far away from me. I never want to see you at this house or around my wife or daughter again, or I will report you to the authorities. Do I make myself clear?"

"Very." Perhaps this hadn't been the best idea, but he had gotten to see Pearl up close. And he had one more test to verify her identity.

R.D. placed the box on the floor in front of the little girl. "What do you say to Mr. Vance?"

"Thank you."

"You're very welcome, Millie."

As the evening dew dampened and chilled Cecile's skin, she hunched behind a forsythia bush across the street from Angel's Home, an orphanage, waiting, watching, wondering. She pulled down the sleeves on her sweater against the cool air.

Day after day during the past week, Cecile followed Miss Tann, always at a discreet distance. Until tonight, she hadn't gotten any answers.

That all changed late this afternoon. Instead of going home, which was Miss Tann's usual practice, she came to this three-story brick Georgian home. Her black Cadillac gleamed in the hazy moonlight, half-hidden by building storm clouds. In the front seat, her chauffeur dozed.

Cecile clutched her chest as if to still the frantic beating of her heart but to no avail. This might be it. Her daughter could be inside this very house.

Light spilled from each of the first-floor windows and a couple of the second-floor ones. The third floor remained dark.

More than two months had gone by since Millie had been kidnapped. With each day that Cecile didn't find her, the chances grew that she would be adopted. Perhaps even out of state. She had to find her. Now.

Overhead, the street lamps flickered. A boy and girl, brother and sister, judging from their identical ginger hair, out walking their dog, stopped beside her. "Whatcha doin'?"

"Playing hide-and-seek. Now be quiet and get going before you give away my spot."

The children moved on, and Cecile resumed her vigil. What could Miss Tann be doing in there?

Enough of this. Cecile was done waiting; she had to know what was going on. Of course, she couldn't march right to the door and waltz in, but she could peek in the windows.

In her mind's eye, she pictured Percy, lying on the street, battered and bloodied. Yes, she knew the cost of crossing Miss Tann. Knew it all too well. She said a prayer for his recovery. In the end though, he was better off without her. Safer. Out of harm's way. When you cared for a man, sometimes you had to make sacrifices. No, it wasn't always easy, but it was right. And with the crushing pain in her chest, this wasn't easy at all. But it was right. She was on her own now, following her daughter's trail by herself.

Keeping low, she crept from behind the bush and, making sure the way was clear, darted across the street and onto the home's brown lawn. The dry grass crunched under her feet. For a moment, she paused. No, they shouldn't be able to hear such a soft noise inside.

She first peeped into what appeared to be a dining room. A crystal chandelier hung above a polished table. This wasn't a room dedicated to children. Still squatting, she maneuvered to the next window. Between the lace of the curtain, the light of a couple of art deco table lamps silhouetted two women. Judging by the size of one, it was Georgia Tann. The other woman, much smaller in stature and girth, gestured.

"You should have had them ready by now. I'm not patient. I have things to do." Georgia's words were loud and impatient.

Dressed in a white nurse's uniform, the other woman answered, but Cecile couldn't make out the words.

"Get those babies now. You can't miss the train."

The nurse hustled from the room and returned with three wicker baskets, carrying two by the handles in one hand and one in the other. The baskets were big enough to hold infants.

Cecile covered her mouth to stifle her gasp.

"Let's get out of here." Miss Tann led the way through the door.

Before Cecile could make a move to hide, the door creaked open. Cecile dropped to the ground and held her breath. Miss Tann and the nurse she'd spied through the window emerged from the home, both holding three baskets. A mewling came from one. Just as she suspected, there were babies in the baskets. Cecile dug her fingernails into the soft ground to keep from crying out. They were smuggling babies under cover of darkness. Did they also take out the older children? Or was it possible Millie was inside the home?

The pair made their way down the walk and to Miss Tann's waiting black Cadillac. The car rolled away.

Maybe this house held the answers she needed. There could be others Miss Tann used, maybe many of them. But it could be a first step. She wouldn't know until she got inside.

Once the street sat silent for several minutes, only the cicadas singing their songs, Cecile rose and took three steps in the direction of the front door. And then someone grabbed her from behind and covered her mouth.

CHAPTER NINETEEN

Cecile screamed, but the hand over her mouth stifled it. It clamped so hard, she couldn't bite down. Though she wriggled and squirmed like Millie, she couldn't break free.

She swung, her breath ragged, but hit only air. Tried to kick but missed again.

What were they going to do to her?

God, help me! I'm sorry, Millie. I'm sorry. Lord, don't let them hurt me.

"Just where are you going?"

At the sound of the smooth, familiar voice, she relaxed. Percy released her. Like a top, she spun around and whispered furiously at him. "What are you doing?"

"I asked you a question first."

"I'm going to get my daughter."

He mumbled something about a stubborn dame.

"And just what are you doing here? How did you find me?"

"I had the same hunch as you. To search the orphanages Tann uses. Imagine my surprise to find you lurking in the bushes. You didn't go to Massachusetts, did you?"

"Please leave. Let me handle this on my own."

"Why, suddenly, won't you let me help you find your daughter? What changed?"

"There's already been one attempt on your life. I couldn't stand it if you were hurt again. Or worse." She gasped at her own words. She'd all but admitted her feelings for him.

He drew her close. "And I couldn't bear to have any harm come to you." He brushed a kiss against her cheek. The kiss was innocent, yet it sparked a flame deep inside her.

"Then we're at a stalemate."

"So it seems." Again, she saw him lying broken and bloodied in the street. No, she couldn't continue to put him in precarious situations. She backed out of his embrace. "I don't want your help."

"You're right. We have to widen our net." He wasn't even paying attention to her protests. "Before, we searched for information specific to Millie. Since we haven't located her that way, if we can get more details on the operation, that might help."

"There is no we." She crossed her arms and stared him down.

"Keep quiet."

A shadow moved behind the filmy curtain upstairs.

She fought to whisper. "I can do this on my own."

"You won't get inside without me. Were you just going to walk right in?"

She ground her teeth. She didn't have a plan, but that wasn't something Percy needed to know. "Why not?"

"Ever heard of trespassing? And they probably lock the doors to keep the kids in."

She sighed. He was right. "Do you have a plan?"

"I'm her lawyer."

"You said she fired you."

"She did, but I doubt the nurse in there knows that."

"No. We'll find Millie another way." If she dissuaded him, she could return later on her own.

"All right. My guess is that one of Tann's associates knows we're here anyway. She has spies everywhere. It's probably safer to leave."

"Separately."

"Exactly."

"Good night, Mr. Vance."

"Good night, Mrs. Dowd."

They parted, each heading in different directions. Cecile rounded the block and continued for several paces before stopping. And waiting. After fifteen minutes or so of standing near a row of bushes along a driveway, twisting the ribbon on her wrist the entire time, she rounded the corner once more and marched toward the house. And in a pool of porch light, there was Percy poised to knock. That sneaky, deceptive man.

Then again, hadn't she done the same thing? She scampered up the walk and joined him. "You gave it a go."

He hissed at her. "Get out of here."

"I'm not going anywhere." Steps sounded from inside. Good. All she had to do was stand her ground until the door opened.

He narrowed his eyes. "I can make up a reason to be here. They'll report you, and Tann will know it's you. You have to stay away. Hide around the corner. I'll let you know what I find."

Cecile sighed. "Fine." She hustled down the steps and out of sight, but she peeped around the corner and listened in.

Before long, another woman dressed as a nurse answered the door and drew her brows together.

"I'm Percy Vance, legal assistant to Miss Tann. She wanted me to check out some of the children for adoption. We have several requests to fill."

"Miss Tann was just here. And why would she send you at this time of day?"

Only Swiss cheese had more holes than Percy's story. "Yes, I know she was just here. But she had to take the children and leave right away. You understand. And these requests are urgent. We need to get these adoptions completed."

The nurse moved to the side to allow Percy to enter. Cecile crept to the front door. Little by little, she turned the knob until she pushed the door open a crack.

A strange odor assaulted her, and it was not a pleasant one. It was more like Millie's diapers when she was an infant. Cecile choked back a gag.

"Are the children upstairs?" Percy motioned to the flight of steps to his left.

"I'll show you." The nurse went ahead of him as they climbed to the second story.

Cecile slipped inside and crouched behind a davenport. The putrid smell intensified. Cecile's eyes watered.

From upstairs came weak whimpers and lustier cries.

"All these babies in a single crib?" Percy's question carried down the stairs.

Cecile's heart pounded. What kind of conditions was he discovering?

Footsteps creaked above her. "Aren't there other caregivers here?" Percy again. His voice carried.

"Others? No, I'm the only one."

"For all of these kids?"

If the nurse replied, Cecile couldn't make it out.

"Let's move along." Percy must not have found what he was looking for in that room.

More floor squeaking, but they must have moved far away enough that Cecile could no longer hear them.

The footsteps came closer again, and then Percy and the nurse descended the stairs.

Percy cleared his throat. "Thank you for your time. Please let me know if you can recall anything about the girl named Millie I told you about. Miss Tann has a special place she'd like her to go. At any rate, Miss Tann will inform you which children we've selected."

"I'll show you out."

Percy left, and the nurse made her way across the living room and through the door into what Cecile had seen was the dining room and probably into the kitchen beyond it. Time for her to get out of here and discover what Percy had found.

As she approached the stairs, a child tugged on her sweater. "Miss?"

Cecile turned to find a sweet, freckle-faced girl of about seven or eight. She motioned for the child to remain quiet. "Yes?"

"That man lookin' for Millie?"

"Yes. She just turned four, has brown hair and green eyes."

"I know her."

"You do?" All the air rushed out of Cecile's lungs. "Where is she?"

"Adopted. A while ago."

No. No. They were too late. Cecile willed her knees to hold her upright. "Tell me everything. Fast."

"She was taken by a pretty blond lady."

"Who was she?"

"I never seen her before."

"Where?"

The girl shrugged. "Something about Memphis. And said her name was gonna be Pearl. That's all. I told Millie to be brave. I always looked out for her."

Tears sprang to Cecile's eyes. She embraced the girl who clung to her. What a gift the child had given Cecile. "Thank you."

Millie was in Memphis. Right under their noses. Now all they had to do was find her.

■ ■ ■ ■

Percy took a deep, clean breath of air as he scampered through the door, down the steps, and out of the horrible place. That terrible, awful home where they stashed children and treated them worse than animals in the zoo.

He inhaled. Cool. Fresh. Sweet. To keep himself from collapsing to the ground, he stood against the trunk of the large magnolia in the yard and panted hard.

A few moments later, Cecile tapped him on the shoulder. "Percy, are you okay?"

How could he tell her? How could he explain to her? Images flashed in front of his eyes. Himself locked in a closet. Dark, so dark. For so long he couldn't control his bladder. The stench had been the same as in the house. He ran to the bushes and vomited.

Cecile held him while he emptied his stomach. Close. Warm. After a while, he stood and wiped his mouth with his handkerchief. "Sorry about that."

"What was it like in there?"

"Four cribs filled the first room. Each crib held three babies, not lying parallel to the cribs' sides but perpendicular to them. Red bug bites covered each of the little ones' faces. And the odor. Indescribable."

"Those conditions inside are enough to make anyone sick. How can a humane person treat children so?"

Only evil, pure evil.

"And to think Millie lived there."

At her words, he straightened and peered into her sparkling green eyes. "What? What are you talking about?" He glared at her. "What did you do?"

She scuffed her shoe in the grass. "I snuck inside and hid behind the couch. Once you left, I got up to leave, but a girl stopped me. She told me Millie had been there."

"What did she say? Tell me everything."

"Not too much. Only that a blond woman took Millie and that they didn't have far to go. They would be in Memphis, and her name would be Pearl."

His stomach, already on an amusement park ride, took another dip. A blond woman. Memphis. His suspicions had to be correct. He had to tell her. And she would be furious when she found out he'd discovered Millie days ago and hadn't said anything. She deserved to know. And only she could identify the child. He wouldn't get anywhere in his investigation without her there to either deny or confirm his suspicions.

If it wasn't Millie, Cecile's heart would be broken. But if it was . . .

"I know a man at the courthouse. The clerk of courts."

"The same one who had the lead about Millie earlier?"

"Yes." He gazed at the house, now almost dark save for a dim light from one of the first-floor windows. A shiver skittered down his spine. He couldn't stand in this yard a minute more. He led Cecile down the block until he could no longer see the house.

"Why did we have to come here to talk?"

"I don't want the nurse in that place spying on us or overhearing our conversation."

She grabbed him by the upper arms. "Please, please, just tell me what you know."

"He is married to a blond woman. And they have a little girl who just turned four years old. A girl named Pearl."

Cecile tightened her grip on Percy. "Where do they live?"

"Don't get your hopes too high. I'm not sure about this lead. But I'll tell you, because as much as I hate it, I'm going to need your help."

"Just tell me before I faint."

"Like I said, I don't know for sure. On a hunch, I visited them and brought their child a birthday present. I wasn't even sure it was the girl's birthday, but I was close. According to Griggs, she turned four a few days after your daughter."

"Birth dates can be changed."

"Yes, they can, but they aren't always. That's one reason why I'm cautioning you."

She slouched. "There's more?"

"As I was leaving, I called the child Millie."

"Did she respond?" Cecile straightened. "What did she say?"

This was the part that made him question the connection the most. "She scrunched up her little nose and told me in no uncertain terms that her name was Pearl."

"Miss Tann could have programmed the name out of her. A child can be made to forget."

Oh, how he had tried to block his childhood from his memory bank. And how unsuccessful he had been. "The girl you spoke to inside. She knew your daughter as Millie?"

Cecile nodded, a frown marring her beautiful face, lines furrowing her brow. If only he could kiss it away and make life perfect for her again.

"There is a chance, but it seems unlikely she would forget her name in such a short time. Still, don't lose hope."

"Can we go see her right now? I have to know for sure. Even if my hopes are dashed, at least I can cry myself to sleep tonight. I'll never get a moment's rest until I know whether this is Millie or not."

"I understand, but it's very late. The entire family is likely in bed."

Electricity sparked in her eyes. "Don't call them a family. If that's my daughter they have, then that's my family."

"After my intrusion into their home, Griggs made it very clear that if I ever made contact again with his wife or the child, he would have me arrested. We have to proceed with caution."

"And how are we going to do that?"

He had no idea.

"If you were a parent, you would understand."

"I do. I know how much you want Millie back. But we have to go about this the right way. Make sure this is Millie before we make a move."

"Fine." She spit the word at him. "We'll do it your way. But for the record, I don't enjoy your way of doing things. You hold back information that would be useful. When were you going to tell me about this girl? Never? Did you want to keep torturing me? Maybe you are working for Miss Tann."

"Of course not. But I didn't want to break your heart."

Why couldn't she see he did it because he cared about her?

CHAPTER TWENTY

A low fog swirled around R.D.'s feet as he placed the last of the suitcases into the car's trunk and slammed it shut. He opened the front door, and light spilled into the inky early-morning darkness. He yelled inside. "Are you ladies about ready?"

This vacation was long overdue. Waiting each day for Tann to arrive on their doorstep and snatch Pearl from them wore on Darcy until she was nothing more than a bundle of nerves. When he told her they were going to Mississippi to visit her family for an extended stay, a light shone in her eyes that he hadn't seen in many weeks.

Pearl bounded down the steps, wearing a frilly pink dress, her hair in what Darcy called sausage rolls peeking from underneath her pink bonnet.

Darcy followed close behind, her hollow cheeks pink. This trip would do her good. When they returned, perhaps all this brouhaha with Tann would be done. They could resume their lives in peace.

She kissed him on the cheek as she went by. "Thank you, darling. I can't wait to introduce Momma and Daddy to Pearl. They're going to love her, don't you think?"

"How could they not?"

They all climbed into the automobile, Pearl snuggled in the backseat with no less than half a dozen stuffed animals. R.D. started the engine, and he backed out of the driveway. After several blocks, he peered into his rearview mirror. Strange, that same Packard had been behind them when they first left home.

Pearl chattered in the backseat, talking to Darcy about tea parties and singing to her baby doll. This trip also took them away from Vance and his prying eyes. He'd been true to his word and had stayed away since he'd brought Pearl that package.

It had startled R.D. when Vance called Pearl by the name of the child he was searching for, the one he'd roped R.D. into helping him find. But maybe . . .

No, God, it couldn't be. Couldn't be that their precious child had been stolen from a woman who loved her daughter and cared well for her. That Pearl belonged to someone else.

He glanced behind him again. What kind of car did Vance drive? The man inside was tall, just like Vance.

R.D.'s mind had to be playing tricks on him. He was getting as paranoid as Darcy. He needed this getaway as much as his wife did. Maybe more.

Before too long, they left the confines of Memphis and rolled into Mississippi, leaving behind the large buildings, the crowded neighborhoods, and the congested roads. Here, the fertile delta soil supported cotton and tobacco, and the fields stretched in front of them, now browning, the ripening cotton balls white in the cloud-studded pink dawn. A cloud snuffed out his view.

And still that car was behind them. Definitely following them.

Pearl stood up behind R.D. and Darcy, between them. "Daddy, I hafta go potty."

"Not now."

Darcy touched his arm. "You don't need to be short with her. A stop would be good."

"We aren't stopping."

"What has gotten into you?"

Pearl sniveled.

"I'm sorry, Miss Muffet, but this isn't a good place to stop."

"R.D.?"

"We're being followed."

"Followed!" A flash of lightning lit the sky.

"I wave." Pearl spun around, but R.D. reached out and nabbed her by the arm, the car swerving as he did so.

His heart thumped against his ribs. "Just sit down and be a good girl."

"But I wanna wave."

"No."

"Pearl, listen to your daddy." Darcy clasped her hands together, her knuckles white. She leaned closer to R.D. "Can't you go any faster?"

He shook his head and focused his attention on the black ribbon of road in front of them illuminated by the headlights. He unbuttoned the top button of his oxford shirt. Sweat poured down his neck.

The vehicle behind them made no move to pass, no matter how slow R.D. went.

"You have to lose them, R.D."

"This isn't the cinema, Darcy. I'm doing the best I can. And if they had wanted to run us off the road or shoot at us, they would have done so by now."

"Shoot?" Darcy quivered.

Oh, he'd said the wrong thing.

"Who do you think these people are?"

"I think it's Percy Vance."

"Vance? Why ever —" She blanched. "No, no. You don't think that she's —"

"I don't know, sweetheart, and that's the honest truth. Miss Tann has had some pretty shady dealings. It's possible." Thunder rumbled in the distance.

"And that's why he came to our house. To see her. To see if that was her birthday."

"And he was close."

Inside, his guts twisted into a thousand knots. Darcy must be going crazy.

"I gotta go potty."

"Soon, baby, soon." Darcy crooned the words to Pearl, who sucked on her thumb.

Did Vance know what was in that file? The one R.D. hadn't had the courage to unseal?

They came to a section of road in the process of being repaired. Instead of asphalt, loose gravel covered the street, and the car's tires kicked up dust, obliterating R.D.'s view of the automobile behind them. Up ahead, he spied a dirt road that turned to the right. This might be their chance to lose whoever was following them. Before they realized R.D. wasn't ahead of them, they might be past the road.

With a sharp crank of the wheel, he turned onto the rough dirt lane.

Darcy gasped. "Pearl, sit down. What are you doing, R.D.?"

"Losing them."

Tires and wagon wheels had etched deep

ruts into the road, if you could call it that. They bumped along, their teeth almost shaken out of their mouths. He spun around to see if Vance still followed them. With the choking dust, he couldn't make out a thing. They hit a large bump. R.D. flew upward. The car tumbled.

The sickening grind of metal against tree rang in Cecile's ears as she stared at the Griggs's car wrapped around an ancient oak. *God, no!* "Millie Mae! My baby!" She grabbed the door handle.

"Where are you going?"

"I have to get to my baby. She might be hurt. Or worse." Cecile couldn't bring herself to say the word.

"No, you aren't."

How dare he? "Don't tell me what to do."

He grabbed her by the wrist. She shook him off.

"Let me go to them first."

"Why?" And then it hit her like lightning from a thunderhead. He believed the worst. Didn't want her to find Millie in such a state. "No. I have to go to Millie. She needs me." She shoved to the back of her mind the pictures of her daughter bleeding. Bruised. Broken.

"I'll signal when you can come."

"I have to go to my baby." Nothing would keep her from her little girl.

"I'm protecting you."

"I don't need protection. I need Millie."

For a moment, he drew her into an embrace. Kissed the top of her head. Spoke soothing words to her. "Let me go. I'm sure the girl is fine, but I want to be the one to check."

And in that moment, she relaxed against him. A caretaker. A protector. An overseer. How she had missed that kind of comfort. Too soon, he released her and opened his door.

"Please —" A sob cut off her words.

"I will."

He understood that she wanted him to make sure Millie was alive.

No sooner had he exited the vehicle, the dark storm clouds overhead released their fury. The wind whipped up the dust, a bolt of lightning lit the roiling darkness, thunder shook the floorboards beneath Cecile's feet. Sheets of rain tamped down the dust and all but obliterated her view of Percy. Through the downpour, she could only make out his silhouette.

He crept along the cars, inching his way forward. He came to the back door on the driver's side, but they had glimpsed Millie behind Darcy. He proceeded to the front door and tugged it open.

Why wasn't he going to Millie? He should have checked on her first. She was just a child, sure to be frightened. Adrenaline rushed through Cecile and propelled her forward. Ignoring Percy's directive, she flung her door open and stepped into the tempest. In short order, it had turned the hard-packed ground into a mud pit. She took three steps and slid, catching herself on the hood of Percy's car. But she had to hurry. Had to get to her daughter. Had to help her.

As fast as she dared move, she slipped her way to where her daughter had been sitting. *Please, God,* was still sitting. She reached the door and tugged and tugged on the handle. It held fast. She braced herself and yanked again. Her feet slid. With a plop, she landed on her backside in the mud, oozing wetness seeping through her dress. None of that mattered. Only her Millie Mae.

Holding to the door handle, she worked to get her feet underneath her, her T-strap shoes not made for messing in the slime. For her next try, she braced herself on the car and put in every ounce of effort. Still nothing. She shuffled to the front door and yanked. It refused to budge.

No. She had to get to Millie now. She could be bleeding, dying. "God, help me!" A crash of thunder swallowed her words. She tried again. And again. And again. "No!" Goose bumps broke out all over her flesh.

As fast as she could without falling, she crossed to the driver's side. Percy had the door open. Mr. Griggs sat slumped over the wheel. Was he dead? What about the rest? Cecile couldn't breathe. "Dear God!"

Beside him, Mrs. Griggs moaned. Percy shook R.D.'s shoulder.

"Percy."

He whipped around to Cecile. "Get in the car."

"I need to see."

"No, you don't."

"Is she . . . ?"

"I can't reach her!" he shouted to her over the gale.

She clawed at her cheeks. If they discovered the worst . . .

"Wh–wh–what happened?" Mrs. Griggs's eyes were glazed over. She groaned.

"Millie? Millie!"

"My baby. Pearl, sweetie? Pearl?"

No answer to either call. Cecile's heart pounded as loud as the rolling thunder. "Let me crawl in the back."

Percy shook Mr. Griggs again. Still no response.

"Is he dead?"

"I don't think so. Just unconscious. Get in."

The wind stuck her sodden skirt to her legs as she crawled over Mr. Griggs and flopped over the seat to the back. "Millie. Millie Mae, it's Mommy. Answer me."

Utter silence.

Trembling from head to toe, she rummaged through piles of stuffed animals, but Millie was nowhere to be found. Had she been thrown from the car? "Millie! Answer me!" She touched warm flesh. Millie's arm. She grasped it. "Millie, can you hear me?"

This time, in response, Cecile got a soft whimper. She released a breath. Millie was alive. Praise the Lord.

"Can you say something to me?"

"I want Mommy."

Cecile's skin prickled. Mommy. Not Momma. Not what Millie always called her. But she might be confused. Had to be. Cecile worked to keep the tremor from her voice. "Do you have any boo-boos?"

"My leg hurts."

"Okay. You stay still. I'll help you."

"Where's my mommy?"

In the storm's inkiness, in the confusion,

in the pain, she must not recognize Cecile. But how did she answer that question?

"Right here, Millie, right here. Everything's going to be okay."

In the dim glow of the auto's interior light, Cecile stared at the child in the backseat of the Griggs's car, her throat gone dry, her arms and legs trembling. Weeks upon weeks had passed since she'd seen her daughter.

Millie wore a pink bonnet similar to the one Cecile had for her but not exactly the same. Her face wasn't as round. Her eyes were a little different shade of green. The mouth, however, was the same. Just the same.

Cecile reached out, her fingers quaking, and brushed the child's soft face. Tears raced down her cheek. "Millie?"

The girl blinked three times.

"Millie!" She reached out to draw her daughter close.

The child shrank against the corner of the car.

"It's okay. Momma's here now." Her chest tightened.

"No, you're not Momma."

Cecile's heart shattered into a thousand pieces.

"No one is going to hurt you if you remember where you came from. If you remember me." What had Miss Tann done to her child? *Please, Millie, dig deep in your brain.* "Do you know our little apartment and how you used to help me make dinner and how you used to draw pretty pictures on the back of envelopes?"

"No." She stuck out her lower lip. When had Millie learned to do that? She'd changed.

"We would go to the park together, and I'd push you on the swing."

"Mommy and Daddy swing me."

The lump in Cecile's throat threatened to choke her. But this was her child. Her voice resonated deep inside Cecile.

"My leg hurts."

Cecile willed herself to stop shaking. There would be time to talk to Millie later. To help her recall her past. Right now, she was in pain and needed help. She needed Cecile to be her mother. "Oh Mills, I'm sorry. Can I have a peek at it?"

"Will it hurt?"

Her speech had improved. Matured. "I promise to be gentle."

Millie nodded.

Cecile lifted a pink and purple blanket from the girl's lap and exposed her stocking-clad leg. "I'm going to have to pull your stocking down. Is that okay?"

Another nod.

As Cecile tugged the black sock, Millie winced.

"I'm sorry, I didn't mean to hurt you." And she was. Sorry for not finding her sooner. "You can hold onto me."

The child gripped Cecile's shoulder, hard enough she'd be left with fingernail marks. "Here we go." Being as gentle as possible, Cecile rolled the stocking down the rest of the way.

An angry bruise had turned the small shin black and blue. Millie's knee was a little swollen but not too much. "I'm going to feel your leg to make sure you haven't broken any bones. Are you ready?"

Millie shook her head.

Cecile chuckled. That was something her daughter would do. "I have to see, so I'm going to do it on the count of three. One, two, three."

Millie sucked in a breath but didn't complain throughout the entire examination.

"That's such a good girl. I'm so proud of you. And I don't think you broke your leg. You have a black-and-blue mark that's going to be sore for a while, but you're going to be fine. Just fine."

Especially now that they would be together

once more. A family, like they should be. No one would ever separate them again. Not ever. She'd never let Millie out of her sight.

While Percy tended to the Griggses, Cecile pulled her daughter close. This time, Millie didn't resist. Oh, how good to hold her in her arms once more. How good to feel the warmth of her little body against hers. How good to again be complete and whole.

She brushed Millie's tangled brown sausage curls from her face. What was that behind her ear? Cecile leaned in for a closer inspection. A dark spot. She tried to rub it away. The mark was about the size of a quarter and raised.

She broke out in a cold sweat.

God, no. No! Don't do this to me. Do you hear me? Do not do this to me.

She closed her eyes. Maybe she was seeing things. The cold was playing tricks with her mind. She opened her eyes. But the spot remained. Millie didn't have a birthmark. Her skin was perfect, unblemished. Her spirit may have been that of a firecracker, but her skin was that of an angel.

There was no denying it. This wasn't Millie.

CHAPTER TWENTY-ONE

"No! No! No!" Cecile cried out, her shrieks bursting with pain.

Her wails pierced Percy to his very core. It was as though a piece of her was being torn away. They were the screams of an animal in utter agony.

Percy climbed over Griggs, over the backseat, and shook Cecile, maybe too hard, because her head flopped. "Stop it. Stop it. What's wrong? Tell me." Was the child hurt? Had something happened to her?

"It can't be. It just can't be. Dear God, no." The shrieks lessened, now replaced by tears.

His breath came in short gasps. "What is it?"

"Please, no." Beside him, she quivered all over.

He drew her close and held her tight. "I need to know what's wrong."

"It's Millie."

His insides plummeted like an out-of-control elevator. "What happened to her?" She hadn't appeared to be too badly hurt, but perhaps she had internal injuries. Had she fainted? Stopped breathing?

No, Lord, not the child. Not when they were so close.

"It's not her."

Maybe Cecile had bumped her head when she'd taken that tumble. "You aren't making sense."

"But I am. I was too blind to see it before, but now it's so plain."

He whispered in her ear. "What is clear to you?"

"This child." Her words were strangled. "She's, she's . . . Oh, I can't even say it."

"You can tell me anything."

She turned in his arms and gazed at him, her eyes shimmering with fresh tears. Her features crumpled. All the fight left her. "She's not . . ." Now the tears rolled down her cheeks as fast and furious as the summer's storm.

"She's not Millie, is she?"

Cecile shook her head.

He kissed her temple, just a brush of his lips against her cold flesh. "I'm sorry." His head drooped. Poor Cecile. She had been through so much. "This is why I didn't want you to get your hopes up. I hate to see you disappointed."

"How could I have been so sure just minutes before? A mother should know her own child. I felt it in my soul, in the deepest recesses of myself, that she was mine. I don't know my own child. How will we ever find her if I don't even recognize her?" A moan tore from within her.

Percy embraced her as she wept deep, bitter, long-overdue tears. Alongside them in the backseat, Pearl cried. From Darcy in the front seat came wrenching sobs. "Give me my baby. My daughter."

Percy released Cecile and handed Pearl over the seat.

Griggs turned around, his brown eyes still glassy. "What is all this hullabaloo?"

"Pearl isn't her daughter." Percy bit the inside of his cheek.

Cecile's cries morphed into hiccups.

"You chased us for nothing? Got us into this situation for no good reason?"

Percy tightened his jaw and sighed. "Not for nothing. Now we know, we all know for certain, that this child doesn't belong to Cecile." He offered Cecile his handkerchief, the monogrammed one Mother gave him for Christmas last year.

"And I'm sorry." He nodded to Griggs

and Darcy. "I apologize for making the assumption, barging into your home, disrupting your lives, causing you this distress. I offer you my deepest regrets."

Darcy offered him a tremulous smile, one that didn't fully absolve him of his culpability. Griggs scowled. Fair enough. It would take time to repair the damage his assumptions had caused.

Cecile wiped her eyes, blew her nose, and tucked a stray, wet, mud-encrusted strand of hair behind her ear. "That leaves two questions unanswered."

"Don't say it." Darcy covered her ears. "Don't say it."

Cecile broke from his embrace and touched Darcy's shoulder. "I'm sorry we caused you such trouble. That wasn't my intention. I had to know, everything inside of me had to find out if this was my daughter. As a mother yourself, can't you understand?"

"She's mine. In every way, she's mine." Darcy snuggled Pearl.

Percy rubbed the back of his neck. No matter which way you looked at it, there was no good solution to the problem Georgia Tann had created. "At least now you don't have to fear anyone taking your child."

"No, we still do." Darcy spun to face

Percy. "So Pearl wasn't Mrs. Dowd's stolen child. How long will it be before someone else knocks on our door, wanting to know if Pearl is their little girl? I can't live like that. As a mother, Mrs. Dowd, you understand."

Cecile rubbed her stomach. "I do. Much as I hate to admit it, I do."

"And you'll return to the city and spread the word about us, won't you?"

Cecile glanced over her shoulder at Percy. What kind of answer did he give? If Pearl was stolen just as Millie was, then didn't the biological parents have the right to get their child back? But what about the Griggs's rights? And the welfare of Pearl, so well adjusted to her new home? "I don't know."

"But the remaining question is even more critical." Cecile pulled up a blanket that had slid from Pearl's shoulders.

"What is that?" Though the question rumbled in his mind.

"If this isn't Millie, where is she?"

No sooner had the sun streaked the sky pink and orange did Gladys jump from bed and pull her old brown work dress over her head. Her only summer work dress, but it didn't matter. Not today.

At church last Sunday, Miz Harper, a

young woman pretty near Gladys's own age, had asked if she might stop by to shoot the breeze for a while. Imagine that. No one ever paid Gladys a visit. What a special occasion for sure. And she was gonna make sure everything was just so.

Willard left for the barn a short while ago. Gladys woke Fanny, the little girl rubbing the sleep from her eyes. "Why're we up so early?"

" 'Member, today Miz Harper is coming for lunch. We gots so much to do. Time to get cracking. Put on your overalls. You can change into your church dress after everything's ready to go."

Breakfast today would be fast and easy. Just oatmeal. Once she had the menfolk fed, she shooed them outside, and she and Fanny got to work.

Gladys handed her one of the loaves of bread they'd baked yesterday and a knife. "Cut them crusts off for the cucumber sandwiches."

Fanny scrunched her face and sawed the knife back and forth over the loaf. Gladys turned to baking the pie she was fixing to make. Apple, the fruit from her very own trees. She cut the butter into the flour for the pastry and glanced at Fanny. What in good gracious? The bread was, was pink.

How had it gotten . . . ?

No, oh no, Fanny was bleeding and hadn't said a word. Gladys grabbed the knife from her and wrapped a towel around her hand. "What happened?"

Fanny shrugged her slim shoulders. "I dunno."

"You cut yourself and bled all over the bread."

"I didn't mean to." Not a single tear leaked from her eyes.

" 'Course you didn't."

"No, she's just the world's biggest genius."

Willard's booming sent Gladys jumping. "I didn't hear you come in."

"But I heard you babying that child again. How's she ever gonna do things right if'n you're always coddling her? I've had about enough and have half a mind to send her back."

Gladys pulled Fanny close. Never, never would she allow anyone to take her child from her. Not this girl that she'd waited for and prayed about for so long. "Ain't no need to do that. There's no harm done."

"No harm done?" Willard scowled, and Gladys backed closer to the warm stove, the heat of it searing her backside. "She's spoiled the food. That don't grow on trees."

"We'll fix it. These fancy sandwiches mean

I got to cut lots of it off anyways. It'll be fine."

"Fine? It'll be fine? Always what you're saying." Willard bellowed so, it was a wonder the windows didn't shake.

"Yoohoo. Anybody home?"

Gladys fiddled with her apron. "There's Miz Harper. You'd best be getting back to the barn if you don't want her to hear what you're saying and spread the gossip all over the county."

Willard hightailed it from the house, almost knocking over the willowy woman as she entered.

"Gracious, where's the fire, Willard?"

By the time she got the words out, he was long gone.

"Miz Harper. You're a mite early. We ain't quite ready yet."

"Oh dear, I'm so sorry. I must've gotten my times confused. But you don't have to worry about me. I can help." She eyed the pink bread. "And it seems like I'm here in the nick of time."

"Thank you, but I hate to put you to work. Fanny and I have it under control."

"I don't mind one little bit. Looks like Fanny could use a hand slicing up that bread. Why don't you tend to her, Miz Knowles, and I'll take care of that?"

261

All Gladys could do was nod and hustle Fanny to the bedroom, where she bandaged her hand and got her changed into her church clothes.

"Am I gonna go home?" Fanny bit her lower lip.

"No. I ain't never gonna let anyone take you from me. You're my little girl for always."

"Even if I'm bad?"

"Even then. I'll take care of you. I promise."

"Oh." And that was it. Fanny showed no emotion. Not a smile or a frown or a tear. Nothing. Just blank. You could never tell what the girl was thinking or feeling. There was something not right about it. But she'd come around in time. With enough love, she'd open up and blossom.

They returned to the kitchen, where Miz Harper had the bread all sliced and piled in a neat stack. She knelt in front of Fanny. "There y'all are. Your momma got you fixed up?"

Fanny stared at her scuffed Mary Janes.

"She's fine, thank you. Why don't you have a seat at the table, and I'll pour you some tea while Fanny makes the sandwiches."

"I didn't come here to be waited on. I'll

make the sandwiches. Let Fanny rest a bit."

"But —"

"I insist."

Willard wouldn't like it if he came in and saw Fanny sitting. But Gladys had no other answer for her guest, so Fanny took a spot at the table.

As the two women worked at the counter, Miz Harper leaned over to Gladys. "I'm concerned about the child, dear. It ain't right how hard she's working. She's so thin and so frightened. I . . . Well, I heard your husband when I pulled up. Is this the best place for Fanny?"

Gladys gazed at the woman, her dark, curly hair parted on the side. " 'Course it is. Fanny's my child, and I'm never gonna give her up. No one's ever gonna take her from me. No matter what."

"I'm just concerned about her is all. And if you can't keep her, Bill and I would be happy to take her. The Lord hasn't blessed us with children."

So, that's what this visit was all about. Nothing to do with being neighborly. Nothing of the sort. Someone just trying to take her child. "All's you gotta do is contact Miss Tann at the Tennessee Children's Home Society. Tell her what kind of kid you want, you know, hair color, eye color, age, everything, and you'll get one of your own."

If Fanny went anywhere, it would be over Gladys's dead body.

CHAPTER TWENTY-TWO

The wind scattered the dry leaves in front of Cecile, and they skittered on the sidewalk in front of her, crunching underneath her feet. For hours and hours upon end, every day she had off work and as soon as she finished her job, she scoured the streets of Memphis, haunting the playgrounds and nursery schools and shops where Millie might show up. Nothing. In a city with a population over a quarter of a million people, what hope did she have of ever finding her daughter? But with each new dawn, she renewed her vow to the little girl she loved more than her own life. She toyed with the pink ribbon she'd tied around her wrist. Millie was always with her.

Cecile rounded the corner, and the nursery school where she worked came into view. A small clutch of women with colorful hats on their heads milled around the school's door. What was going on? It was early. Early enough that she would be the first teacher there.

Cecile approached the low-slung white brick building. Why, it was Faith's mother. And Virginia's and Norma's.

Cecile squinted. They didn't have their daughters with them. She twisted the ribbon on her wrist. Something was wrong. She picked up her pace and reached them in short order. "You're here at the crack of dawn. And on a Monday morning, no less." She worked to keep her voice casual and natural.

Faith's mother, a tiny woman with dark hair, turned to Cecile, holding a handkerchief to her nose. "It's our girls."

Cecile frowned. "I don't understand." She refused to allow herself to understand.

"They never came home from school Friday."

"All three of them?"

The women nodded.

Cecile tapped her knuckle against her mouth. "We sent them on their way as usual. I watched them until they turned the corner. You all live in the building just down the street. How could they have not made it home?"

"That's what we'd like to know." Faith's mother dabbed at her eyes. "What happened to them? We've contacted the police, and they're no help. We spent the weekend scouring the city. We don't have the number to telephone Mrs. Quinn. She's not listed in the directory."

Norma's mother fished her hankie out of her white pocketbook. "We've spent the weekend combing the city, turning the town upside down, searching everywhere we can think they might be. No sign of them, not a trace. They've vanished. Thought maybe you knew something. Saw something."

"No, I knew nothing of this until just now." A thought struck Cecile. An awful, horrible thought. "Did you notice anything unusual last week? Any strange cars or people around the neighborhood?"

Norma's mother, a large-boned woman, gasped. "Yes, I do remember now. A few days last week, at different times of the day, I saw a black Cadillac limousine cruising up and down the street."

The other two women concurred.

Cecile stumbled against the building's rough brick exterior. "Are you sure?"

The rotund woman nodded. "This isn't a hoity-toity neighborhood by any stretch of the imagination. No one around here has the money for such luxuries, especially these days. That's what made the car stand out.

Such a strange sight."

"I think I know who has your children." Cecile inhaled, long and deep. "Let's go inside, where we can speak more privately." She undid the lock and led the way inside, the room smelling of paint and glue.

As soon as they stepped inside, Faith's mother grasped her by the arm. "What do you know?"

"I know that automobile. I've seen it before, and I know who drives it."

"Who?" Each of the women stepped closer to Cecile. "Who?"

"Have you ever heard of Georgia Tann and the Tennessee Children's Home Society?"

Virginia's mother nodded. "Yes, I have. They do wonderful work for disadvantaged children and families."

"Is that what you think?" Then again, if Cecile hadn't known better, she might have believed the same. "That's not what they're about. Miss Tann kidnaps children and sends them to be adopted. If they survive."

A strangled cry came from Faith's mother. "How do you know?"

"Because it happened to my daughter a few months ago."

"You mean she's not visiting your parents?"

"I haven't had contact with my parents in more than five years. They don't know of Millie's existence. I didn't want you parents to think I'm not fit to raise my daughter. She was snatched from my neighbor's house when I was out hunting for a different job. I have reason to believe she's somewhere in this city, but I don't know where."

"And you think that's what happened to our girls?" Norma's mother's voice trembled.

"I can almost guarantee it. They send out spies to case places like this school to find children to sell."

"Sell?" Faith's mother grasped her handkerchief, her fingers turning white.

"You don't think Miss Tann does this out of the goodness of her heart, do you?"

"My baby, my poor baby." Norma's mother slumped to the floor.

Cecile grabbed her before she hit her head. With a paper she snatched from a nearby table, she fanned the chubby-cheeked woman. Mrs. Brown's eyes fluttered open. "My Norma."

Cecile helped her sit. "Are you all right?"

"All right? How can I ever be when my daughter is who knows where? You have to help us find our girls. Surely you know where Miss Tann took them."

"I don't. If I did, I'd have my Millie with me. But I've been searching for two months without success. I wish I could help you, but the reality is that I need help myself."

"Can't we talk to this Miss Tann?" Faith's mother knelt beside Mrs. Brown. "Just ask her to return our children. There must have been a terrible mistake. We aren't bad mothers. We take good care of them."

"None of that matters, only that the girls were pretty and out of sight of an adult for a few moments. I'm sure that's all it took for her to lure them to her vehicle and spirit them away."

"We have to try." Virginia's mother hardened her features. "Don't we owe it to the girls to at least try? My heart has been ripped from my body. I need it back."

"You'll take us to see this Miss Tann?" Mrs. Brown pleaded with Cecile.

Cecile rocked back and sat on her haunches. "I will. I'll try to help, but I'm warning you that it won't be easy. And probably won't be successful. But we'll try. Maybe if we all go together and make enough of a fuss, she'll listen to us. Perhaps for your daughters, it's not too late."

But was it too late for Millie?

"Fanny! Fanny, where are you?" Gladys

stepped onto the farmhouse's front porch. Ten minutes ago, she'd let Fanny go to the outhouse, and the cotton-pickin' kid hadn't come back. Hopefully, she wasn't sick or nothin'.

Gladys made her way to the small rectangular wood building, but the door swung open in the early fall breeze. "Fanny, you come out from wherever you're hiding. This ain't funny. You don't wanna go gettin' me mad." But only the lowing of the cows in the pasture beyond answered her.

The privy couldn't be more than fifty yards from the house, with nothing between the two. Fanny couldn't have gotten into trouble between the two places. Maybe she'd gone to visit the kittens in the barn. One day last week, when Willard had run to town for something or another, Gladys had taken her to see the new litter. For the first time since Fanny came to live with them, her little face lit up. She didn't say much, but she squealed and held the littlest of the bunch in her arms for the longest time.

Once Gladys's eyes adjusted to the inside of the dark barn, she searched high and low for the girl. "Come on, Fanny. You gotta finish dustin' the parlor and then make some biscuits. Daddy'll come in from the fields soon and won't like it if his dinner ain't ready." Even that threat brought no response from Fanny.

Gladys climbed the ladder to the hayloft and found the momma cat and her kittens on a bale in the corner. But Fanny was missing. Gladys called and called until she was hoarse but got no answer. Her arms tingled. Where could the child have gone?

As fast as she could, she flew across the yard, through the apple orchard, and down to the little brook. "Fanny! Fanny!" A bird twittered in the tree above her, but no little girl's voice answered. Where could she be? She had to find her before Willard discovered she'd run off. He'd have both their hides for sure.

Where else could a child hide herself? Gladys searched the cold cellar, the cotton barn, and all the other outbuildings on the property. No Fanny.

Maybe she'd gone back to the house. Gladys might've just missed her. "Fanny? You in here?" She peeked into the parlor and in the lean-to where Fanny slept. Empty.

She blew out a breath. "God, you gotta help me find her." But though she peered in every wardrobe, behind all the curtains, and underneath each of the beds, she didn't see Fanny. She wasn't inside. She wasn't outside. Where on earth could she be? Gladys parted the curtains at the kitchen window and looked through it. Movement in the far field caught her attention. Willard and Quinn were on their way back to the house. She had to find Fanny. Now.

Once again, she went outside to search. A long, straight dirt road ran in front of their property. She shielded her eyes from the late afternoon sun and glanced both ways. There, in the distance, was a shadow. Small. Tiny, in fact, against the big, open sky. But it might be Fanny. She was headed in the opposite direction of town, but the girl didn't know any better.

Gladys would never reach her in time to retrieve her and get her home before Willard finished in the barn. She grabbed the keys to the Chevy truck from the hook by the back door and headed for the shed where Willard stored it. After a few cranks, the motor turned over, and she puttered her way in Fanny's direction. About five minutes later, she pulled over beside the child and set the parking brake. "Fanny Knowles, you get your behind in this car right this minute."

The round-faced girl gazed at her through tear-stained lashes. "No. I wanna go home."

"Well, that's where I aim to take you."

"Not there. I want my momma." Her cascade of tears cut ditches through the dirt on her face.

"This is your home. I'm your momma. You got no other momma. She didn't want you."

"No! No!" Fanny stomped her feet then fell into a sobbing heap on the ground.

Leaving the truck idling on the side of the road, Gladys went to her daughter and gathered her into her arms. "Oh Fanny, my Fanny." She stroked the girl's silken hair. How much heartache had she seen? But how could she love a mother who neglected her so? Her life here might not be easy, but at least she had someone to watch over her and plenty of food in her belly. "How were you gonna get home?"

"I dunno."

"It's much too far for you to walk. And your momma won't even be there. She don't miss you. I'm sorry about that. But I'd miss you if you left me. So will you come home and stay with me?"

With those green eyes that melted Gladys's heart every time, Fanny stared at her. "I don't wanna."

"Come on." At least the child still weighed next to nothing, making it possible for Gladys to scoop her up and carry her to the waiting vehicle. How was it possible for a six-year-old to be so small?

Fanny fought her with everything she had. Gladys thumped her in the backseat and turned the car for home.

"No! No! I want my momma. Please, please, I want my momma."

CHAPTER TWENTY-THREE

By the time Cecile and the three women arrived at Angel House, where Percy and Cecile had searched for Millie, Cecile's stomach had wound itself into knots. She closed her eyes. If only she could be anywhere else on earth besides here.

Too much misery.

Too much suffering.

Too much horror.

A chill wind blew through her threadbare brown coat, and she drew it closer. They'd come here because it was certain Miss Tann would never admit them to her office. On the outside chance she did, she'd never volunteer any information.

Cecile opened her eyes and stared at the three-story brick Georgian home. So innocuous on the outside. No clue from here about the secrets on the inside.

She risked returning, not for Millie but for the three ladies next to her, each of whom was missing a child. And for the countless other women who had lost children to Georgia Tann.

Cecile drew in a deep breath and swallowed hard. As the four women made their way up the walk to the front door, her palms sweated. She braced herself for the sights and sounds and smells she would encounter.

She turned to the others. "This isn't going to be a pleasant experience. Conditions inside are deplorable. I want you to be prepared. Are you ready?"

Virginia's mother nodded, her face jiggling. "I'll endure whatever I have to if I can just bring my daughter home."

Cecile rang the bell.

When the nurse who opened the door saw the group on the step, she widened her gray eyes. "Can I help you?"

"Please, ma'am. You care about people, otherwise you wouldn't be a nurse. And you want to do right. I have reason to believe these women's children were brought here last night. Please, if we can just have a look around and take them home, that's all we're asking."

"Absolutely not." From the scowl on her already dour face, it was doubtful she truly wanted to do what was right. She moved to close the door.

Cecile stuck her foot on the threshold. Pain shot through it when the nurse attempted to squeeze the door shut. She couldn't allow her to cut them off. "Aren't you a mother? Can't you understand?"

"No, I'm not a mother, and I don't ever care to be. These children are nothing but trouble."

"Then let us take a few of them off your hands. It will make less work for you. Wouldn't that be nice?"

"And what would Miss Tann have to say?"

Why did it always, always have to circle around to that woman? If a few more people in this city stood up to her and Judge Kelley and Crump, none of this would be happening. Mothers would be holding their little ones close, telling them silly stories and singing them sweet lullabies. Children would be sleeping in their own beds tonight, dreaming peaceful dreams and growing up happy and secure.

"If nothing else, let me inside, just me alone. Let me search for the girls."

"I'm telling you, no one is to be allowed inside. Not any of you. Their children aren't here. We didn't get any new admissions last night. That's the honest truth. If you know what's good for you, you'll leave. Right now."

Cecile strained and shoved the door wider. "We aren't going anywhere until at least one of us is admitted to check for ourselves. If, as you say, you don't have the girls, you have nothing to fear."

Faith's mother whispered. "Good for you."

"None of you are getting into this house." The deep voice came from behind Cecile and sent every hair on her arms standing straight.

Miss Tann.

Cecile spun around.

The large woman narrowed her blue eyes. "And all of you have something to fear."

Percy pulled his Packard to a screeching halt in front of Angel House. From the sound of Cecile's voice over the phone, there was no doubt something was wrong. Why was she even here? He bounded from the car, up the walk, and to the door. The half-opened door. Without stepping inside, he leaned in and studied the scene. Tann held Cecile and three other women in a corner of the room, her pistol pointed at them.

He was walking into a trap. But he couldn't turn his back on Cecile and the other ladies. Before Tann realized he was here, he had to formulate a plan to disarm her.

"Nice that you could join us, Mr. Vance." The uniformed chauffeur pushed Percy through the doorway. He spun around and fisted his hand, but before he could raise his arm for the punch, the click of a pistol being cocked sounded in his ear. The hard, unforgiving metal of the barrel pressed into his temple.

"Welcome, Mr. Vance."

At the sound of Miss Tann's voice, Percy went cold all over.

He shuffled into the living room, the dark wainscoting and dark brown floors sucking the light from the room. The women huddled together in the corner to the side of the brick fireplace. The heaviest of the ladies whimpered.

"Now I have you just where I want you." Tann circled the room like an eagle eyeing its prey.

"And what do you plan to do with us?" Though Percy's pulse pounded in his ears, he kept his voice unwavering. No need in frightening the women more.

Tann tapped her whiskered chin. "I haven't rightly decided. Perhaps I should make you disappear as I did with the children."

"Please," the small, dark-haired woman squeaked from the corner. "Just tell us where our children are. We'll never say anything to anyone about you. I beg you."

Tann gave a single guffaw. "Begging. Nice touch. But it doesn't sway me."

He needed a plan, a way to at least get the women out of here. If they banded together, they could overpower her. The problem was the firearm. With just a few shots, they would all be eliminated.

Cecile stepped forward from the clutch of women. She directed her venom on Tann. "I know you have my daughter. I've been here before, and one of the little girls here told me about Millie. She told me Millie was going to Memphis. You have to tell me where she is. How cruel can you be? To know she's so close and I just can't get to her . . . it's torture."

Memphis. At the sound of that word, Percy's world came to a sudden stop. A fog enveloped him. He couldn't breathe. Sweat bathed him. His heart throbbed.

"I demand to know where she is."

Cecile's words cut through Percy's haze. The room spun and tilted.

"You're in no position to be making demands. You will never, ever see your daughter again." Tann's gaze swept the

281

room. "None of you will. I would rather see them dead than returned to you."

The walls closed in. Percy couldn't breathe. He loosened his tie and licked the sweat from his upper lip. He held up his hands. "Listen, no one wants a confrontation. Just let us go, and we won't say a word to anyone."

"That's not going to happen." Miss Tann nodded at her chauffeur. "You know what to do." She looked at each one in the room. "Good riddance." As she headed out, three towheaded boys raced into the living room, followed by their huffing and puffing nurse.

"What are these hooligans doing in here?" Miss Tann's face turned tomato-red.

"The rascals got away."

Whooping like Indians, they darted around the room, over the furniture, and tackled Miss Tann. She wobbled and dropped her pistol to the ground.

"Is that a real gun?" One of the boys bent over it.

"Now!" Percy screamed. He grabbed Cecile by the hand. She grasped one of the other women, and the five of them dashed for the door.

"Get back here! Stop them!"

CHAPTER TWENTY-FOUR

Percy and the four women raced down the walk from Angel's Home. Behind them, Tann screamed. Two shots fired. On and on they raced, not slowing until they had gone several blocks and turned the corner. Tann's shouts faded. Percy's lungs burned.

Cecile tugged on him. "Stop. I can't . . ."

He pulled to a halt, the women accordioning behind him. "I think we're safe. I never did see the Cadillac come after us."

Cecile's hand trembled. "I don't feel safe. Look, here's a café. Why don't we get some tea and rest? Think about what we're going to do next."

The other women agreed with her plan. This way, they were off the street and out of sight of Miss Tann and her uniformed guard. No telling when they might come cruising down the road. They entered the small restaurant. Cecile and Percy occupied one table in the back, the other mothers at a different one nearby. They sat away from the glass windows and near the kitchen door in case they needed to make a quick escape.

"You gave me a scare. What happened?"

"I know where Millie is."

She gasped. "You know?"

"Yes."

"For how long?"

"I just figured it out now."

She furrowed her brows.

He blew out a huge breath and sipped his tea. "I grew up in Walls, Mississippi. Just a dot on the map right next door to Memphis . . . Mississippi."

"There's a Memphis in Mississippi?"

Would he ever forget that town? Or that day?

A blaring hot sun had beaten down on him, searing him. At eight years old, he'd had enough. Enough of the belittling. Enough of the darkness. Enough of the beatings. He was going to do something about it.

He wasn't big enough to fight his pa. All his ma did was cry 'cause she got beaten too. And Tenny. His big sister could never fight again. Pa had robbed him of her forever. That left him with one other choice. He was going to run away from home.

On that sweltering hot summer day, under

the big Mississippi sun, he set off down the dirt road toward freedom. The loose soles of his shoes beat a steady rhythm on the hard-packed ground.

Memphis wasn't that far from Walls. Pa went there to drink all the time. If he could walk there, so could Percy. The coins he stole from Pa's sock drawer, the money Pa kept for his liquor, jangled in Percy's pocket. It had to be enough to see him through until he got a job. After all, he was a man. Ready to take on the world and leave behind the life he despised. The people he feared. The nightmares he dreaded.

Memphis was a big city, at least that's what he'd learned in school. There were lots of tall buildings and trolleys that ran on tracks in the streets. Crowds were everywhere. They even had a zoo. Maybe once he got himself settled, he'd visit and see the exotic animals.

After a while, his toughened feet ached. His parched tongue stuck to the roof of his mouth. Yet he persevered. Nothing was going to stop him from getting to Memphis. Maybe Pa got there faster cause his legs were longer, but Percy would make it sooner or later.

He trudged on. Heat shimmered from the road, and cicadas chirped in the cotton fields. A group of sharecroppers sang a rousing spiritual as he passed one farm. How much farther could it be?

A little group of houses appeared on the horizon. Yes, now he was getting somewhere. Memphis must be close. Though sweat dampened every piece of clothing he wore, he picked up his pace. He was almost free.

But the little bunch of homes was just that. No big city. No tall buildings loomed on the horizon. So where was Memphis?

A shrunken old man rocked on his porch, whittling a piece of wood. "You lost, boy?"

"Yes, sir. I'm lookin' for Memphis. Gonna make my way in the world there. But I don't rightly know where it is. My pa walks there and back all the time, so maybe I went the wrong way."

"You Ike Vance's boy?"

"Yes, sir."

"Well, you done found Memphis."

Percy pivoted on one foot. "This ain't Memphis. My teacher told me it was a big city with lots of tall buildings and automobiles. I don't see none of that here."

"This is Memphis, Mississippi, not Memphis, Tennessee. You can't walk all the way there. It's too far for anyone to walk, even your pa."

Like a cornstalk in a drought, Percy

drooped. And when he turned around, there had come Pa swinging a willow switch.

"Percy?" Cecile touched his hand, drawing him to the present. "Are you okay?"

He nodded and gulped. "Yes. Memphis, Mississippi, has a population of less than a hundred. Just a few houses at a crossroads. A nothing place. No one outside of the area would know of its existence."

"What about that place upsets you?"

He gave a couple of small shakes of his head, more of a shiver, and worked to unclench his hand. He couldn't talk about it. Ever. "Nothing."

She rubbed his forearm as he fiddled with the handle of his teacup, warm against his cold flesh. She leaned closer. "You can tell me anything. You know all about me, but I don't know much about you. Whatever you say won't go further than this table."

"I did not have a happy childhood. Can we leave it at that?" He worked to block out Tenny's cries the day Pa snuffed the life out of her because she had tried to save Percy.

"I'm sorry. I can't imagine. Mine was idyllic. At least until Nathaniel came into my life. Then my parents warned me he would never amount to anything and turned their backs on me. On us. Every child deserves a youth like I had, a good life."

287

"I would have loved to have been adopted. If Tann came and took me away from my parents, I would have been the happiest child in the world."

"So that's why, when I first met you, you believed she was doing good for every one of those children."

"And she could, if she handled her business aboveboard. There's a right way to go about helping hurting, innocent little ones, and there's a wrong way. Obviously, she's chosen the wrong way.

"I grew up with nothing. Nothing materially, nothing emotionally. I swore my life would be different."

"You've lost all you've worked so hard for."

"I've had to put my house up for sale before I lose it to foreclosure. Not that there are many buyers."

"Helping me has cost you everything."

He nodded.

"How you must blame me for yanking away the security you had managed to build."

How could he blame her, when he'd been the one to turn a blind eye to Tann's schemes? "But my life was built on sand. Sure to collapse." He grimaced. The reality of it stung.

He shook himself, pulled a few coins from his pocket, and slapped them on the table. "What are we wasting our time sitting here for? Let's tell the other women you and I are going to get your daughter."

"Those are the most beautiful words ever." She pecked him on the cheek.

He could only pray it would be as easy as he made it sound.

R.D. pushed the papers around his desk and rubbed his throbbing temple, still smarting from the accident. Even though he and Darcy had the assurance that Pearl wasn't Mrs. Dowd's daughter, neither of them could sleep. Any moment, R.D. expected Tann or one of her underlings to appear at his home and wrench Pearl from them. If only these headaches would stop. If only he could close his eyes for a few moments of rest. If only he had the assurance his family was safe.

"Griggs!" A wild pounding sounded at his counter. *Vance!*

The pain behind his eyes intensified. What could the man want? He'd promised to leave them alone.

Vance continued to pound. You had to give the man credit for his persistence. "What?"

"Do you remember any adoptions to Memphis, Mississippi? Any at all in the past two months?"

Strange, but he did. Several recent adoptions went through his home area. His and Vance's home area. He gave a slow nod.

"Names. Do you remember any of the names?"

He squeezed his eyes shut, but no matter how hard he thought, he couldn't recall a single name. He shook his head.

"But aren't you still familiar with the area?"

"What is this about?"

"I have reason to believe Millie Dowd is in Memphis, Mississippi. I left so long ago, I don't know anyone there anymore." Vance bit his lower lip. "But if you go back more often, you might have connections. People there wouldn't be willing to give up information to Ike Vance's kid, but they might be willing to open up to you."

"You're right. They aren't about to tell you anything."

"Then we need your help. Cecile is waiting in the car outside. We don't have any time to lose. If Tann figures out that I know, and I have a feeling she does, then she'll do whatever she has to do to stop us. We have to get to Millie first."

R.D.'s head hurt so much. How could he decide what was right with this pounding in his temple? To help rip away a child from her adoptive parents. Was that the thing to do? If Pearl's birth mother showed up on his doorstep, demanding her back, and she was a decent woman, how would he feel? The answer to that question was clear. It would devastate him. Maybe even kill Darcy. They'd run once. They would run again.

R.D.'s skin prickled, and he glanced behind him. Landers stared at him. He had to decide. Now. Shut out Vance for good. Save his job. And his family. Or get out of his chair. Go with Vance. Change his life forever. Lose his job. Possibly his daughter. Nothing would ever be the same. He glanced around for Landers. No sight of him.

As R.D. stood, his hands trembled.

Percy held his breath as the expressions on R.D.'s face changed as fast as the weather in summer. One moment, he almost smiled. The next, he frowned. His eyes lit then dimmed.

Percy had put him in an impossible situation but a vital one. Without R.D.'s help, they may never find Millie, even in a town as minuscule as Memphis. Gossip got around. People would know who had just adopted a girl. But they weren't likely to share that with the son of the town's most hated man, even if that man was now cold in his grave.

To go, however, would cost R.D. everything. How well Percy understood that dilemma. Like he'd told Cecile in the cafe, just like the men in the Bible parable, without the right type of foundation, nothing in this life was secure. He was doomed from the start when he aligned himself with Tann and the Crump cronies. He shouldn't have been surprised when his life imploded.

Okay, Lord, You have my attention. I need to rebuild on Your foundation. Right now though, we need R.D. to help us. Cecile won't be able to reconstruct her life without his aid.

If R.D. walked out of this office, he could never return.

Percy could do nothing more than pray. In his entire life, he had never prayed harder. Cecile needed this. And for them to make a life together, he needed this too. But more important than anything else was Millie's welfare.

R.D. rose from his chair, stiff like an old man. Would he turn away or come with them?

Sweat broke out on R.D.'s brow, much as it did on Percy's. Taking baby steps, R.D. moved toward the exit. Left the office.

Percy released his pent-up breath.

R.D. joined him in the hall.

"Thank you." Percy choked out the words. "You're doing the right thing."

"Let's get out of here." R.D. hustled toward the door.

Once outside, they ran for the car idling on the side of the street. When Cecile spied them coming, she clasped her hands together. A wide grin, the biggest Percy had ever seen from her, broke out across her face.

Oh, she was beautiful when she smiled. Lovely all the time but especially gorgeous when her face shined like the sun.

Both men jumped into the car, and Percy roared away from the curb. He had urged the other women to remain in Memphis, and they had complied.

Cecile turned in her seat to address R.D. "Thank you. From the bottom of my heart, thank you. You're doing the right thing."

R.D. cleared his throat. "I have to stop and telephone Darcy. She has to get out of the city immediately. While I'm willing to help you locate Millie, I couldn't stand it if anything happened to Pearl."

Percy nodded. In the same situation, he might feel as conflicted as R.D. must. "Wait until we're on the edge of the city. Then we'll find a telephone booth."

"No. We don't have time to waste. We can't stop." Cecile fidgeted beside him, squirming like her daughter.

"We owe him that much."

"But —"

"He's willing to help. We have to give a little."

She slumped in her seat and turned her attention to the passing city.

They paused for a short time to allow R.D. to make his call then continued their race to Mississippi. Behind them in the distance, a cloud of dust appeared and gained on them with amazing speed. Then it passed them. A black Cadillac.

CHAPTER TWENTY-FIVE

"Was that . . . ?" Cecile stared at the dark vehicle passing the Packard in a ball of dust. She coughed. Her throat swelled closed, but not from the dirt swirling through the window.

"I think so." Percy stepped on the gas. The car lurched forward but didn't match the Cadillac's speed.

"They're getting away. Hurry. They'll beat us there." Her heart pounded faster than the tires turned.

"I'm going as fast as I can. They have a bigger engine."

Griggs grabbed the back of the front seat and leaned forward. "Give it all you have."

"I am. I can't push it anymore. We're going to lose them." He smacked the steering wheel.

"No." Cecile couldn't allow that to happen. "We can't let them out of our sight."

"I have the gas pedal to the floor. There's

nothing more I can do."

They hit a bump, and all three of them flew from their seats. Cecile knocked her head on the car's ceiling, and pain shot down her spine. "Oh!"

"Sorry. The road isn't the best."

"Don't worry about me. Just keep up with that Cadillac."

She stared at the car ahead of them, willing it to slow, praying for something, anything, to stop it. Though Percy did his best, the car grew smaller on the horizon.

Then a puff of white came from the Packard's hood followed by several more white clouds. Then a steady flow of either steam or smoke bellowed from underneath the hood. The car sputtered.

"No, God, not now!" Cecile hugged herself and rocked back and forth.

The car continued to sputter.

"It's not going to make it. I have to pull over."

"You can't. Millie." She went to rub the ribbon on her wrist. It wasn't there. Where had it gone? No, oh no. The last piece connecting her to Millie. Missing just like her daughter.

"He's blown the engine." Mr. Griggs's words were flat.

Percy steered to the side of the road, green

grass swaying in the wind. From behind a fence that ran parallel to the street, a cow peered from her munching, her eyelashes long, and lowed at them.

The car halted.

A cicada screeched.

Cecile leaned against the sun-warmed dashboard. "Now what? How are we going to get to Memphis? To Millie? Miss Tann is going to beat us, and no telling what she's going to do or where she'll take Millie." She worked to push away the images of that woman's hands on her daughter.

Percy hopped from the driver's seat. "Let me see what I can do."

She exited the vehicle as did Griggs. The three of them stood over the car's engine, staring at it. She glanced at the men. "Do either one of you know anything about automobiles?"

Both men shook their heads. Percy slammed the hood shut. "Even if I did, I doubt there would be much I could do. I imagine it needs a mechanic."

Cecile banged hard on the hood, bruising the side of her hand. "We were so close. I could almost feel Millie in my arms. So close."

Percy pulled her into an embrace. "They would have passed us anyway. My car

297

doesn't have the ability to keep up with theirs."

"No, no." The world spun around her.

"We aren't about to give up. Not yet. Not ever. I promise." Percy's breath was warm on her neck, his arms strong.

She leaned into him. "Is it close enough for us to walk?"

"No."

"Then how will we get there?"

A car appeared in the distance, another puff of dust on the horizon. Percy ran into the street, waving at the approaching motorist.

The car came closer and closer but never slowed. As it was about to zoom by, Percy jumped out of the way to avoid being hit. He gave Cecile a stiff smile. "We'll flag down the next one."

But car after car went by without stopping, no matter how hard they waved, no matter how loud they shouted. The sun crossed the sky and headed toward the western horizon.

Would no one help? Had all kindness left the world? She paced in circles. Her tongue stuck to the roof of her mouth. They needed water. Food. But most of all, Millie. "By now, Miss Tann must be to Memphis."

"This next one. I promise you." Percy

rubbed her shoulders, his touch strong and sure. How could he be so positive? He'd said that for the past fifteen minutes.

A short eternity went by before another vehicle appeared on the horizon. This one, a farm truck, so covered in dust it was impossible to discern its color. The three of them scrambled into the middle of the dirt road, jumping, waving, yelling. Never moving out of the way. Forcing the truck to slow then stop.

Percy ran around to the driver. "Please, sir, we need a ride up the road just a bit. To Memphis. It's urgent. A matter of life and death."

"Well, son, I wasn't figuring on going all the way to Memphis, seeing as my farm is half a mile down the road, but if'n you want to jump in, I figure I can take you there."

Not giving the man a chance to change his mind, Cecile climbed aboard. Percy joined her, and she had to sit on his lap for the three of them to fit. Even then, they crowded close to the sweat-soaked, dirt-smelling farmer, only the stick shift separating them. R.D. climbed in the pickup's bed.

She leaned against Percy's chest, willing some of his strength to flow into her.

Percy tapped the dashboard. "We'd be obliged if you'd go as fast as you could. I'll make it worth your while."

The farmer wiped his damp brow. Spit a stream of tobacco out the window. "Well then, let's see what this old girl's got left in her."

They sped down the road, the windows wide open, the dust gagging Cecile. But they were moving once more, and she couldn't complain about that.

God, just don't let it be too late.

Percy held tight to her but directed his words at the farmer. "Do you know anything about a brown-haired girl of three or so who just came to the area?"

The man shook his head. "Nope, sure don't. Ain't heard nothin' about new folks."

"Not new people. The girl would have been adopted by a family." Maybe they could jog his memory.

"Don't know about no adoptions. Word gets around. If'n there was, I might've heard about it. But I don't go to Memphis often. Not much there."

The ride might as well have been ten hours instead of ten minutes, but at last they rolled into Memphis. Or what they called Memphis. Did the small collection of a dozen or so homes constitute a town? Finding Millie should be easy here. They only had to knock on a few doors. One of these broken-down places, most of which needed a coat of paint, held her daughter.

The farmer braked to a halt at the edge of the settlement. "Here y'all are. Don't rightly know what y'all want, but I hope y'all find it. Memphis ain't nothin' much."

Cecile leaped out of the car, just about sprinting to the first house.

"Hang on." Percy pulled his wallet from his pants pocket and peeled a few bills from the cash inside. "We're mighty grateful to you." A drawl tinged his speech.

She couldn't wait for him. Had to get to Millie. Now. If she was still here. She raced for the first house. White clapboard yellowed with age. Up the rickety steps. Across the uneven porch. Pounded on the weathered door. No answer. Banged again. Nothing but the call of bullfrogs. Peered into the dirty, cracked window. Empty.

She raced next door, almost bowling over Percy and R.D. This one was a shop. A few items displayed in the plate-glass window. A shovel. A woman's hat. And a bonnet. A pink bonnet. One with frills on the brim. And a white flower on the side.

As Cecile peered into the shop window, her face blanched, and her knees buckled. Percy caught her just before she hit the ground. She trembled in his arms. An ache to protect her, take care of her, almost overwhelmed him.

"What is it?"

Shaking, she pointed to the bonnet in the window. "That's Millie's. I'd know it anywhere. When I was waiting for her birth, I took it out of the box every day. I memorized each stitch. It was the only thing of her own she had with her when Miss Tann kidnapped her."

"I remember it too." Percy took a deep breath in and blew it out little by little. "We're in the right place."

"So it would seem." Griggs pressed his nose to the glass. "Let's see if the proprietor knows where it came from."

A tinkling bell heralded their entrance into the dim, dingy store. A bent plow sat in the middle of the room. The shelves behind the counter brimmed with Mason jars of rusty nails and screws, empty oil cans, and frayed engine belts. Brown cardboard boxes, all unmarked, lined the other three walls and spilled onto the floor. Even the glass display case, which constituted the counter, was stuffed full of broken children's toys.

No one answered the bell. Upon spying a doorway in the middle of the boxes, Percy threaded his way there and opened the door. "Hello. Anyone here?"

"Hello," came the scratchy reply from the back.

The floors creaked, and several minutes later, a heavyset man in a white shirt, black pants, and black suspenders lumbered through the doorway. The musty smell he emitted reached Percy long before he did.

"What can I do you for?"

Cecile sniffled. She wouldn't be able to answer the man. Percy stepped forward. "We'd like to inquire about that pink bonnet in your window."

"Perty, ain't it?"

Beside him, Cecile nodded.

"You folks from outta town?"

"Do you remember where you got that bonnet? Did someone bring it in for you to sell?"

"Yes, that'd be correct. Either I pick up items I find layin' around or things folks just don't want no more. That's what mostly happens. But every now and again, a body'll come in here and just wanna get rid of something."

"And that was the case with the bonnet?"

Cecile leaned over the counter. "Who? Who gave it to you?"

The man stepped back, even though there wasn't much extra space for him to do so. "Now, I don't cater to giving out personal information, you see."

Cecile almost lay across the glass display case. Percy pulled her back so she wouldn't strangle the man. "It's very important we find the person who gave this to you."

"People 'round here don't cotton to strangers bargin' in on their business."

"This is urgent. A matter of life or death. A little girl's well-being hangs in the balance."

Cecile strained in his arms. "You have to tell us. My daughter was kidnapped. That's her bonnet. I'd know it anywhere." Tears streamed down her face.

Griggs stepped forward. "Aren't you Mr. Edmunds?"

The man nodded.

"You don't remember, probably, but I'm Henry Griggs's son, R.D."

"Well, now, I do recall you as a tyke. Sat across the church aisle from you folks most Sundays."

"That's right. So you know I don't mean to cause any trouble. But this lady here needs this information, and if you could give it, we'd appreciate it."

The man combed back the few strands of graying brown hair he had remaining. His large belly shook as he spoke. "I suppose it won't do no harm to tell y'all. Don't like them people none, anyway. Mrs. Knowles from outta town a ways brung it to me. Said she don't need it no more."

Percy shook his head and frowned. Cecile slid in his arms. He supported her and kept her upright.

She burst into blubbering sobs. "She doesn't need it?"

"No, ma'am. That's what she done told me."

They were too late. Something awful had happened to Millie. Percy rubbed his eyes. Now what?

Griggs managed to keep his head, the least emotional of the bunch. "Would that be Willard or Herbert Knowles?"

Good. He knew the family.

"Willard."

"Still on his daddy's place?"

"Yep, shore is. But I'd be right careful if'n I were you."

Percy handed Cecile his handkerchief.

She wiped her eyes. "Why's that?"

Percy could've answered the question, but Mr. Edmunds stepped in. "Willard Knowles ain't the friendly type, if'n you know what I mean. Best watch your step around him, or he's likely to set his shotgun on you."

Griggs sighed. "Still the bully, sounds like."

"Thanks for the warning." Still support-ing Cecile by her arm, Percy led the group from the store.

Griggs grunted. "It'll be getting dark before we walk all the way there."

They needed a ride. Already, they'd wasted too much time. Tann had too large of a lead. Percy spoke in Griggs's direction. "Stay here with Cecile. I'm going to see about getting us an automobile to use."

Griggs narrowed his eyes. "How do you aim to do that?"

"Never mind. I have my ways. Just make sure she's all right." This had to be a great strain on Cecile. The woman's words, the one who brought the bonnet, didn't instill confidence that Millie was alive or even still with these people. If only he could take her in his arms and reassure her. But he didn't have the words. And he didn't have the time. Back inside, he called for the shop-keeper. "Hey, mister, are you still here?"

He must not have gone far, because he returned within a few moments. He snapped his suspenders. "Didn't think I'd be seeing y'all again, least not so soon."

"I need a favor."

"Well." The man drew out the word.

"Do you own a car?"

"Yes, sir, I most certainly do." He puffed

306

up at that declaration. "Own three of them, to be exact. When I'm not busy running this place, I like to tinker with the engines. Got one to purring right nice."

"I need to borrow it."

"Well." Another drawn-out word.

Percy reached into his billfold. The stack of cash inside was dwindling fast. But so were their hopes of locating Millie alive and well. He slapped a generous amount of money on the counter.

The man picked it up and counted it. "Don't know if'n this'll cover the gas you'll use."

Percy slapped down another few dollars. "That's it. I'll return it to you in the same condition you have it now, and I'll fill the tank with fuel. I'll be needing that pink bonnet too." *God, lead us to the girl that belonged to it.* Cecile was sure to want it to keep her hope alive or, heaven help her, mourn.

"Then I reckon you have yourself a deal."

The man told him where to find the car and handed Percy the keys and a box. He raced from the building and motioned to R.D. and Cecile.

He thrust the box at Cecile. "Millie's bonnet. You'll want this when we find her."

"Oh Percy, thank you."

"Don't thank me yet. Let's go."
They didn't have a moment to lose.

CHAPTER TWENTY-SIX

Swish, swish, swish. Fanny worked at sweeping the parlor while Gladys dusted her bedroom. "Come on, Fanny girl, time to get crackin'. It's a big, important day. My sister's getting married. She's your aunt now. Yours and Quinn's. And she ain't the only one with a pretty little girl. We gotta hurry and get these chores done."

The whisper of bristles against pine wood floors stopped. "I go fast."

"I know. Just get it done real quick like, and then you get to take a bath, just like it was Sunday."

"I don't wanna bath. I don't wanna go."

"Oh, you're gonna have so much fun. You'll meet your passel of cousins for the first time and get to play with them. Why, when I was little and me and my cousins got together, we made the best of it with relay races and tag. Once we finish feeding the men lunch and getting the kitchen cleaned, it'll mean no more chores for the rest of the day."

Gladys left out the part about how much moonshine Willard was sure to consume and what state of mind he would be in when they returned home. She pressed on her stomach. She'd have to keep Fanny away from him. Herself too, if that were possible.

"Play?" Was that a hint of a smile in her voice? Those were as few and far between as a two-headed cow. When she did smile, it sure made the tyke pretty enough.

"I suggest we shake a leg."

The swish started again, this time with more speed. Hopefully, Willard wouldn't inspect her work.

Soon the menfolk came in from the barn and plunked down at the table for lunch. Willard wasted no time in trying to spoil her day. "Don't see why we have to drive for an entire hour just to see your sister say I do. For the third time. Woman can't keep a husband for nothing."

"We're all going, and that's the end of that discussion." Gladys set the coffee in front of her husband with more force than necessary, and it sloshed over the side of the cup.

"Watch what you're doing, woman. Can't you even put down a cup the right way?

Hard to believe I've stuck around all these years."

He stayed because he knew he wouldn't find another wife who would put up with his treatment of her like she did. "Sorry. Just a bit excited. I think this time it'll all work out for her. Can't you just be happy for one day?"

Quinn stabbed one of the slabs of ham off the serving platter and dropped it onto his plate. "I don't wanna go to no dumb old wedding. Just a bunch of sissies all dressed up."

Willard whacked the boy on the back of his head. "If'n your ma and I say you're going, then you're going."

"I don't wanna go."

Gladys almost dropped the hash browns she was carrying to the table. This had to be one of the first times Fanny had ever spoken in Willard's presence.

Willard slapped her across the cheek. "Like I done told your brother, you gotta go. We all gotta. Just for mouthing off, you don't get no lunch. How's that suit you?"

In answer, Fanny slipped from the chair and left the room.

Gladys sighed. "Why'd you have to go do that? Don't ruin this day for me. Goodness knows, I get few enough of them."

"You don't do no work. Quit your belly-achin' and get me more ham. I need forti-fyin' for this wedding."

They finished the meal in near silence, and Quinn and Willard went to the barn to bathe. Once they were out the door, Fanny appeared in the kitchen and picked up a dish towel to dry.

Gladys ruffled Fanny's butchered hair. She'd tried to cut it herself and hadn't done the best job because Fanny wouldn't sit still. Even so, the girl was cute as a kitten.

Fanny was wiping the last plate when a black motorcar roared by, stirring up a cloud of dirt. It halted just beyond the house. A large woman in pants and a man's shirt stepped from the auto. A flash of recognition shot through Gladys. What was Georgia Tann doing here? They hadn't seen her in weeks, not since they'd completed Fanny's adoption. She locked her knees to keep them from knocking together. She snatched the plate from Fanny's hands and pulled the child to her side.

Miss Tann pounded at the door. Gladys turned Fanny around. "Go to your room. Don't come out."

Hardly able to put one foot in front of the other, Gladys went to the door. "Miss Tann, what a —"

"Where's the kid?" Miss Tann pushed her way inside the house, breathless.

This was no social call. The woman's eyes were large behind her round glasses, wild, like a lion on the hunt. For whatever reason, she wanted Fanny.

But Gladys would never give her up. "She's not here." Gladys stared at the floor and worked on putting on her saddest face.

"What do you mean she's not here?" The volume level of Miss Tann's voice was sure to burst Gladys's eardrums.

"She got a fever." Gladys swiped at pretend tears. "We took her to the doctor and all, but it was too late. Poor little thing up and died just a little more than a week ago." She sniffled for effect.

Miss Tann took three giant steps in Gladys's direction, backing her against the still-warm stove. "Where's the grave?"

Gladys swallowed hard. Miss Tann was smarter than her by a mile. Now what was she going to do? There was no grave.

Just then, Willard and Quinn burst through the door, wet hair slicked back. Willard eyed their visitor. Either he didn't recognize her or he chose to ignore her. "Ain't you ladies even had your baths yet? You told me we needed to get there early. Get Fanny and start moving. I don't wanna

313

miss the food."

Gladys dared to peer at Miss Tann. If possible, her face turned redder than a Mississippi sunset. "You lied to me."

"Please, what do you want with my girl?"

"Where is she? I'll find her."

Miss Tann set off for the parlor, her heavy orthopedic shoes clunking on the floor.

Gladys grabbed Willard. "Make her stop. Tell her she can't have Fanny."

"What've you done to bring her here?"

"I don't know. Honestly. But she can't take Fanny. I won't let her."

Two seconds passed. Miss Tann emerged from the lean-to. Under her arm, like a football, she carried Fanny. The child screamed. Twisted. Kicked. But to no avail.

Gladys blocked the door. Willard watched from the other side of the room.

"Gimme my baby."

"Get out of my way." Miss Tann clipped her words.

Gladys stood her ground.

"If you know what's good for you, you'll let her pass." Gladys spun around. A colored man held a dull black gun and aimed it at her heart. Her lungs burned.

Miss Tann shoved Gladys to the side. "There will be a grave now."

Through the door. Out of the house. Into

the car. Away from Gladys.

At the crossroads in Memphis, Percy turned the car right just as Griggs instructed. The back wheels skated as he kept his foot on the gas. He clung to the steering wheel.

"Keep it steady." R. D. hollered from the backseat.

"But keep going as fast as you can. We can't be too late. We just can't be." Cecile bit her lip and gripped the door handle, her knuckles white.

He patted her knee. How his heart broke for her. Somehow, he had to give her hope. "Don't think the worst. All the woman said was that she no longer needed the bonnet. That could mean anything. Millie might have outgrown it. Perhaps the woman had other bonnets she preferred. There could be a million reasons. You have to keep fighting for your daughter. Don't give up until you have solid proof it's time to stop."

She turned away from him and stared out the window. She rubbed the side of her leg. "I'm afraid."

"I know. Me too." His hands sweated on the steering wheel.

"What if . . . ?"

"Don't play that game. I left home at thirteen. Up until that point, my life had

315

been nothing but a what-if. But that wasn't the way to live. Dreams don't come true unless you act on them. To make my way in the world, I had to believe in when. When I got a job. When I got a place to live. When I had it all."

"But you don't. Have it all, I mean. Not anymore."

"Oh, but I think I might."

They bumped along for a minute or two more. Up ahead, rising from the cotton field, was a low-slung gray house. A long porch hugged it. A bramble of wild roses covered in pink blooms ran up a trellis on one side of the dwelling.

Griggs gave a single clap. "This is it."

Cecile slid forward in her seat. Ready to pounce.

Percy braked, sliding to a halt. The three of them burst from the vehicle. Cecile dashed up the three steps and across the porch to the door. She banged.

No answer. In the yard, a rooster crowed.

Percy got to her side. Pounded on the door. "Hello."

Silence. A donkey brayed.

"Hello, hello. Is anyone home?" Cecile knocked with her fist.

Griggs joined them. "Open up, Willard. We have urgent business."

But still no one came to the door.

Holding the screen to the side, Percy tried the knob. It turned. He pushed it open.

Griggs held him by the shoulder. "What are you doing?"

"Acting like a gumshoe." He stepped inside.

Cecile followed him. "Do you think Tann did something bad to them?"

"Remember what I said about what-ifs? Think about when we find her."

"I am. Trying, anyway."

His throat dried out. Swallowing was difficult. "Then keep it up."

The kitchen, small as it was, was neat. Tidied, though dishwater filled the sink. He tested the temperature. It was still warm. They hadn't been gone long.

Griggs moved from the kitchen. "I'll search the parlor. You check the back bedrooms."

Percy peeked into one, a bright quilt over a wrought-iron bedstead. A lace runner covered the walnut bureau. It was like the kitchen. Simple. Clean. Nothing here. No clues.

"This is a boy's room." Cecile exited the adjoining bedroom. "Not one helpful item."

They joined R.D. in the parlor. Another spic-and-span room. "No items out of place

317

as far as I can tell." He rubbed his mustache.

Percy slammed his fist against his palm. "I thought for sure we'd find something here. If not Millie, an idea of where she might be."

"Tann has her. I just know it. She's come and taken her. We'll never find her now."

Percy embraced Cecile and whispered in her sweet-smelling hair. She was so small, so fragile, so vulnerable in his arms. "Fight, Cecile, fight. Now is not the time to give up. Millie needs you more than ever. Don't disappoint her."

"Look over here." R.D. interrupted the moment. "I think I found something." He pulled aside a light purple flower-sprigged curtain.

Percy squinted. "What's that? Some kind of closet?"

"A lean-to, I think. Looks like it's been converted into a bedroom."

Cecile broke free of his hold and crouched to enter the tiny, cramped room. Percy peered over her shoulder as there was not enough space for them both. A small mattress covered the entire floor, a thin pink blanket balled up at one end. Two hooks hung on the wall. One held a white nightgown. The other, a mint-green dress.

Cecile cried out. "This is for a girl." She

pulled the dress from the hook. "One about Millie's size. I don't recognize it. It's not the one she was wearing the day she was kidnapped, but it would fit her."

"Then we do know a small girl lives here."

"But look at this room. So tiny. She has nothing. I gave her more than this. How could Tann rip her away, look me in the eye, and tell me she was giving Millie a better life? This isn't better than what I offered her."

"She doesn't vet the adoptive parents like she should. If they can pay her exorbitant fee, that's all she cares about." Percy sighed.

She thrust the dress at him. "Money. Always about the money. Riches trump even the welfare of children."

R.D. stepped aside as Cecile exited the tiny space. "So we know Millie was here. And the family isn't."

Cecile swayed. "Perhaps they ran when they knew Miss Tann was coming."

"That's a guess." R.D. adjusted his glasses. "Let's deal with the facts. Maybe they went out for the afternoon."

"That's another guess. And would they leave with the water still in the sink?"

"Could be that someone forgot to drain it." Percy made a circuit of the parlor. "Maybe a neighbor knows where they are.

They might even be at the neighbor's or in town, for all we know."

R.D. nodded. His bowler slipped. He righted it. "Good place to start."

They retraced their steps through the kitchen. The screen door squeaked open. A bear of a man filled the doorway. He brandished a rifle. "What're you doin' in my house?"

CHAPTER TWENTY-SEVEN

Cecile stared at the giant man filling the doorway. A deep frown covered his pock-marked face. He took long, heavy breaths. She bunched her skirt in her hand.

"I asked y'all, what're you doin' in my house?" He cocked the rifle.

Mr. Griggs stepped forward. What was he doing? He was going to get himself killed. "Willard. Good to see you. We're sorry to barge in."

The bear of a man wrinkled his forehead. "Who're you?"

"R.D. Griggs. Don't you remember?"

"Aw, yeah, weird little kid, always acting too big for his britches."

"Again, I apologize for the intrusion."

"You'd better have a good reason for being here."

A frumpy woman in a baggy yellow dress, her oak-brown hair a mess, appeared behind the man. "Willard, what's this?"

"These people was just about to explain why they broke in. Then I'm gonna shoot 'em."

Cecile darted from behind Mr. Griggs. Willard pointed the rifle between her eyes. She clutched her chest in a vain attempt to still her racing heart. She stared down the barrel then forced herself to gaze at his dark brown eyes. "Please. We're here because we're searching for my daughter. Miss Tann was here earlier, wasn't she?"

"That ain't no business of yours."

Sweat trickled down the side of her face. "I've had dealings with the woman."

The lady behind Willard, possibly his wife, ducked under his arm. Red rimmed her eyes. "She was here."

They had the right place. Cecile fought to keep herself standing. "You have a daughter."

The woman gave a slow nod.

Willard exploded. "Don't you tell these people nothin', Gladys. Do you hear me? They're just causin' trouble, is all."

Cecile maintained her attention on Gladys. "We aren't here to cause trouble. Just the opposite. We're here to right a wrong."

"What wrong might that be?" Gladys whispered.

322

"Miss Tann kidnapped my daughter a few months back. She was just three at the time."

Gladys puffed out a breath. "Then you have the wrong place. Our daughter turned six a few days back." She chewed her upper lip.

Percy spoke over Cecile's head. "Brown hair. Bobbed. Round cheeks." He pulled Millie's picture from his coat pocket. He carried it around? How beautiful. He really cared about finding her.

Gladys grabbed it from him. Stared at it for a moment. Shook like a poplar tree in a windstorm. "Hard to tell. That's an old picture. Fanny's six." With trembling hands, she reached into her dress pocket and pulled out a photograph. "This is the one Miss Tann showed us of Fanny."

For the first time in months, Cecile stared into her daughter's eyes. "That's her."

Gladys crunched the photo in her hand. "No. No. You can't take her from me. Don't do this to us."

Cecile fell backward against Percy. He held her up, his arms strong. They had found Millie. *Oh Millie Mae, Momma's here for you.* "Where is she? Let me see her."

Gladys handed the bent picture back to Percy. "Like you said, Miss Tann, she was here earlier. Like a house afire. Come in and swiped Fanny right from her room. Carried her outta here."

"In her black Cadillac?"

Gladys nodded, sweat dotting her upper lip.

Mr. Griggs approached Willard, reached out, and pressed the gun lower. "Which way did they go?"

"I dunno."

"I don't think they went back toward town, that's for sure." Gladys wiped her forehead with a yellowed handkerchief. "We've been lookin' and lookin', and no sign of neither of them. Nor of that pistol-packin' man she had with her."

Cecile grabbed Gladys by the upper arms. "You have to help us find her. Miss Tann will kill her. You know that."

Gladys's eyes filled with tears. "I know. She done said just that."

Cecile's throat closed, and darkness threatened. She forced air into her lungs. "Then let's go." She marched from the house, not caring who was following, if anyone. If she had to, she'd find Millie by herself.

But Percy, R.D., and Gladys traipsed after her. Once in the borrowed motorcar, Cecile turned to Gladys. "Where is a likely place

Miss Tann might have gone? Somewhere you haven't searched yet."

"Another family down the road a few miles also adopted a kid from that lady. Just got her last night. Maybe she's gone there."

Cecile hugged herself. "That makes sense. Percy, head that way." Could this other girl be one of the children from the nursery school? Maybe Cecile would have good news for another mother as well as herself.

Now she was jumping ahead too much. First, they had to locate Miss Tann. Then they had to get Millie back. Alive.

Percy tore off down the rutted road. Cecile finger-combed the tangles from her hair. She prayed, begging God to return Millie to her in one piece. She kept a vigil out the window, eagle-eyed for any sign of Miss Tann or her car. But she saw nothing but cotton. Fields and fields of the crop. The bolls whitening, the field hands picking the ripened fluff.

Several precious minutes ticked by. They came to a house much the same as Gladys's. This one was white. A little girl played in the yard. Blond and curly-headed with a pink bow in her hair. Wide blue eyes. Faith. But Cecile couldn't allow the child to recognize her. This woman who now had her might take off with her. Cecile turned her face away.

Gladys led the way to the door. She called through the open screen. "Earlene, are you home?"

A young woman answered, freckles dotting her fair face. "Gladys. What can I do you for?"

"Is your girl here?"

"She sure is. Where else would she be?"

"Miss Tann been around your place at all today?"

Earlene shook her head. "Why?"

"Fanny's missing."

"Her name is Millie." Cecile stepped in front of Gladys. "She's my daughter. Miss Tann kidnapped her from me in Tennessee a couple months ago. Now she took her from Gladys. Have you seen her black Cadillac today?"

"No, I sure haven't. Would've remembered it if'n I had."

Percy tipped his hat. "We're much obliged, ma'am. If you see Tann, let us know."

Earlene nodded.

The foursome traipsed from the porch to the car. Cecile confronted Gladys. "That's another one of the girls Miss Tann stole. Now tell me where else might they have gone."

"I dunno. Maybe back to the city. I don't

have any clue. We done searched everywhere."

Cecile shook Gladys's arm. "You must
have some idea. Think, please think."

R.D. stood away from the car as Cecile got
more forceful with Gladys. "You have to tell
me. You must have some idea where Millie
is."

"I done told you, I have no clue. If'n I
did, don't you think I'd be there now to get
my Fanny?"

He directed his attention to the farmhouse. The lace curtains blowing in the soft
breeze at one of the windows parted. A
sweet-faced child peered from behind them.

R.D. loosened his tight collar and forced
himself to swallow. The child popped her
thumb in her mouth. Waiting to be rescued.
Rescued. The word took him aback. Since
when did he believe these children needed
rescuing?

The girl leaned against the weathered
window frame. The afternoon's sun caught
the glint of a tear on her cheek. And a little
of the ice around his heart melted. How
could it not?

Earlene stepped from the house and
joined the convocation beside the auto. As
if an invisible string pulled him in, he moved

toward the little girl in the window. The yard's green grass softened his footfalls. Even Vance was intent on the discussion. No one paid R.D. any mind. He approached the child and flashed her a tentative smile. In return, she lifted one corner of her mouth.

"Hello."

She waved, her fingers slim and white.

"What's your name?"

"Faith. I'm not Harriet."

"I know." What was Pearl's given name? She'd never mentioned it. Had she forgotten it? Or just buried it so deep inside she couldn't recall? Or didn't want to? Before he'd come over here, he'd heard Cecile's words. This was another stolen child. "You'd like to see your mommy again?"

Little pocks appeared in her chin, which quivered. "Yes."

"I'm sure you do. Was she a nice mommy?"

Again, Faith nodded, her blond curls bouncing with the movement.

"Was she nice to you, or did she beat you?"

"Mommy only spanks when I'm bad. And not hard. Mommy hugs me. She loves me. God loves me and wants me to be a good girl."

He had to know more. Her first home wasn't abusive. Just the opposite. From the sound of it, the home was filled with love. "Did you have enough to eat?"

She puckered her rose-red lips. "Yes. I like peanut butter and bananas."

He chuckled, and so did she, her laugh rivaling the wind chimes ringing in the background. "I like that too. Do you have a daddy?"

At this, she shook her head. "Daddy runned away. But Mommy loves me. I just wanna go home."

He couldn't blame her. Despite not having a man in the home, she had a good life, from the sound of it. She didn't deserve to be ripped away from her mother, a mother who loved her and was willing and had the ability to parent her.

Was that what Pearl had? Was there a woman out there who longed for her? To feel the weight of her in her arms as she fell asleep? To kiss her soft brow when she tucked her in at night? To laugh at all the silly antics Pearl pulled?

He further loosened his tie. "Do you know why that lady is here?"

"Her little girl got taken just like me."

"That's right." What an awful, awful experience for a child. If the biological parent couldn't care for their child, that was one matter. Adoption could be a beautiful experience. It could join an unwanted child with a family who wanted her above everything.

But what about those who already had loving homes? That was a different matter altogether. "Did you see any strangers around here today?"

"Yes, sir."

His mouth fell open. "Oh. Who?"

"You people."

He chuckled. "Any others?"

"No, sir."

"How about a big black car? Did you see one like that today?"

"Yes." She gave such a vigorous nod that the pink ribbon in her hair slipped out. "Like that car that brung me here. I told the lady."

He sucked in a breath. So, Earlene had lied. Probably so she didn't lose the child she now called her own.

"Where did that car go?"

She pointed in the direction they had been traveling. "That mean lady came here."

"She was at this house? Today?"

Another nod.

"Did she have a little girl with her?"

Another nod.

"What did she say?"

"Where was I. I was in the outhouse, but I peeked and heard 'em. The mean one said she was gonna take us someplace fun. With candy. And a Ferris wheel. But this lady said no."

Through the screen, R.D. tapped her nose. "Thank you very much for the information."

"Okay." Faith stuck her finger back in her mouth.

He broke into a flat-out sprint back to the car. "I know where Tann took her."

Mrs. Dowd's green eyes widened. "Where? Is she close? Is she alright?"

"I don't know the answer to that last question, but I think I know where Tann was headed. Get in the car. I'll tell you on the way." The last complication they needed was for Earlene to discover they knew she'd been lying.

The four of them piled into the vehicle and, with a spin of the tires, Percy stepped on the gas. "Which way?"

"Same way we were headed. According to Faith, Millie was with her. And alive."

"Alive?" Cecile breathed the word.

"For now."

Chapter Twenty-Eight

Percy set a breakneck speed as they bumped over the dusty dirt road toward town. "Griggs, I have to hand it to you. Talking to the girl was brilliant. We all ignored her, but you recognized she knew more than Earlene was saying."

"Your bickering with Mrs. Knowles provided me the perfect opportunity to question Faith."

Cecile sat beside Percy, clutching Millie's pink bonnet, her leg brushing his, setting his limb on fire.

Percy sighed. "But why would Tann say she was taking them somewhere fun?"

R.D. shrugged. "Probably to get Earlene to give her Faith. It's the best lead we've had all day."

"You're right there." They had to get to Tann while Millie was alive and before Tann harmed her.

"Y'all are wrong. There ain't nothin' fun

'round here. No carnival or fair. If'n there was, I'd sure know about it." Gladys sat farther back in her seat and crossed her arms over her skinny chest.

Percy concentrated on his driving. "We have to find out for sure. Otherwise, we have nowhere else to search."

Gladys grunted and frowned.

Cecile leaned against the black dashboard as if she could push the automobile to go faster. "Keep going, Percy. Go to the town. But please, please, hurry. Please, Lord, let Millie be there. Keep her safe. Watch over her."

He prayed along with her whispered requests. If it was the good Lord's will, they would locate Millie in time.

The endless ribbon of road stretched in front of them. Browning fields of cotton fanned out on every side. The dying leaves rustled in the wind, the noise of it just audible over the auto's engine.

Ahead, a dirty young boy wearing nothing more than patched overalls led a skinny cow by a frayed rope. He waved as Percy skirted him.

"Faster, Percy, faster." Cecile urged him on.

"I'm giving this old girl everything she has and then some. We don't need to break down again."

"But if we miss her . . ."

"We won't. Keep praying we won't."

Off in the hazy distance, a cluster of buildings rose from the fields. Little by little it grew until it filled the entire bug-splattered windshield.

Percy steered the car down the main street, brick buildings lining the roadway. A bank rose three stories above the town. The marquee of the theater proclaimed performances of the movie *One Sunday Afternoon.* A woman with a passel of children, all holding hands, scurried across the street in front of them. A stooped old lady wearing a long black dress and leaning on a cane shuffled from the mercantile to a waiting wagon.

Cecile strained forward in her seat. "I don't see a black Cadillac. Are we in the wrong place?"

They ground to a halt at a stop sign. A tall, thin man dressed in a white suit and a white bowler hat nodded at them as he exited the bank.

Cecile leaned out her window. "Excuse me, sir. We were led to believe a black limousine was headed this way. Do you know anything about this?"

He clutched a corncob pipe between his yellowed teeth. "Nope, don't rightly do. This here's such a remote area, simple folk. If'n there was a car like that, the whole town'd be abuzz about it. And I ain't heard a thing."

"Thank you very much." As the man continued on his way, Cecile tapped the dashboard. "Now what? A dead end. Another one. Each time I think we're getting close to Millie, we end up farther away than ever."

Percy grasped the steering wheel. "Now, now. What we do know is that the child isn't here. Mrs. Knowles, do you have any other thoughts?"

She shook her head.

Griggs cleared his throat. "Faith did say she saw the Cadillac headed in this direction. We're on the right track."

"And Faith wouldn't have made that part up. She had to be telling the truth." Cecile clutched the bonnet even tighter.

Percy swung a right-hand turn. "Then I say we keep searching this town until we come up with some clue, some indication of where they might have gone. Someone here must have seen Tann's car. It stands out too much to go unnoticed."

They drove the few streets that comprised the village. Every now and again, Percy stopped the car, and Cecile jumped out to ask the residents if anyone had seen a black

Cadillac. After the third or fourth such stop, she returned to the car, a bead of sweat on her red forehead, a tear on her cheek. "Nothing. She's managed to disappear into thin air."

"We'll find them. Someone has to have seen them."

"Lemme ask over yonder at the hat-maker's. Y'all ain't from around here. Nobody's about to give you information, but they might talk to a local." Gladys patted her brown hair.

They moved down the street until they arrived in front of a white clapboard building with the name HABERDASHERY stenciled in gold on the big display window.

Gladys slid from the car and entered the shop. No sooner had she disappeared inside than movement caught the edge of Percy's sight. A purring noise. Then something dark slithered by. The late afternoon sun glinted off the windshield.

"That's it! There they are." He started the engine and peeled into the road.

R.D. piped up from the backseat. "What about Mrs. Knowles?"

"We don't have time to wait for her. We have to catch them. Now. Before we lose them again."

"Was that Miss Tann's car?" Short of

breath, Cecile clung to the edge of the car's seat.

"We've got them in our sights now." Percy stomped on the gas pedal, and the car lurched forward. "I'm not going to lose them this time."

R.D.'s voice sounded in her ear. "Isn't it strange that she would be driving around the area, especially if she knows we're here?"

How could he have said that? "Don't steal my hope. I know it's just a sliver, but don't yank that from me." She had to keep believing they would find Millie and find her alive, or else she would dissolve into a puddle on the floor.

Percy glanced at her. "She's gotten sloppy. It's our chance to catch her."

"Thank you." His reassurance rang hollow though. He too believed it was unusual for Miss Tann to be in the area when she knew they were tracking her.

"Or else she's taunting us."

Percy glanced behind him. "That's enough, Griggs. Hold your tongue."

He turned back and hunched over the steering wheel, clutching it with both hands, eyes straining in the dying light. Off in the distance, a flash of lightning brightened the coming night.

The Cadillac didn't speed like it had

before but drove at a normal rate. Percy was able to keep up with it without pushing their vehicle.

Cecile's stomach danced. R.D. might be right. Something was rotten. Miss Tann wouldn't want them to catch her. Not after she'd spent all day dodging them. If she still had Millie, she'd want to get away and not allow them to discover her. After five or ten minutes, the Cadillac pulled off the main road and down a lane flanked by soybean fields. Ramshackle sharecropper cabins dotted the field. The car ahead of them came to a stop. No one inside moved. Percy clicked his door open.

Cecile reached out and pulled him back. "Don't." Her mouth went dry. The word squeezed between her tight vocal chords.

He drew his eyebrows into a *V.* "Why not? This is what you've been waiting for. Your daughter is in that car. Let's go to her."

"It's too easy." Her skin prickled.

"You've let Griggs influence you. Don't listen to him."

"I just said it all feels strange. Wrong." R.D. pushed his glasses up his nose.

Percy sighed. "Stay in the car if you like, but I'm going to get Millie." He slid out and slammed the door.

Cecile inhaled and ignored her premonitions. Millie might be in the car. Within reach. She had to get her daughter. She followed Percy to the driver's side of the Cadillac. R.D.'s footsteps sounded behind her.

The uniformed chauffeur exited and stood in front of them, legs akimbo. "So you found me."

"It appears we have." Percy moved forward.

With a shove against Percy's chest, the chauffeur pushed him back. "Where do you think you're going?"

"To get Mrs. Dowd's daughter."

James gave a wry chuckle. "I don't think so."

All of Cecile's muscles twitched.

"Let me take her, and we'll be on our way."

James shifted, and the glint of the gun at his hip caught Cecile's eye. Had Percy forgotten the man was armed?

Percy pushed forward and bent into the open door.

James pulled his pistol and stuck it into Percy's back.

Cecile's knees dissolved to mush. Griggs caught her.

"Get in the car." The driver waved the gun at them as he kicked Percy in the backside and shoved him inside. "Let's go, let's go."

"Millie!" Cecile cried out as she obeyed James's order. A few moments passed. Her eyes adjusted to the dim interior. Tufted leather seats. Wood accents. But no child.

"Where is she? Where is Millie? What have you done with her?" Cecile fired the questions at James.

"Don't worry none about her."

She climbed over R.D. to get out. "Tell me right now where she is. Where is Miss Tann? Are they together?"

James pressed the gun against her breastbone. "You ask too many questions. Shut up and sit back."

R.D. wiped sweat from his forehead. Moisture trickled down Cecile's spine. She shivered.

James started the car and pulled back onto the road. Cecile leaned against Percy's shoulder. He pressed her hand to his chest. At least she wasn't alone. She had God. She had Percy. But she didn't have Millie. Would she ever have her? With each passing moment, the likelihood dimmed, a flickering flame in danger of dying out.

From outside the car, the crickets tuned up. Fireflies danced above the crops. A cool breeze drifted through the open window. The window. She whispered in Percy's ear.

"Could we jump out?"

"Quiet back there." The chauffeur's roar filled the compartment. Driving with one hand, he brandished the gun. He was in control.

Percy shook his head. "Too dangerous."

"I done told y'all to shut up."

"Are you taking us to Miss Tann? To Millie?"

"You'll see Miss Tann."

She held her breath. Despite the breeze, heat rushed through her, Percy and Griggs too close to her.

God, what has happened to my baby? She can't be dead. Please, don't let her be dead. Even if Miss Tann kills both of us, give me one more chance to see my daughter alive. To hold her in my arms again. To tell her I love her. Let me cradle her and keep her from being afraid.

Don't let her die alone.

CHAPTER TWENTY-NINE

"Come back, come back." Gladys tightened every muscle in her body. The car carrying the people in search of her daughter pulled away. How could they go off and do that to her?

She turned to the owner of the hat shop. "I gotta go after them. They were taking me to Fanny. Where's your man's truck?"

"He's out with it. Done gone to pick up a load of wood."

"No. I gotta have one now. If'n they get to Fanny first, I'll lose her forever."

Another puff of dust rolled down the street and neared the shop. Maybe she could flag down the driver. They could give her a ride. Go after those people. The ones trying to destroy her life.

A few minutes later, Willard's dirty red truck pulled up. "Dad blame it, woman. Where you done run off to? Been looking all over DeSoto County for you."

"Willard, Fanny's gonna get killed. I just know it. Feel it in my bones. We gotta find her before anyone else does. Them people from the house done took off without me. Left me here."

Under his breath, Willard mumbled something about good riddance. But once Gladys climbed into the cab, he gave the truck the gas, and they took off. "I seen 'em go in this direction." She pointed to the right.

"Do they have much of a lead?"

"A good bit. Stranded me there at the haberdashery."

"I spent a fair of piece of money on Fanny, and I ain't gonna have that wasted."

Gladys ground her teeth together and willed herself not to get worked up. No matter what reason Willard had for searching for Fanny, at least he was willing to fight to get her back. That was most important. She'd take it.

They hadn't driven far enough to be out of sight of town when a black car pulled in front of them from a narrow lane. Willard had to stand on the brake to keep from hitting them. He swore.

"That's them! Get after them. Don't let 'em out of your sights."

"The things I do for you, woman."

She suppressed the sarcastic laugh that

begged to be released from her throat.

They drove for the longest time, just able to keep up with the expensive, once-shiny, now dust-covered car. "You're losing 'em, Willard. She'll kill Fanny for sure, if she hasn't already."

Darkness pressed on them, a physical weight. Seeing the car ahead of them was difficult.

Willard slowed the truck. "We ain't gonna be able to follow 'em anymore. Gettin' too dark."

"Don't stop. Whatever you do, don't stop."

"But we'll never find 'em."

"I don't care. We can't give up on Fanny. You said yourself she cost a big chunk of money. Don't throw that away."

He backhanded her across the cheek. "I can't do the impossible, woman."

Her face stung, and tears burned the back of her throat. How had he ever charmed her? How had she allowed herself to fall in love with such a beast?

Whatever emotions she'd had toward him had long ago evaporated like the morning mist. "My Fanny." All she had left that was good in this world.

Then, with the moonlight slanting through the clouds, she glimpsed the big car turning off the main road into a piney grove. "There they are."

"I can't go in there. I'd scratch up the truck."

"You have to. For Fanny."

"It'd be cheaper to get another kid than to get another truck."

"Then let me out. I'll run after them."

He came to a stop, the gravel on the shoulder crunching underneath the tires. "Do what you want, woman. I ain't waitin' around for you. I'm going home. You and the brat can find your own way."

"We will. Oh, you'd better believe we will." Once she had Fanny in her arms, she'd never subject herself to Willard again. She'd find Quinn, and the three of them would run.

She jumped from the cab and raced into the thicket. Though she tried to follow the car's path, she lost it in the undergrowth. Branches reached their twiggy arms toward her, gruesome shadows in the moonlit darkness. They clawed at her face. Slapped her cheeks. Tripped her. As she hit the ground, the hard-packed earth smashed all the breath from her lungs. The world teetered. She drew in air and clambered to her feet.

Twigs cracked. An owl hooted a warning. A possum's beady eyes shone in the black velvet of night. She lunged forward. Decaying leaves softened her footfalls. The rotten-egg odor of death hovered in the air. Her lungs begged for air, her legs cried for relief. On and on she ran until a stitch in her side radiated pain through her midsection. Sweat bathed her, making her wetter than any rainstorm would.

And when she couldn't take another step, she burst from the unholy canopy above into a clearing. Like a spotlight at a stage show, the moon beamed on the rough, unpainted cabin in the middle of it. She climbed the steps. Underneath her feet, they creaked. She shivered and walked through a spider's web, the sticky threads clinging to her hair, face, and hands.

As she entered, someone covered her mouth, stifling her screams and holding her fast.

Percy leaned against the back of the Cadillac's tan upholstered seat and stared at the ceiling. He halfway smiled at Cecile's suggestion they leap from the moving car. Her plan was bold and gutsy, that was for sure. But it was not going to work. James traveled too fast. They traversed the empty, uneven road.

For three of them to escape before James turned to fire was impossible. Before they could run far enough to be out of pistol range, he would shoot. And not miss. A tremor raced through him.

No, they had to stay put and go along with what James had planned. He suggested he was taking them to Tann. All the better. They'd confront her. See Millie. Perhaps at some point, a true path of escape would open. They would leave with the child, and this nightmare would end.

Cecile nestled against him and clutched at his hand with a death grip. He held her trembling body close. Her breath tickled the base of his neck. It was warm. Soft. Inviting. His heart flipped and flopped. If he could deliver Millie to her, if he could grant her the greatest desire of her heart, would there be a chance for them? Would either of them ever find joy again?

His joy had evaporated the day he'd assisted Tann in kidnapping Millie. He'd believed he'd had it all. Everything necessary for happiness. Wealth. Prestige. Social standing. In that moment, however, it all morphed to sounding brass.

Obtaining wealth didn't justify this kind of cruelness, this level of violence. Nothing did. The life, welfare, and happiness of children and their parents was priceless. Jesus had already purchased their lives with

His blood. They were no longer up for sale.

James directed the car off the dirt road and onto a path into a dense stand of trees. The darkness around them deepened. Only thin slivers of moonlight peeked through the thick branches, highlighting the night's blackness. Twigs extended their menacing fingers and screeched along the side of the car. Percy's arms broke out in goose bumps. Cecile covered her ears.

They traveled on, encased in a cocoon of trees and vines and night. *Thunk.* James swore. "Possum." Percy recoiled. They'd run over the animal.

Humidity and dampness pressed on Percy. Sweat covered his forehead, his upper lip. Cecile's bare arm was cool but clammy.

The trees parted. Before them ran a narrow stream, a silver snake slivering through the ink. In one motion, James cut the engine and spun around. Training his gun on Percy's heart, he shouted, "Hands up. Get out. All of you. Now."

Percy emerged from the car as a breeze caressed his cheek and mussed his hair. Cecile, letting go of his hand, came after him, followed by Griggs. "Now what?"

James sneered. "Anxious, aren't you? Ready to die?"

No, God, no. Not like this. Not before they

found Millie. Not before he acted on his desire for Cecile. He bent over to her, pressed his lips against her ear. "I love you. I'm sorry I did this, put you in this situation. I could have prevented it."

With a touch of her finger against his mouth, she hushed him. "I love you too."

"Let's go." James's command broke the spell. "Over there." He waved the gun, indicating they should move to the creek bank.

The boggy, marshy ground silenced their steps. A fishy odor permeated the heavy air.

Cecile stumbled and fell to her knees. He pulled her to her feet and helped her along, steadying her. If only he could steady himself. Inside, he quivered. James intended to kill them. Murder them.

"Line up!" James barked the order.

A small cry escaped Cecile. "No. Please, let me see my baby. Don't let me die without holding her one last time. Just so I know she's safe. Well. Happy. That's all I need. Do what you want with me, but keep my daughter from harm." Her voice broke.

A tear trickled down Percy's own face. He'd failed her, himself, and Millie. At the end of the day, he was an utter failure.

"Shut up. You ain't gonna see that kid ever again. No one is." A ghost-like apparition shadowed against the car's headlights, James lifted the pistol.

Their lives couldn't end like this. Not in this manner. Not without a fight. *Lord, show me the time. Give me the opportunity. Don't let Tann and her kind win.*

He squeezed Cecile's hand. Sucked in a breath. His last?

From the forest behind them came a rustling. Snapping of twigs. Crackling of branches. A huffed breath. A deer bounded into the clearing.

"What the . . . ?" James spun around.

Opportunity. Percy powered forward, tackling James to the ground. With an *oomph,* they both hit the leaf-covered dirt. Percy pinned James's arms to the ground, but James pushed back stronger than Percy anticipated. James flipped Percy, now with his back against the earth.

Cecile screamed. Griggs pounced on James. With a kick to the groin, James sent R.D. sprawling. Meanwhile, Percy rolled away and tried to stand. The world tilted in front of him. Returning his attention to Percy, James shoved him to the ground and punched him in the left temple. The stars before his eyes mingled with the ones in the sky. They merged into a single bright light. Percy blinked. Blinked again. His vision cleared. The gun. James held it in his left hand.

Cecile screamed again. The stillness-shattering sound bounced in Percy's head. Didn't stop. The gun. The gun. He focused. He grabbed James's left wrist and banged it on the ground hard. James yelped, releasing the weapon. Percy grabbed for it and touched the cold, hard metal. He reached it at the same time as James did. They both held it and rolled. Left. Right. Back again. Neither let go of the gun. Then, a single shot rang out.

Chapter Thirty

"Well, well, well, you aren't the person I expected to show up." Miss Tann's voice in Gladys's ear sent goose pimples breaking out up and down her arms. "This puts me in a tight spot. What am I going to do with you?"

With the woman's large, fleshy hand over her mouth, Gladys couldn't answer. She worked to maneuver herself from Miss Tann's grip, but she couldn't any more than she'd been able to overpower Willard.

A dank mustiness hung over the place. The small oil lamp on the table in the middle of the room didn't illuminate much. Shadows writhed in every corner, reaching out, inviting Gladys to their macabre dance. She stomped on Miss Tann's foot. The woman howled like a coyote and shoved Gladys. She fell against the rickety table. The lamp tilted then righted.

Gladys pivoted to face Miss Tann. The

flickering light carved deep, dark crevices into her features, hardening them more. Miss Tann moved forward. Gladys was trapped.

Miss Tann grabbed her by the neck. "You're nothing but trouble. Helping them. For that, you're going to lose your daughter."

Gladys attempted to squeak a few words through the narrow opening in her throat. She failed. What was the point? Miss Tann already had Fanny. Had stolen her out from underneath her. The pungent odor of burning oil churned Gladys's stomach. Was Fanny here? In this house?

Pink dots scattered on the blackness in front of her eyes. For Fanny, she had to fight. Couldn't stop until she won. With everything she had left, she shoved Miss Tann off her. Gladys stumbled and teetered, falling against the wall.

She righted herself. "Fanny. Fanny, where are you?"

Miss Tann charged her, the scrape of the soles of her shoes on the warped wooden floor the only sound.

"Fanny!"

"You'll never find her. I won't let you."

"You won't stop me. Not ever."

Three doors led off the main room. Fanny

must be behind one of them. Gladys flung one open. It was a narrow pantry with a few cans of Campbell's soup dotting the shelves. With a burst of energy, she raced for the next. Her hands sweated, and she couldn't take hold of the knob. Heavy footsteps came up behind her. Using both hands, she turned the knob. A rush of cool, damp night air washed across her. A chorus of bullfrogs. A trickling of water. The back door.

Before Gladys could turn inside, Miss Tann thrust her out the door. *Click.* It locked.

No, she couldn't leave Fanny alone. Not with that woman.

She raced for the front of the cabin. Her right foot landed in a hole. It twisted, and she felt burning pain. She cried out. As she came to her feet, she bit her lip. The pain of it equaled that in her ankle. Broken or not, she had no time to figure it out. Wincing, she limped the rest of the way around the building. Grabbing the wobbly handrail, she hopped up the two steps and tried the front door. Barred.

Now what? She had to get inside. Had to. No telling what Miss Tann had in store for Fanny. The woman was out of her mind. Crazier than a rabid dog.

Gladys leaned against the loose porch rail. The doors were locked. Even if she had two good feet, she could never kick them in.

Oh, why was she so stupid? If she had half a brain in her skull, she could figure this out and get Fanny back. But not a thought came to her. Willard was right. A tree stump was smarter than she was. The ache in her ankle worsened. She covered her mouth to keep from yelling. Squeezing her eyes shut, she blocked out the agony. She had to figure out how to get inside to rescue her baby.

The rail moaned. Cracked. Splintered. Fell away. Gladys caught herself on the post and clung to it for dear life. In the thin light from the window, she gazed at the pieces on the ground below. Then she glanced at the window and back at the rotted timbers.

Wouldn't Willard be surprised? She wasn't so stupid after all. Two hops down the steps, a few over to the broken rail, and she snatched one of the posts. Using it as a cane, she hobbled to the window.

Miss Tann peered at her through the glass. Her eyes blazed in the lamplight.

With a mighty screech, Gladys hammered the post through the window. Glass shattered, tinkling as it hit the floor inside. Miss Tann jumped back. Gladys withdrew the rail then struck the window again. And again. And again.

Only a few shards remained, glinting in the light. Ignoring the pain in her ankle, Gladys climbed through the window, dragging the post in with her. One sharp piece of glass dug into her palm's calloused flesh. Miss Tann approached. Still holding the wood, Gladys raised it above her, her chest heaving. "Gimme my girl."

"I gave her to you once. I can take her away if I want." Miss Tann's hands trembled as she held the oil lamp.

Gladys approached. The room burned red. She clenched the post. "No one takes Fanny from me. No one. Not even you. I done protected her these past months. I'll never stop."

Miss Tann grimaced, her ugly face even uglier. "You didn't protect her. I took her. For keeps."

"This ain't no child's game. This is a girl's life we're talking about. She needs a momma. I'm her momma." Forget about that other woman. "Now tell me where she is." Gladys could hit Miss Tann, but then she'd never find out where Fanny was.

"Some kind of mother you are. Ha. You don't even know where the girl is. Can't keep track of her. You deserve to lose her." Miss Tann's eyes glowed yellow like those of a wolf about to spring on its prey. "You deserve everything that's coming."

Miss Tann flung the lamp to the floor. The chimney broke. Oil and fire spilled from the base. Flames leapt in front of Miss Tann, separating her from Gladys. Heat seared Gladys's legs. She swung the post but hit nothing more than air. She swung it again, but it flew out of her hands. The flames rose higher.

"Fanny!"

"Percy!" The scream ripped from Cecile's throat. R.D. held her back, but she shook him off. She rushed forward then dropped to her knees on the soft ground beside Percy, the man she loved. Tears clogged her throat and rolled down her cheeks. She couldn't live without this man. She wouldn't lose another beloved.

"Percy, Percy!"

James groaned.

Percy pushed the driver off him. James's body flopped to the ground. He moaned. Percy came to his feet and stood over James, the revolver pointed at James's heart.

Cecile grabbed him. "Did he shoot you? Are you hurt?"

"I'm fine." He cocked the gun.

Was he about to kill James? "Don't." She

yanked down his arm.

"Let me go. Let me finish him off."

"No." How could he think such a thing?

Percy turned to her. "He tried to kill us."

"This isn't the way. It doesn't justify taking his life." No matter what he'd done, he might have a family, a wife and children who needed him. "There's been too much loss."

"But —"

"Give me the gun." Her hands trembled as she reached for it. In the distance, an owl hooted. The heavy mist dampened her face, chilling her to the core.

"He'll come after us again." Percy clung to the weapon.

She glanced at James. Blood seeped from a shoulder wound. His eyes flickered shut. The car's headlights cast a yellow pallor on his skin. "He's not a threat anymore."

"Don't bet your life on it."

R.D. joined them in standing over James. "Be reasonable, Mrs. Dowd. It's our lives or his." From the creek bank, frogs croaked their warnings.

"I won't have it. Percy will be indicted for murder." The metallic odor of car exhaust sickened her. She swayed on her feet. All she could focus on was the gun.

Percy inched his arms down. He gazed at Cecile.

"Please, give it to me."

"Are you sure? Eliminate James, and we'll have one less worry."

"We can take the weapon in case he wakes up and comes after us."

His hands shook as he leaned forward and passed the revolver to her. The warm barrel touched her flesh, and she shivered. The weight of it tugged on her. Just a lump of metal with the potential for so much destruction.

She drew herself to her full height. "What are we standing here for? Let's get going before he wakes up."

They piled into the idling Cadillac, Percy in the driver's seat, Cecile beside him. She slid the revolver under the bench, out of sight. She sucked in a few steadying breaths. They'd come so close. So close to death.

If it weren't for leaving Millie behind, she might have welcomed it. To be rid of the world's trials. No more pain. No more suffering.

But then she stared at Percy, who turned the car around and headed down the narrow drive. If James had killed them, what else might she have missed? The joy of loving a man again? For she did love him. No matter what he'd done in the past, she did care for him a great deal. He'd proven time and time again that he'd changed. The man she met in the hallway of the Goodwyn Institute a couple of months ago wasn't the man that steered this car.

He was different.

So was she.

And she was ready to love once more.

Percy inched the car down the road. What there was of it.

"Hurry. Hurry."

Percy blew out a breath. "I know. I know."

"Where do we look?"

R.D. piped up from the backseat. "I have a feeling she isn't far."

"How do you know?"

"I don't. Just intuition. She sent James after us. Makes sense he would bring us to her."

Percy nodded.

Cecile tried to relax against the seat, but that proved impossible. Instead, she slid forward, her forehead almost touching the windshield. Up ahead and to the right, an orange aura danced against the soot-dark sky. A burning odor floated in through the open window. The hairs on her forearms stood on end. "Is that a fire?"

Percy didn't even shift his attention in that

direction. "Probably a hobo's camp."

"No, it's bigger."

"Cecile's right. That's more than a camp-fire." Griggs, at least, was on her side.

Now Percy did turn. The eerie glow deep-ened the hallows of his eyes and cheeks. "Something's burning. Just through the woods here." He halted the car. They jumped out. He led the way through the bramble.

Trees, bushes, and raspberries unleashed their claws on her, scratching her legs, her arms, her face. She tripped on a half-buried root and stumbled against Percy's back, but she stayed upright.

Without warning, the dense undergrowth thinned, and the pines gave way to a clear-ing. A small cabin occupied the middle of the opening, a door flanked by two win-dows, fronted by a half-collapsed porch. Clouds of white smoke and angry red and orange flames burst through one of the win-dows.

"Help me! Help me!" A woman's shrieks came from inside.

Percy raced forward.

"Percy!"

"I have to get her."

Millie. If this was Miss Tann, Millie might

be with her inside that house, facing those flames.

Cecile sprinted after him. They entered, smoke choking them. It was so black, they couldn't see anything. Couldn't breathe. Couldn't think.

"Millie! Millie!"

"I'm over here."

Not Millie. Maybe Gladys? "Keep talking."

The woman coughed. "Have to get to Fanny."

"She's here?"

"I've got Mrs. Knowles." Percy's voice came from the same direction as Gladys's.

"Let go of me. I have to get Fanny."

"Where is she?" Cecile had to shout to be heard over the crackle of the flames.

"In the back room."

A wall of flames blocked the way.

A creak.

A groan.

A crash.

The ceiling fell in.

CHAPTER THIRTY-ONE

Heat seared Percy's face, the burning intense. He grabbed Mrs. Knowles. Then, with a great creak and groan, the roof caved in.

"Millie!" Cecile's screams penetrated the roar of the fire. "Millie!"

"My Fanny, my Fanny!" Gladys's screech rivaled Cecile's.

"Let's get out of here."

"No!" the women screamed in chorus.

"We can't get to her this way." He gagged on the noxious fumes. "I'll go through the back."

"Door is locked." Gladys fought him.

"I'll get in. Don't get yourself killed." He scooped up the lithe woman and headed in Cecile's direction. The smoke obscured his path. "Cecile!"

"Here. By the door."

He followed the sound of her voice and bumped into her. "Out. Now!"

"Millie!"

"Out!" This was not the time for her to be stubborn. He nudged her with his elbow. She moved. He followed. Several steps, and they were outside.

Griggs climbed up the rickety porch and grabbed Mrs. Knowles from Percy's arms.

"I'm going for Millie."

"Fanny." Mrs. Knowles hadn't lost her spunk.

He raced down the steps and to the back of the house. Cecile came right on his heels. "Go back."

"She's my daughter."

What if they found Millie but not alive? She didn't need to see that. "Don't risk your life."

"You are."

They were wasting precious seconds. "I don't want you hurt."

She pushed by him. He caught her and flung her to the side. Like Gladys said, the door was locked. He took three steps backward then kicked with all his might. Nothing. He kicked again. A small budge. A slight crack. One more kick. With a crash, the door gave way. Heat rushed at him, propelling him away. He fought his way forward.

Cecile was at his side. "Millie! Millie! Millie!"

Each of her cries was answered by nothing but the whoosh of flames. He flung off his jacket and tossed it to her. He covered his mouth with his shirt sleeve. He pressed on, but the heat intensified. His eyelashes were singed. "Can't keep going."

"Have to." Cecile coughed, her words weak.

"Not here."

"Gladys said."

Total darkness covered him. He couldn't find anyone, and his skin was blistering.

He pivoted. "Must leave."

"No! No! My baby!"

As with Gladys, he picked up Cecile and slung her over his shoulder like a sack of flour. She beat his back. Every blow hurt because he was already bruised.

They burst through the door. He gulped fresh air as he dropped Cecile to her feet. He bent over, gasping to breathe.

Cecile sputtered. Wheezed. He rubbed her back. Tears ran in rivulets down her soot-stained face. "Millie. God, where is she?" She fell to her knees.

He knelt beside her. "Not in there. She would have answered. Would have called to you."

"She's gone." The whisper barely reached his ears.

"No. Don't think that. Don't give up. We'll find her. We will."

For a few moments, he allowed her to grieve. To release her fear. To calm herself.

She gazed at him, nothing but questions and confusion in her eyes.

"Believe. God takes care of His own."

"He does. Yes, He does." She spoke as if comforting herself.

He kissed her temple, her hair smoky. "Let's go to the others. Maybe Tann is there with Millie."

She widened her watery eyes. "Maybe?"

"Could be." He lifted her to her feet and clasped her by the hand as they rounded the cabin. They came into view of the others. Griggs stood with Mrs. Knowles at the edge of the clearing, both intent on the disaster in front of them. Another figure kept watch closer to the house. A larger, rounder person. The light from the flames illuminated her face. Miss Tann.

Cecile must have realized who it was at the same moment he did. She lunged forward at Tann, knocking her over and sitting on top of her. "Where's my daughter?"

"Get off me." Tann flailed and writhed.

"Not until you give me Millie." Cecile

pinned down Tann's beefy arms.

"Never."

"Is she in there?"

"Yes, yes!"

Cecile released the woman, leaped up, and headed for the burning cabin.

Percy caught her by the collar. "No! You can't get to her." Flames now burst through the back of the house.

"But my baby. My baby."

He held her fast. "It's too late." Just a little too late. Maybe no more than a few minutes. All this effort, all this time, all this hope. For naught.

"No! No!"

He embraced her. Every muscle in her body was taut. "I'm so, so sorry." He stroked her hair, a cloud of ashes snowing from it.

She broke free and returned to Tann, who had struggled to sit. "You killed my child." The ice in Cecile's cold words could have extinguished the fire. "There is a special place in the afterworld for people like you."

Tann scooted back, and she rose. Was she going to try to escape?

Percy turned to Griggs. "Don't let her get away. Where's the gun?"

Cecile stood nose to nose with Tann. "In the car."

His heart hammered. "I'll get it."

From the shadows, a silhouette appeared beside Cecile.

The cock of a pistol.

"No one is going anywhere."

At the click of a gun, Gladys flinched. A sound she'd heard too often. One that haunted her at night. In that moment, time froze. Like she watched a talking picture show set too slow. Even the voices were distorted, low and blurred, like when the film in the projector was breaking.

The fire burned, but not with the same fierceness as before. The flames performed a slow dance in the skeleton of the building.

"No one is going anywhere." James pointed a pistol at Miz Dowd and winced. Blood dripped from a shoulder wound.

Behind her, Mr. Griggs shouted, "We should have killed him! We should have killed him! I told you so."

She inched forward, closer to the action.

All color had drained from Miz Dowd's face. She was as white as the cotton in Willard's field and about as wilted as it got in a summer's drought. "My baby's dead! You killed her!"

Cold raced down Gladys's spine. That couldn't be. Fanny couldn't be gone. Not that poor child. Not that sweet girl.

"I'm glad of it." Miss Tann sidled next to James.

A sob broke from Gladys's throat. Her head pounded. Her ankle throbbed. She closed her eyes. Saw Fanny in the flames. Fighting. Falling. Flying away. Leaving Gladys alone. Utterly alone.

She could never return to Willard. Even without Fanny, she never would. She could never be used and abused in such a manner. Perhaps she would sneak back and get Quinn. He shouldn't have to live like that either.

The flames had consumed the one good thing in her life. From the corner of her eye, Gladys caught sight of Mr. Vance moving around the back of the cabin. Was he going to try to get in once more? See if Fanny was truly dead?

She limped after him, trying to stay on her tiptoes. Leaves crunched under feet. He spun around, motioned her back. She shook her head.

He nodded and came her way. "I have to sneak behind him." He hissed his words. "If you're with me, that's too much chance of getting caught. They might already realize we're gone. Go back."

With a lump in her throat, she obeyed his command. What good was she going to do

him, anyway? If only she could help, do
something, anything to make Miss Tann and
the people involved pay for what they did to
an innocent child. They had so much blood
on their hands. It was a wonder they weren't
permanently stained. Maybe they were, and
Gladys hadn't noticed.

She returned to the front of the cabin.
James held the gun trained on Cecile's
temple with both hands. He shook. That
shoulder wound had to be bothering him,
hampering him. Perhaps that would give
Percy a chance to overpower him. Get the
gun away before anyone got hurt.

Movement came from behind James. It
must be Percy. Gladys held her breath. Her
pulse pounded in her neck. A breeze stirred
the mist. Percy lost his cover.

"Just pull the trigger, and get it over with."
Miss Tann spoke with all the emotion one
would have if giving directions to wrap up
rotten fish and dispose of it.

James trembled from head to toe. Maybe
he'd pass out.

Percy wasn't far behind him now.

James blinked once, twice, three times.

"Oh, for heaven's sake, if you can't do it,
give me the gun." Miss Tann spun a quarter
of a turn. And spied Percy. She yanked the
pistol from James and pointed it at Miz

Dowd. Percy pushed James to the side.

Gladys shot forward. She had to get Miz Dowd out of the way. An ear-splitting crack rang out. There was a firework-like bang and a flash of light. In her midsection, there was a tugging, pulling sensation. No pain. Just release. Sweet release.

CHAPTER THIRTY-TWO

The retort of the pistol rang in Cecile's head. Before her eyes, Gladys crumpled to the ground. A ring of crimson spread from the middle of her chest. She gurgled a few times then fell silent.

Percy bounded forward but missed tackling James. He grabbed Miss Tann by the upper arm and squeezed hard. She dropped the gun. Mr. Griggs scooped up the weapon.

James and Miss Tann headed for the thicket. Griggs fired and missed. He gave chase, but the forest swallowed them.

Cecile slumped to the earth, the silty dirt sticky with Gladys's blood. Covering her head, Cecile wailed. It was all too much. Too much loss. Too much grief. Too much burden to bear.

How could she go on without her beloved daughter? It had been hard enough to be separated from her, but at least she had the hope that Millie was alive and well somewhere in the world. Now, in a single stroke, Miss Tann had extinguished that hope.

Percy knelt beside her. "God, why did it have to come to this?" He breathed the prayerful question. "She gave up her life to save yours, Cecile."

She wiped away a tear, even though another one took its place. "Despite how she came into Millie's life, she loved my little girl. Loved her like her own. And when she knew Millie was gone, there wasn't anything left to live for."

Percy drew her close, and she nestled into his shoulder. His bare shoulder, his shirt torn and his jacket lost in the fire's commotion, his skin smooth and cool. "Just cry. Let it out."

"If I start, I might not stop."

"I'll be here."

And so she opened the floodgates and allowed the dam to burst. Great, wracking, heaving sobs exploded from the depths of her soul. The full weight of her loss settled on her shoulders. Millie was part of her. Flesh and blood. Half of herself, half of Nathaniel. Together, a whole new little life. Cecile hadn't lost someone she loved. She'd lost a piece of her very being. Without Nathaniel, without Millie, the puzzle would never be complete. What was the point in finishing it?

"I'm here. I'm here." Percy. Solid. Steady. Sure. A safe place, someone to lean on. Depend on. "And God is here."

God. Millie was seeing Him face to face now. For her daughter, there was no more pain or suffering. No more cruelty. No more fear. All her troubles had ended. Perhaps she bowed before the Lamb's throne next to Nathaniel. How happy they must be. Part of her family was together. Whole and complete. Unblemished.

With that thought, her weeping slowed, her tears not a rushing river but a trickling creek. She even managed a small laugh. "She's perfect."

"I know she was."

"No, not in this life." She turned up the corners of her mouth. "She was an imp. A little scamp. Funny and fun-loving, but a girl with a mind of her own. In heaven, she's perfect. Nathaniel doesn't have to scold her."

Percy's shoulders shook. "That's beautiful."

"I'm so sad. This pain is horrible. Horrendous. Worse than losing Nathaniel. But I only grieve for myself. Not for her. Because she's with both her fathers. With Nathaniel. And with her loving heavenly Father."

Throughout the long night, Percy held her. He spoke soft, soothing melodies into her ear. The words weren't important. Just that he was here with her.

The crackle of the fire diminished and ceased. Wisps of smoke emanated from the blackened remains of the cabin.

The simple, repetitive songs of a cardinal broke the predawn hush. Right on cue, the world came to life again. Maybe someday Cecile would too.

As morning dawned, her cries subsided into hiccups. Once the sun had broken free from the hold of the trees, Cecile eased back from Percy's embrace. He wiped her eyes with his handkerchief. "I'm going to owe you a new box of them."

"I wish I could do more."

"Just stay with me. That's all I ask."

"I'm not going anywhere." He hesitated, as if wanting to say more but not sure how to go about it.

"I love you, you know."

His countenance brightened. "I love you."

Her knees ached from being on them so long. She rocked back. "Now what?" Difficult as it was to tear herself from this place, they couldn't stay here forever.

"We notify the authorities."

"And find Millie." The thought tripped

over her tongue. She flicked her attention to the home's hull. "Will you help me search for her body?"

"Stay here. I'll do it."

"I have to get my baby."

"It's better this way. You don't want to see her. Instead, remember her as she was."

All the fight drained from her body. She nodded.

"Let me take you back to the car. I'll get a blanket to cover her."

"No. I want to stay here. I want to be with Millie when you find her."

He helped her to a stump some way from both the cabin and the dead woman. She didn't let him out of her sight as he sifted through what was left of the place. Thorough. Meticulous. But it shouldn't be that hard to find her, should it?

She swallowed the vomit that rose in her throat. "Oh Millie. My Millie Mae. I promise your death won't be in vain. Somehow, we'll bring that woman to justice. She won't get away with this."

Percy bent over the burned building for quite a while. Cecile succumbed to the numbness. Time didn't matter anymore. A shadow fell over her. She peered into Percy's face. His smiling face. He was smiling?

"What?"

"There's no trace of Millie. Nothing to indicate she was ever here. And certainly no body." He knelt in front of her and clasped her hands. "I don't think Millie is dead."

Cecile's heart stopped beating. "Not dead?" She must have heard wrong. This was a dream too good to be true. Had she mourned her daughter for nothing? Could this puzzle yet be completed?

"I don't know for sure, but I'm not seeing anything that would lead me to conclude Millie perished in the fire. Nothing."

"Another one of Miss Tann's tricks?"

"She's capable of it. We've seen it before."

"For what feels like the thousandth time, I have to ask, since she's not here, where is she?" Could she still be with Miss Tann somewhere?"

Percy coughed, no doubt from the film of smoke that hung in the air. "Both she and James were busy. They had their hands full with us. My guess is they didn't have time to deal with Millie. If I had to bet money on it, I would bet they stashed her somewhere. Somewhere close."

Cecile glanced around their location. Other than the cabin, or what was left of it, there was nothing but trees. The breeze stirred the trees' leaves and needles, a kind of natural wind chime. In the distance, a crow cawed.

"I know I'm just repeating myself, but where? Why can't we get the answer to that question once and for all?"

Percy stroked her arm. "We will. Eventually, we will. And that might be more than any other woman will get."

"Argh." She rose from the stump and stomped around him. "I feel sorry for those women. I most certainly do. Many of them haven't had the support and encouragement and help that I've had. I'm blessed to have you to assist me. To keep me from giving up. But right now, those other women aren't my concern. Only Millie. She's my single focus."

Percy squeezed her shoulder. "I understand. Maybe that wasn't the best thing to say."

"No, I'm sorry. I'm just worried. Too many emotions, ups and downs, in a short span of time."

"And no sleep." Percy rubbed his eyes, emphasizing his point.

She stared at the gray-blue sky. "If you believe Millie is still alive and near, then what are we waiting for? Let's go find her."

The crackle of twigs breaking underfoot broke the morning calm.

Mr. Griggs returned, his blue oxford shirt

ripped, leaves clinging to what little hair he had. Cecile had almost forgotten about him. In his hand, he clutched the gun. "They got away."

"Away?" Percy rubbed his forehead.

"I chased them for a while, but in the dark, I couldn't get a good shot. In the end, I got tripped up and tangled in vines, and they disappeared. They must have made it to the car, because it's gone."

Cecile's chin trembled. Miss Tann would live on to kidnap and abuse other children. Millie was nothing more than another unfortunate casualty.

"When I was chasing them, we came across a small shed. They slowed down and started toward it, then turned back and kept running. Something tells me that they've hidden a secret in there."

"My secret?"

Mr. Griggs nodded. "The shed is locked. I've been trying to open it to no avail, so I came back to see if I could find a tool to get in it."

"Could you find your way again?" A tiny bubble built in Cecile's chest. She popped it before it could grow into full-blown hope. Already, she'd had too many disappointments.

Griggs nodded. "We trampled the vegetation, so it should be easy to follow."

Percy returned to the ash heap that was the cabin and retrieved a metal bar. "The bolt from the front door. This should work on the shed."

Mr. Griggs headed the group into the woods. They had cleared a distinct path through the trees and vines and bramble. Still, branches scratched her arms and face. She slapped away a few mosquitoes.

In time, they stumbled on a shed set back from the path. Vines grew up the sides, almost obscuring it. Dark green and brown moss covered the wood-shingled roof that threatened to collapse. The greenish-brown paint camouflaged the building, almost indistinguishable from the surrounding forest.

Cecile tried to get ahead of Percy on the narrow path. He turned and held her by the shoulders. "No. You stay here. There's no telling what we'll find. You promised me once already to let me do the looking. I haven't released you from that promise."

"But —"

"Tell me you'll keep put. Don't waste time arguing."

She nodded and held on to the trunk of an oak tree to support herself. The men opened the door little by little. Each squeak of the rusty hinges sent goose bumps over Cecile's entire body. They peered inside. Then disappeared into the tiny building. Cecile held her breath. And there, in the entryway, the faded green door hanging at an angle, was Millie. The early sun cast its pink rays over her round face, coloring her cheeks. Her brown hair glowed yellow, a halo of sorts.

The woods, the birds, Percy and Mr. Griggs, everything around Cecile faded into the background, a piece of fabric washed out by years of scrubbing. The narrow pathway in front of her transformed into a tunnel leading to her daughter. Her breath rushed from her lungs and stole all conscious thought. Like the magnolias bending in the wind, Cecile doubled over, dropping to her knees. Twigs dug into her tender flesh. "Millie Mae. My Millie."

The child, her child, rushed toward her. Stumbled. Fell. Cried.

Cecile leaped to her feet and sprinted to her daughter. She gathered her soft body into her arms. "Oh my sweet, sweet Millie. Hush now. Momma's here. Momma's here and is never going to leave you again."

"Momma. My momma."

Like the missing puzzle piece now found and slipped into place, Millie fit perfectly into Cecile's arms. A part of her soul, once torn away, was now restored. She was whole again. Complete. The raw, gaping wound in her heart was now scabbed over and healed.

Dampness from Millie's tears soaked Cecile's thin dress. Her own tears bathed Millie's forehead. The light breeze ruffled the child's hair, carrying the scent of soap and strawberries.

She was home.

CHAPTER THIRTY-THREE

Percy's throat tightened as he stood at Cecile's side. She hugged Millie, nestling her child to her body. Both of them wept. Touched each other's faces. Kissed. They should never have been separated. This mother, this child loved each other with an overwhelming love, a love that knew no bounds, no limits, no ends.

Until now, he hadn't understood the unshakable, unbreakable bond a parent had with a child. But there was nothing like a mother's love, other than God's love for His own children. Fierce. Determined. Protective.

In this small miracle in front of him, lit by the morning's rays, a perfect picture, he at last saw true, unconditional love. And it stole his breath. It was so beautiful, he had to turn away and wipe a tear from his eye. What he would have given to have had a love such as that. He thought of all he had missed out on. But he did have that kind of love now, that kind of love with his heavenly Father. It was more perfect, more beautiful than any love on earth. Holy. Sacred.

And he embraced it, allowing the full extent of his Father's love to flood his soul. For the first time in his life, that heavy weight of not belonging, of not having a family, lifted from his chest because he belonged to the family of God.

He returned his attention to Cecile and Millie. They clung to each other as if clinging to a rope over a chasm. As if they would fall without each other.

He glanced at his chest. What a wonder that his heart didn't pop his shirt's buttons, because he had another family. Or he prayed he would have this woman and this child for his family soon. God had granted him an earthly love. A love beyond measure. Also unconditional. For both the mother and the child.

He knelt beside them in the pine needles and gathered them close to him. Millie backed away, but Cecile nestled into him. He relished the belonging. He'd come home.

After a time, Griggs cleared his throat and broke the spell. Percy and Cecile laughed and wiped their eyes. They stood, lifting

Millie to her feet.

The girl hid behind Cecile. "Go away, man. You don't take me from my momma."

All the happiness of the past few minutes drained from Percy's body. Of course, she would be afraid of him. He'd stolen her from Cecile. Ripped her from her mother. He didn't blame her.

He squatted in front of her. "I'm sorry I took you from your momma before. I was wrong. I shouldn't have done that. Your momma loves you very much, and I'm going to make sure you stay with her forever."

Millie gazed at Cecile with those big, beautiful green eyes. Cecile nodded. "It's true. He is very sorry for taking you away. He helped me find you. Without him, I would have never gotten you back. He's a very, very good man." She smiled at him. "One I love."

"And I love your momma."

Millie stared at the ground and didn't make eye contact with Percy.

Cecile touched his bicep. "Give her a little time. She'll see. She'll forget about before and come to love you as much as I do."

He nodded, but the luster had worn off the day. Yes, he had to be patient, but that wasn't his strong suit.

Griggs stepped forward. "We have to

report Tann and James to the sheriff. We can't wait any longer. It'll be a long enough walk to town."

Griggs was right. "Let's get going."

Percy and Griggs led the way down the forest road. "Do you think Gladys came to terms with losing Millie?"

Griggs adjusted his glasses. "I suppose she saw no reason to go on. When you lose a child, the effects can be devastating."

"You speak as one who knows."

"I do. Even years later, it's difficult. The ordeal almost cost me my wife too. I can understand why Mrs. Knowles did what she did. If she couldn't raise Millie, she wanted Mrs. Dowd to. She did it to keep Millie from Tann's clutches."

By the time they returned to the town, it had come to life for the day. A few cars were angle-parked along the main street. People went in and out of the drugstore. But Percy drove beyond the commercial district to the sheriff's office. They piled out of the automobile and entered the dark red brick building. From the back room came a tall, broad young man in a brown shirt and pants, a gold star on his chest. "Sheriff Lisle. What can I do you for?"

Percy explained the situation. Cecile and Griggs chimed in to add their own details.

While they spoke, the lawman scribbled notes. By the time he finished, Percy had no more energy.

Sheriff Lisle pushed his white Stetson hat from his eyes. "That's a mighty interesting tale."

"Not a tale, sir, but every word the truth."

"Now, I don't think Miss Tann would ever engage in that kind of activity."

Pain pulsed behind Percy's eye. "She did. Here are three witnesses to that fact."

"Just hearsay. Can't go and make an arrest on that."

Had they stumbled on another man in Crump's back pocket? "Two witnesses in the Bible were enough to convict."

"Ain't that nice? But the laws of Mississippi are a little different. That of the United States too. I'm sorry, but I can't bring a case against her. For all I know, you're the ones who killed that woman."

Percy shook his head. "Of course not. That's crazy." How could the man accuse them?

"We'll see about that. I'll call for my deputy and the mortician to go and take care of the body."

The day dragged on as Sheriff Lisle investigated the case, taking detailed statements from each of them. Separately. When they weren't subjected to the inquisition, they took turns napping on the cot in the open jail cell.

By the time the sheriff concluded his interviews and cleared them, darkness once again covered the land. Percy got in the car and slammed the door. Hard. "So they're going to get away with it. Again."

From the backseat, Griggs mumbled something unintelligible.

Cecile leaned against Percy, Millie asleep in her arms. "For now, I want to go to a safe place. Away from all this craziness. Forget about Miss Tann. Forget about everything that's happened. Just enjoy having my daughter in my arms again."

"But we can't let her get away with this. With kidnapping, abuse, and murder."

"Who's going to listen to us? We tried. If we go back to Memphis, no one will pay any attention to us or take us seriously. Our lives might even be in jeopardy. Please, tell me we won't go back there. Please."

He bit the inside of his cheek. She did have a point. They could never return to Memphis. But he couldn't let Tann win. "I'm not giving up the fight. We have to protect these precious children."

She touched his hand, hers warm and soft against his. Would she ever do that without his skin zinging? "We will. We'll get Faith and return her to her mother. And maybe it's time I go home to my family. See if I can restore the relationship I used to have with them. Let them meet their grand-daughter."

She wanted to leave? Without him?

No. He couldn't allow that.

R.D. leaned his head against the back of the bus seat and closed his eyes. Beside him, Faith slumbered, a light snore escaping her thin lips. Poor kid. All she had been through in her short life. Even the past couple of days, for that matter.

Every limb ached, and every part of his body screamed for sleep. Yet his mind refused to slow down, to allow himself to absorb all that had happened. Faith. Millie. Pearl. All victims. But did that mean he was under an obligation to locate Pearl's birth parents and return her? After all, he did have her adoption folder. Still sealed. But how could he part with that ray of sunshine, his Miss Muffet? She'd become a piece of him. As essential to him as a heartbeat. And who was to say she hadn't been abused?

There was only one conclusion. Adoption was messy. It consisted of brokenness, loss, and heartache. For one family to gain a child to love, another had to give up that child.

The bus arrived at the depot in Memphis, and Faith's mother waited at the bottom of the steps. She swept up her daughter, and for the longest time, they held each other close.

A lump welled in R.D.'s throat. He'd never been one given to emotion, but these reunion scenes were too much to bear. He turned away so the women wouldn't catch the tears in his eyes.

Faith's mother came to him and pecked him on the cheek. "I can't thank you enough for bringing Faith home to me. It means everything. I never thought I'd see her again." Her voice was thick. "In a way, you brought her back from the dead."

"I did no such thing."

"Trust me, you did. You will always hold a special place in our hearts. Thank you, thank you for the greatest gift."

He patted her back and walked away before he broke down. As he left the depot, Darcy and Pearl met him on the street outside. His daughter ran to him and jumped into his arms. "Daddy, Daddy, you're home. I missed you."

He kissed both cheeks, her chin, her forehead. "And I missed you, Miss Muffet."

She giggled, the sound pure as a church bell. "Don't go away, Daddy. Mommy and me were sad."

"I was sad too. But I had to go and help Mrs. Dowd."

"Did you?"

"Yes."

"You're a good daddy."

What was wrong with his eyes today? Maybe allergies. He pushed aside the thought that it wasn't even allergy season. "And you are the very best daughter ever. I love you."

"I love you, Daddy."

Darcy inserted herself between the two of them. "I hate to break this up, but I'd love a kiss from Daddy too."

Pearl sighed.

R.D. and Darcy laughed then kissed. "I'm glad you're home safe."

She tasted like whipped cream and sugar. Smelled like candy. Sweet. Pure. "Me too. The Lord was watching over us. Making sure we got our families back the way they belong." He set Pearl down, and she skipped to the car.

Hand in hand, he and Darcy followed. "And what about our family?" she asked.

"We're in an impossible situation. Who knows how Tann went about getting her for

391

us? But is it fair to rip her away from our home, our arms, our love? She's happy and settled. To disrupt that might be more than she can handle. We can provide her with love and happiness and security."

She squeezed his hand. "We both know what is right."

God help him, he did. He gave a single slow nod.

"We'll try to find her? Pearl's birth mother?"

Again, another nod. The hardest thing he'd ever done. "I have Pearl's file. I took it the night I broke into the records room to dig up information on Mrs. Dowd's child. We'll open it. See what it has to say."

She rubbed his arm. "That's what's best for all involved. Once we find her, we can decide what to do from there."

He stopped, turned her to face him, and drew her to his chest. He kissed the back of her neck. "Have I ever told you what a wise woman you are and how much I love you?"

She nuzzled him. "Many, many times. But I never get tired of hearing it."

"In the meantime, if we want to protect Pearl, we can't stay in Memphis. Tann and Kelley and Crump are too powerful, and I know too much. They'll be after all of us."

"Then we'll leave. I've always wanted to

live in the country. We were going to go to Lookout Mountain before. Let's do it now. Find a quiet, out-of-the-way place to settle where Tann won't find us."

"You won't miss the city's society?"

She caressed his cheek. "I have all I need."

And so did he.

CHAPTER THIRTY-FOUR

Water droplets splashed on the mirror above the washbasin in the boardinghouse as Cecile washed her face. She and Percy had come here last night after everything was settled. Today, she was going home. While her bath yesterday evening had been nothing short of heaven, the charred odor of smoke and soot clung to her. The water helped to erase the horror of the past few days.

Millie sat on the edge of the bed, her legs dangling. She folded her hands in her lap and stared at the black Mary Janes she wore. What had happened to the bright, mischievous little girl Cecile had known?

She dried her face on a towel and sat beside her daughter. "What is it, Millie?"

She shook her head. "I be good. I promise."

"Oh sweetheart, none of this happened to you because you weren't a good girl." So much guilt for a four-year-old to carry. "It happened because Miss Tann is a bad, bad woman."

"I didn't listen. Mrs. Ward didn't like me."

"She had no right to take you from me. That's not what I wanted. I wanted you to live with me always. You're my girl. Nothing could ever change that. I'll love you forever, no matter what."

"Even when I bad?"

"Even then. I promise that no one is going to ever take you away from me again. I'm not going to let you out of my sight. We'll be like we're glued together."

A slight smile crossed Millie's not-quite-so-round cheeks. Cecile would see they plumped again.

"How would you like to go meet your grandma and grandpa?" If her parents wouldn't welcome her, she didn't know what she would do. But those were decisions for later.

"Grandma and Grandpa?"

Cecile touched her chest. It had been difficult for her to speak of her parents, but had she really never mentioned them? "Yes. They live far away where it snows in the winter all the time." Perhaps Millie even had cousins.

"I like snow. You eat it."

"If it's white." At the sight of Millie's scrunched-up face, Cecile chuckled. But inside, she ached. When she'd mentioned going to Massachusetts, Percy never said anything to her about them being together. Hadn't he truly loved her? He had said the words, but did he mean them? Perhaps it was fine when she didn't have Millie, but maybe he didn't want children. Or didn't want Millie.

How wonderful it would have been to have a complete family for her child, a mother and a father. Two people to love her. Siblings someday. And how wonderful it would have been for Cecile to have someone to share her life with, her hopes and dreams and ambitions. Together, once they were settled, they might have even continued to fight Tann. To shed light on the corruption that ate away at the fabric of Memphis society. But it was not to be. She swallowed hard, having shed enough tears in the past few months to last a lifetime. Sorrow had come to an end. The time had come for joy.

She would return home. Family meant everything. She had Millie back. Now she would work on getting the rest restored to her.

With great care, she slipped on the dress provided by the woman who ran the boardinghouse. Cecile would pay her for it once she reached home. She pinned on her hat and peered in the mirror. Dark half-moons still hung from her eyes, but there was nothing she could do about that. From the box the shop owner in Memphis had packed it in, she withdrew Millie's pink bonnet. Though scrawny, Millie had grown while away. The bonnet wouldn't fit her much longer. Cecile slipped it on Millie's head. For the first time today, Millie flashed a genuine smile. How good it was to see it on her daughter. The trauma of this ordeal would fade. The real Millie would reappear in time.

They met Percy in the parlor. He'd shaved, though the scent of smoke hung about him. He pecked her cheek and patted Millie's head. "You look rested."

"I could have slept another ten hours, but I'm anxious to get going." The longer she stayed, the more difficult it would be to leave. And he'd given her no reason to hope for a future for them.

"Are you sure?"

She nodded.

"And you, Miss Millie Mae, are you ready?"

She eyed him, but neither nodded nor shook her head.

He offered Cecile his elbow, and they walked in silence to the bus depot a few blocks away. Did the same ache fill him that almost consumed her? After Nathaniel died, she believed she'd be on her own forever. But she'd healed and fallen in love again. He told her yesterday he loved her. Then why wasn't he stopping her?

They reached the red brick depot, and she purchased their tickets. Once she had them in hand, they located a bench in the almost-empty lobby to sit and wait. She leaned against him. Even though he smelled like burning wood, he also smelled of pine. A sweet and pleasant odor, one she would remember him for.

"I'm going to miss you."

His quiet words startled her, and she bolted upright. "I'm going to miss you too." Was there more to come? She gripped the tickets so tight she crumpled them.

"I'll try to keep in touch."

"That would be nice."

A heaviness fell over her, and her shoulders slumped. "Thank you for everything you did for me and Millie. I know what it cost you. I can never repay you."

"There's no need. I may have lost a great deal, but I gained so much more. You have given me the life I didn't realize I desired.

You have given me true happiness and wealth."

Then why was he letting her walk out of his life? "And you've restored my daughter to me. That's everything. Absolutely everything."

The call came for her bus to Atlanta then on to Boston. The three of them rose and made their way to the vehicle. As they stood by the bus's folding door, he grabbed her, embraced her with such fierceness, and kissed her. Hard. Long. Passionately.

And she responded. Poured her gratitude, her love, her desire into that kiss. Drank him in like a thirsty desert-dweller at an oasis. Impressed this moment in her memory to last a lifetime.

He pushed her away. A rush of cold came over her. She took Millie by the hand and started up the steps. She pinched the bridge of her nose, her feet leaden. She willed herself to climb another step.

"Wait!"

Percy's call stopped her. Spun her.

He rushed to her, grabbed her, pulled her from the bus. "Don't go. Please, don't leave me. I don't ever want to be without you and without Millie again. You've brightened my life in a way that no one else ever has. Now, forever, I want to show you how much I love you."

Right there on the asphalt in the parking lot, he dropped to one knee. "Cecile Dowd, will you marry me?"

Though she vowed she'd had enough of tears, she couldn't stop them from streaming down her face. She joined him on the ground, kneeling in front of him. "When no one else believed in me, you did. When I gave up hope, you gave it back to me. When I was at my lowest, when it was the darkest, you brought light.

"I'm the one who can never repay the debt I owe you. Not only did you return my daughter to me, but you brought love back into my life at a time when I didn't even know I needed it. I love you, Percy Vance. I love you as much as I could ever love anyone."

She leaned in to kiss him, but he stopped her. "You haven't answered me."

She laughed. "Yes, Percy, yes. I'll marry you."

Now he drew her to himself. This kiss was soft, gentle, but full of promise for the future.

Millie tapped Cecile's face. "Momma, you're crying."

"These aren't sad tears. They're happy

tears. I'm going to marry Mr. Vance. He's going to take care of us, very good care of us. He will help keep that bad lady away."

Millie pulled down her brown eyebrows. "You promise?"

Percy touched Millie's cheek. "I promise. No one is ever going to take you away from your momma and me. We'll go together to meet your family. Start a new life there."

Nothing in the world sounded better to Cecile than that.

Millie wrapped her arms around their necks and entered their circle, the brim of her pink bonnet against their foreheads.

AUTHOR'S NOTE

When I set out to write *The Pink Bonnet,* I knew it would be difficult for me to write about the kidnapping and sale of children because I am the mother of three children who came to us through adoption. I wanted to tell the true story of Georgia Tann and the Tennessee Children's Home Society without casting a black shroud over adoption in general.

Georgia Tann was a woman who ran an adoption agency in Memphis, Tennessee, from 1924 until 1950. It is estimated that, in that time, she kidnapped over five thousand children and sold them to the highest bidder. She even advertised the children in the newspaper, especially around the holidays. Some of the nation's biggest celebrities adopted through Miss Tann, including Joan Crawford, Dick Powell, and June Allyson.

It was a frightening time to be a parent in

Memphis. You didn't dare allow your children to walk the streets alone or play in the park by themselves. You kept a watchful eye for Tann's black Cadillac limousine, which was said to cruise the streets. She caught women still groggy from anesthesia after giving birth and tricked them into signing away their rights.

Complicit in her heinous acts were Judge Camille Kelley and E.H. "Boss" Crump. Though Crump had moved into state and national politics years earlier, the city's former mayor still held considerable sway in Memphis, and he wasn't afraid to wield his power. Judge Kelley rubber-stamped Tann's adoptions. Her lawyer, Abe Waldauer, also worked with her to accomplish her dirty deeds.

An investigation was opened in 1950 into Tann's crimes, but she died of cancer before any conclusions were reached. No one was ever held to account for their actions. Very few, if any, of the children sold illegally were ever recovered.

Tann did have a chauffeur, though James is a character who springs completely from my imagination. All of the other characters in the book are fictional. While in 1933 Tann did have homes throughout the city that served as orphanages, Angel House is not a real place.

And though it is critical to highlight that the black market continues to operate in adoptions (I have seen it with my own eyes), it is also important to know that most adoptions today, both domestic and international, are aboveboard. These are truly children whose parents, due to a variety of circumstances, are unable to care for them. Today's social workers strive to ensure that children are placed in good, loving homes where they will be allowed to grow and thrive.

At its very best, adoption is messy. It is a series of losses for everyone involved — the birth parents, the children, and even the adoptive parents. Along the way, there is grief, and there can be healing. Adoption is a beautiful way to build or add to a family. There is an orphan crisis in our world. There are 160 million children who don't have loving families. If only 7 percent of the world's Christians adopted, the crisis would be alleviated. If you have been considering adoption, please contact your local agency to find out more.

Even if you can't adopt, please consider sponsoring a child. In addition to our three, we have a sponsor daughter we have gotten to know over the years and love as much as our other children. Adoptive families also appreciate your monetary support and your prayers.

ACKNOWLEDGMENTS

This book would never have come to be without a good number of people who supported me throughout the entire process. First, thank you to my amazing crit partner, Jen Crosswhite. You, my friend, know romantic suspense. Thank you for standing by me when I tore my first draft to shreds, and thank you for helping me put it back together. I still say your name should be on the front cover. Thank you also to Diana Brandmeyer for your wonderful critique work. You have a sharp eye, and I'm so grateful for you.

Thank you to my agent, Tamela Hancock Murray. You convinced me I could write this book, so thank you for being such an encouragement to me. I appreciate how you have walked through this process with me and for all the wonderful advice and help you've given me throughout the years.

Thank you to the fabulous team at Barbour Publishing. I've written five novellas with them, but this is the first full-length novel. Thank you, Becky, for taking a chance on me. I loved writing this story. Your idea for this series was phenomenal, and your helpful hints for this book were spot on. Thank you to my editor, Ellen Tarver. I've enjoyed working with you. You have some great suggestions! Thank you for helping me grow as an author. Looking forward to next time!

And as always, thank you to my family. I know life these past two years has been crazy, so thank you for allowing me to take this crazy ride. Doug, you are my rock and my anchor. Thank you for telling me that I've done enough for one day and for closing my laptop when I needed a break. Thank you for putting up with all this insanity. I love you! Thank you to Alyssa, for taking care of Jonalyn so I could stay at the cabin and rework this book. It means the world to me that you are willing to do that for me. I'm so proud of the woman you are. God has great plans for you. And Brian, even though you didn't get to share in this writing whirlwind, thank you for always making me laugh just when I need it most. You don't know how many times you've kept me from tears. And Jonalyn, thank you for being you and reminding me what is most important in life.

Most importantly, thank You, Lord, for Your abundant blessings. Without Your sustaining grace in life, I would be able to do nothing. You have given me far more than I deserve. Soli deo Gloria.

ABOUT THE AUTHOR

Liz Tolsma is a popular speaker and an editor and the owner of the Write Direction Editing. An almost-native Wisconsinite, she resides in a quiet corner of the state with her husband and their youngest daughter. Their oldest daughter is a college student. Her son proudly serves as a US Marine. They adopted all of their children internationally, and one has special needs. When she gets a few spare minutes, Liz enjoys reading, relaxing on the front porch, walking, working in her large perennial garden, and camping with her family.